Immortal

Nicole Conway

Month9Books

D1160799

EPub ISBN: 978-1-945107-25-2 Mobi ISBN: 978-1-945107-24-5
Paperback ISBN: 978-1-944816-53-7

Published by Month9Books, Raleigh, NC 27609
Cover design by Beetiful Book Covers

Month9Books

To my mom and dad.

Immortal

PART ONE

FELIX

one

I lost Jaevid and Mavrik in the fray almost immediately.

In front of me, my partner, Lieutenant Darion Prax, was leaning into his dragon's speed as we made our final approach. Behind me, a dozen more riders were following us in. Below me, the city of Barrowton boiled with the fury of battle. Our lines of infantry were broken, but trying to reform. The gray elves fought like savages, wielding spears, bows, and scimitars. Some of them rode on the backs of jungle monsters, others were zipping around us through the sky on creatures called shrikes—our natural enemies.

Prax gave me a few brisk hand signals, instructing me to move into place and get ready. I twisted my saddle handles slightly, applying a bit of pressure under the saddle. With a few heavy beats of her wings, my dragon caught up with him and flew right underneath him. Nova was a big girl, bigger than most male dragons twice her age. But what she lacked in speed she made up for in other ways—something the gray elves were about to figure out first hand.

We dropped down lower. Arrows sailed past my helmet. One bounced off my breastplate and gave me a scare. I leaned down closer to Nova's body for shelter from the hail of fire coming from below. Unlike most of the other dragons, gray elf arrows couldn't pierce her thick hide.

I checked Prax out of the corner of my eye. He was giving me one finger and a closed fist. First target. Time to hit hard. I clenched my teeth and twisted the saddle handles, giving Nova the signal.

Prax and I dove as one, our dragons spiraling in unison towards the ground. We pulled out of the dive flying side-by-side, barely a hundred feet off the ground behind the enemy lines. I squeezed Nova's sides with my boot heels, and I felt her take in a deep breath.

Together, our dragons showered the ground with a storm of their burning venom.

Gray elf warriors screamed. They fired at us with everything they had. But our rain of fire didn't end until Nova had to stop for another breath.

We broke skyward and began preparing to make another coordinated pass.

But the second time wouldn't be so easy. The trail of flames and burning corpses we'd left behind had gotten the attention of a few warriors on shrikes. I spotted four of them heading straight for us.

I gave Prax the news—we had company.

He quickly replied with a plan.

I was slower, so I was bound to be their first target. But that was fine; I was ready.

When his volley of arrows failed, the first gray elf rider had his shrike attack us outright. The bizarre creature was like a furious mirage of mirrored glass scales. It wrapped around Nova's neck and started clawing at her eyes. Nova roared and slung her head back and forth. The shrike's rider was twisting in his saddle, drawing another arrow that was aimed right at me.

"Better make that shot count," I yelled and drew my sword.

Suddenly, Prax blurred past us.

There was a crunching sound and a shrike's yelp of pain as his dragon got a tasty mouthful of the monster. I saw the gray elf rider fall from the saddle and begin to plummet toward the ground. A very small part of me felt bad for him. The rest of me still remembered he'd just tried to kill me.

Another shrike hit Nova. Then another. One was wrapped around her head again while the other hit much closer to the saddle—closer to me—right at the base of her tail. I twisted the one saddle handle I was still hanging onto and Nova pitched into a violent roll. She spun, getting faster and faster.

The shrike on her head lost his grip. He flew backwards, bouncing along her body and whooshing past me. One well aimed thrust of my sword made sure he wouldn't be coming back around for a second try.

The last shrike and rider were a problem, though. She was trying to cut my saddle straps. Clever. Effective, too, if she managed it.

But I wasn't about to give her that chance.

I sheathed my sword and twisted the handles again, hanging on for dear life. Nova snapped her wings in tight against her body and dropped from the sky like a giant, scaly stone. The further we fell, the faster we went. The wind howled past my helmet. The ground was getting closer and closer.

I bit back a curse and looked back. It was working. The shrike was losing his grip, sliding further away from me down Nova's tail.

I squeezed my heels against her ribs.

Nova spat a burst of flame directly in front of us, and I hunkered down against her as she wrapped her wings around herself. Everything went dark. I could smell the acrid venom in the air. It made my eyes sting. I could feel the heat of the flames as I panted for breath.

Dragon venom is funny stuff. It's sticky like sap and highly acidic. It'll burn through just about anything—except a dragon's own hide.

Nova flew through her own burst of flames, shielding me with her wings. When we came out the other side, she flared her wings wide and caught the air like a kite. Below us, a shrike-shaped fireball crashed into the ground.

Prax appeared next to us, giving me hand signals again. *You okay?*

I gave him a thumbs up.

Good. Time for another pass.

The battle was over.

The shouting voices and clashing blades had gone quiet. Now, there was only the crackling of the flames still smoldering in what was left of Barrowton. It was a wasteland – barely more than a charred crater littered with the bodies of the fallen.

Yet another ugly scar on Maldobar's landscape.

We'd only just gotten back to the citadel at Northwatch—our little slice of paradise where the forces assigned to protecting the northern border were housed. Group after group of dragons and their riders continued to land on the platform and file into the tower. One hundred proud warriors had left to retake the city only a few days before. Less than forty of us returned.

Still, I was only looking for one.

"Where is he? Does anyone see him?!" I shouted at the top of my lungs and shoved my way through the other dragonriders. I called his name over and over, hoping to spot him or his blue dragon making their way down the corridor ahead of me. They must have fallen behind.

I searched every bloodied, war-beaten face that came walking in from the rain. Before I knew it, I was standing back at the open gateway that led out onto the platform.

Jaevid Broadfeather was nowhere to be found.

Someone grabbed my shoulder. A bolt of hope shot through me as I spun around, hoping to see him standing there.

It wasn't him.

It was my riding partner, Lieutenant Prax, standing over me like a giant in blood-spattered battle armor. He was much older than I was and a far more seasoned rider. That's why the look on his face absolutely terrified me.

"No one saw him or Jace depart with us."

I was instantly sick. I couldn't accept that. Jaevid wouldn't just roll over and die—not this easily. We'd made it this far, gone through all of our dragonrider training together from beginning to end – so I knew he could fight. Sure, I'd teased him plenty about sucking at hand-to-hand combat, but I'd never met anyone faster or better with a blade. He was half gray elf, for crying out loud. Granted, he hid it well, but I knew he had that elven killer instinct buried down deep in his soul. I'd seen it surface once or twice before when someone pushed him too far.

I had to believe he was here somewhere. I just hadn't found him yet.

I turned around with every intention of standing out on the platform in the driving rain until I saw him land. Boy, was he in for it. That little jerk should have known better than to pull a stunt like this after our first battle, the one time I hadn't been standing right next to him while we did something ridiculously dangerous to make sure he didn't get killed.

Prax grabbed my arm to stop me. There was no shaking off his grip. "We can't go out there. They want the platform clear for the riders still landing. We'll have to wait in the stable."

I stole another glance out of the gateway. The skies were choked with rumbling black storm clouds and the rain was falling hard enough to obscure the city below. Every couple of minutes, the ominous, dark shape of a dragon appeared through the gloom, wings spread wide and legs outstretched to stick the landing. As they landed, infantrymen rushed out to help the riders dismount and escort them inside. Some of them had to be carried because of their injuries. Their cries of pain were drowned out by the sound of the thunder.

"Come on." Prax shook me a little to break my trance. "You need to look after your lady. Then I'll wait with you back at his stall."

I didn't like it. I wanted to be standing right here when Jae finally dared to show his face after making me stress out like this. But Prax was right. My dragon, Nova, was still dressed in her saddle and I needed to get her settled in before I did anything else.

The work was distracting. It kept me from staring at the gateway every single second while I unbuckled her saddle strap-by-strap and checked her over for injuries. Thankfully, she was unharmed. Her scales really were as strong as iron plates. And judging by a few nicks and scrapes I found around her chest and neck, that trait had saved her life more than once.

Once she was fed and nestled into a bed of hay for the night, I closed the door to her stall and immediately made a break for the platform. I had every intention of waiting there again. I didn't make it there, though.

Everyone was waiting on me. The other surviving riders in Emerald Flight had gathered outside Nova's stall.

"They still haven't come back yet?" I looked at Prax, expecting an answer.

He didn't have to give a verbal one. Once again, his expression said it all. Jaevid and his senior partner, Lieutenant Jace Rordin, still hadn't returned.

So we waited.

Sitting outside Jaevid's empty dragon stall, we watched the rest of our dragonrider brothers tending to their mounts like I had. It wasn't looking good. The elves had made an impressive stand at Barrowton and our ranks had taken a beating. Less than half of us had returned and many of those were wounded or grounded because their mount had been injured. The riders landing now were barely able to limp in out of the rain. Some of them even had to be carried.

I watched one rider who had to be dragged off the platform by the infantrymen. He was shouting like a madman, still crazed from battle. I couldn't figure out what he was saying or why he was so upset until a big group of soldiers rushed past us to help restrain him. Then I heard why.

His dragon had managed to carry him back safely to the tower, but the creature had died on the platform shortly after.

The rider's grief-stricken screams mingled with the constant rush of the rain. It was a sound I'd never forget.

I couldn't watch anymore after that. I leaned against the stall door with my eyes closed, trying not to think about or imagine anything. Then, infantrymen rolled the iron grate down over the passage that led out onto the platform. It made an awful clanging sound.

That was it. The last of us who survived the battle had landed.

It was over. We all knew it, and yet none of us wanted to be the first to get up and leave.

It didn't feel real. I didn't want to believe it was. There had to be some kind of mistake. He was going to pull off another miracle, come wandering in with that weird, self-conscious smile on his face and start apologizing—he *had* to. It wasn't supposed to end this way.

"Jace was set on going head- to- head with that gray elf princess again." Someone finally spoke up and broke the heavy silence. "He must've dragged Jaevid into it, too. Poor kid wouldn't stand a chance in a skirmish like that."

I pushed away from the door and started walking away. I didn't want to hear this. I didn't care how he died. He was gone. The *how* didn't matter.

I thought I managed to get away without any of them following me. But I should've known better than to think Prax would let me go. I heard his heavy footsteps and the clinking of his armor as he fell in right behind me.

He waited until we were well away from the others, standing just inside the stairwell that spanned the full height of the fifty-story tower, to catch me by the shoulder. "I'm sorry, boy."

"Sorry won't bring my best friend back from the dead. Sorry never did anyone any good. It's a waste of everyone's time," I snapped.

He let me go. I could see sympathy in his eyes as he stared down at me. It pissed me off. For a few seconds, neither of us said a word. Then he shook his head. "We've all lost someone today, Felix. Every last one of us. So go do whatever you have to do. Work it out. Then clean up your armor and get ready again. You and I are some of the few who are still battle-ready."

I already felt like a total failure for letting my best friend down. I'd let him die alone in battle. And now I felt worse knowing I'd offended Prax, although there wasn't a lot I wanted to do about it right now. All I knew was that my insides hurt. I couldn't think beyond the rage that was burning in my body like hellfire. I could practically taste the flames crackling over my tongue. I needed a way to let it out.

Three days. That's how long it took Prax to resurface and try talking to me again.

I knew he'd be coming. I was already on borrowed time. At any given moment, orders could come down and I'd be sent back to the battlefront somewhere to kill more elves in the name of peace and justice. A bunch of crap, really. Neither existed in my world.

My knuckles were bleeding through the strips of bandages I'd wrapped them in. It probably had something to do with me facing off with a sparring bag every day at dawn, pounding at it with all my strength until I was too weak to stand. I didn't stop to eat and sleeping was totally out of the question so I didn't even bother trying.

Honestly, I didn't know what else to do. I was asking myself a lot of hard questions while whaling against the sand-filled training bag, and most of those questions I no longer had an answer for.

Why was I here? Punch. *What was this all for?* Punch. *Could I even justify not being at my estate now?* Punch.

"Felix." Prax's voice interrupted the rhythm of my internal interrogation.

I stopped and let my arms drop. They were so numb I couldn't even feel my fingers anymore. I turned around, wiping away the sweat that was dripping into my eyes.

I expected to see Prax there, giving me one of those cautious, sympathetic gazes. But I hadn't expected to see the guy next to him. I didn't know him. Rather, I'd never laid eyes on him before. But I knew right away who he must be.

Jae had never been all that chatty when it came to his family. I could sympathize. My own family life hadn't been great, but it didn't hold a candle to what I suspected Jae had put up with.

When we'd first met, he looked like a pulverized, half-starved puppy. Some of the other guys training with us liked to pick on him because he was one heck of an easy target—but they weren't the cause of all those bruises. Some of those marks had been older. Much older. He'd gotten them long before he'd darkened the door of the dragonrider academy. So I went out of my way to ask Sile about them. Needless to say, the answer had been unsavory.

My father had never beaten me, even when I probably deserved it. He didn't have the strength or the audacity. He popped me across the cheek a few times for mouthing off, sure, but that was more embarrassing than anything else.

Jae, though? He probably weighed eighty pounds soaking wet when we first met. And that father of his had been beating him mercilessly for years, according to Sile.

Now I was looking at the one person who should have stuck up for the little guy whenever his dad decided to use him like a doormat. I knew this had to be his older brother. The family resemblance was strong, even if this guy wasn't a half elf like Jae. Same piercing eyes. Same strong jawline.

"Roland, I presume?" I glanced him up and down. He was taller than me, unsurprisingly. Chalk that up to yet another Broadfeather family trait. "You look like hell."

It wasn't an insult. He really did look awful. His right arm was sealed in a crude plaster cast all the way up to his shoulder and he had bloody bandages wrapped around a wound on his head. He was obviously one of the lucky infantrymen who made it back to the citadel from Barrowton—the uniform tipped me off. Except for the stubble on his chin, he looked so much like Jae it would make anyone stop and take a second look. Granted, this guy had a lot more muscle to throw around, but he had the same squared jaw and high cheekbones.

"I don't believe we've met." He was looking at me cautiously. I suspected being in the dragonrider quarters was making him uneasy. Infantrymen weren't supposed to be up here.

"We haven't," I replied. I left it at that, hoping Prax would take the hint that I wasn't really up for a heart-to-heart discussion with this guy.

I walked past them to a corner of the sparring room where I'd stashed a few of my things, including a towel to wipe myself off with. I could hear them both following me.

"Colonel Bragg has issued his official statement. Medics swept the battlefield at Barrowton looking for any remaining survivors and taking record of the dead," Prax spoke up.

I stopped. All the little prickly hairs on the back of my neck stood on end. "And?"

"They never found his body—or Jace's for that matter. But his dragon was sighted in the area with an empty saddle," he answered quietly. "Some of the other riders report having seen them engaging the gray elf princess in aerial combat. They saw her shoot Jace's mount down. Jaevid was right on his tail, so … we can only assume …"

"—That he's dead. Yep. Thanks. Figured that much out on my own, you know, when he didn't come back." I scowled at them both, hoping it would be enough to stop this conversation from going any further.

It wasn't.

Prax turned his attention to the silent infantryman standing next to him. "We cleaned out their room. There wasn't much left behind, but Jae's brother here insisted you should have it."

That's when I noticed Roland was holding something. It was a mostly empty burlap sack. He held it out to me with a tense expression. "They tell me you two were close."

I didn't want to take it. Just the thought of seeing what was in there made me start to feel nauseated all over again. "Shouldn't this be given to his family?"

"That's why I'm giving it to you." Roland fixed his gaze right on me. "I know how you must feel about me. And you're right to despise me. I can only imagine the things Jaevid told you about me let alone the rest of our family. I won't deny any of it. But I never laid a hand on him. Not even once."

I snatched the bag away from him. "Some might argue that joining in and just standing by and watching it happen are basically the same thing."

Roland hesitated. Slowly, his eyes moved down until he was staring at the floor. "We were both trapped in that house, both suffering at the hands of the same man. Jaevid never knew how many beatings I took for him, how many nights I would sleep by my bedroom door so I'd hear if Ulric went outside after him. My every waking thought was about how I could get out of there. But I couldn't just run away and leave Jaevid there alone. I would have never done that to him. So I waited until Ulric came back from Blybrig and told us he'd been adopted by the dragonriders. Then I left."

An uncomfortable silence settled over us. I'm sure Prax was learning a lot more about the Broadfeather family than he ever cared to. After a few seconds I cleared my throat, crammed the bag of Jae's belongings under the rest of my gear, and nodded. "Actually, he didn't talk about his family life much."

"I suppose that shouldn't surprise me," Roland sighed. "I just thought, since you were closest with him, you ought to have what was left of his things. He'd probably want it that way. And considering the circumstances, I wanted to thank you in person."

"Thank me?"

"Yes. I'm not trying to be condescending. But I am grateful that you were willing to step in and befriend him. Someone of your social standing—"

I stopped him right there. "That never had anything to do with it. It wasn't charity."

He nodded. "I understand. I'm just saying that there aren't many others who would be willing to jeopardize their reputation. You're a better man than most. And I want you to know I appreciate that."

"Ah." This was beginning to make me really uncomfortable. I began picking up my stuff and planning a quick exit.

"I also wanted to ask if there was anyone else we should inform," Roland added, as I slung my bag of gear over my shoulder. "Did he ever mention having a lover?"

Once again, my body locked up involuntarily. I hadn't even thought about *her*. Did she know? Who was I kidding … of course she didn't know. I cursed under my breath and flashed Prax a telling glance. Someone was going to have to tell Beckah Derrick what had happened.

"I'm willing to do it," Roland offered. I guess he could read my expressions well enough to tell what I was thinking.

I clenched my teeth. "No. I'll do it. She should hear it from me. I'm the one she'll blame."

The trouble was, I didn't know how I was going to find her. Beckah lurked on the edge of every battlefield, haunting our blind spots like some kind of avenging angel. To my knowledge, she'd been keeping her distance from the riders otherwise, which was smart since she was playing a dangerous game. Being the only female dragonrider wasn't something to be proud of. It might earn her the hangman's noose or the business end of a sword if anyone found out her real identity.

If anyone could actually catch her, that is. Being paired up with a king drake, the biggest and baddest of all the dragons in Maldobar, put her at a big advantage over the rest of us.

I had my work cut out for me. As soon as I managed to shake

off the pity brigade, I headed straight for my room and started thinking of ways to get in contact with her. I didn't know where she was hiding out between battles, though. Jae might have known, but if they had a secret lovey-dovey rendezvous spot, he'd never spoken a word about it to me. That sneaky devil.

I decided to look for clues when I got back to my room. I dumped out the burlap sack of his belongings onto my bed and began to look through them. There wasn't much. It was mostly spare uniform pieces and a few bundles of letters tied together with twine. I hesitated to go through those because that kind of stuff was probably pretty personal. What right did I have to go digging around in his private life?

Then again, what did it matter now? And one of those letters might contain a clue about how to get in touch with Beckah.

Hesitantly, I untied one of the bundles and opened up a few of the letters. None of them were helpful, really, and going through them gave me an eerie feeling. It just felt wrong.

Finally, I came to one that looked like it hadn't been opened in a while. The address scribbled across the front said it was from Saltmarsh, a town down on the southern coast. I'd never been there, never had a reason to. It was a port city, home to mostly fisherman and hired hands looking for shifts on the merchant ships that came and went from the harbor.

Seeing that address struck a chord in my memory. Jae had mentioned to me before that Beckah and the rest of her family lived there. He'd visited them before the start of our avian year. When I opened up the letter, I found only one line scribbled inside. There wasn't a signature, either. Just two initials:

— B. D.

They had to be Beckah's.

I knew she wouldn't be there. It was a long flight between Saltmarsh and Northwatch, too long for her to be going back and forth every time there was a battle. Heck, I couldn't even be sure her family still lived at that address, either. Sile struck me as kind of a shady character, like he had something to hide. He might just pick up and leave without saying anything. But this was the best lead I had. I was going to have to start there and hope for the best.

I lit a candle and took out a few sheets of fresh paper. I wrote three letters. The first one was to Sile Derrick, letting him know what happened and where he could find me. The second one was to my commanding officer, Colonel Bragg, who was in charge of all the dragonriders here at the citadel.

And the last one … was to my mom.

two

"Is this what you nobles do? Tuck your tail and run every time something doesn't go your way?" Prax was looming over me, yelling loudly enough to get the attention of everyone in the dining hall.

I'd just told him and the rest of Emerald Flight what I intended to do. I'd thought it over. After sleeping on it for a few nights, I was sure. I was turning in my formal resignation to Colonel Bragg first thing in the morning. It was time to go home.

Obviously Prax didn't agree with my decision. I guess he thought yelling and embarrassing me in front of everyone would make me change my mind. Heh, yeah right. My dad had tried that too, when he was alive. It didn't work.

"I'm not running." I kept my cool. I knew Prax could crush my neck like an overripe banana if he wanted to, but I was willing to chance that he wouldn't actually hit me. "I'm just done, that's all. I don't have to justify myself to you or anyone else."

His glare was smoldering. "You're making a big mistake, boy."

"Probably. I've made a lot of those recently."

"These are your brothers. You're abandoning them," he fumed, gesturing to the rest of our flight.

I have to admit—that sort of got to me. I had to bite my tongue to keep from flying off the handle and giving him the all-out brawl he was probably hoping for. "No. My brother is dead. The rest of you will be fine without me."

I looked around at the rest of the riders in my flight. There weren't many of us left. Six, counting Jaevid and Jace, were gone now. Those of us left behind would never be the same. I guess that was why I didn't get the same resentful sense from the rest of them that I was getting from Prax. I hoped they understood, but told myself it wouldn't matter if they didn't.

Either way, I was as good as gone.

And why not? The war was more or less over. Barrowton had been the last outpost of enemy forces on our soil. That's why the elves fought so fiercely to keep it, and why we'd been so determined to take it back. Driving them out meant sending what was left of their army fleeing back into the god-forsaken jungle they'd come out of. Not even their legendary battle princess could turn the tide now. I didn't know what the king's next move would be, if he'd pursue them any further or not, and I had no intention of sticking around to find out. My work here was done.

"I appreciate everything you've done for me," I told him. Then I offered to shake his hand. Prax didn't respond except to narrow his eyes at me threateningly.

As I walked away, I could still feel the heat of his glare on my back. I'm sure there was a lot more he wanted to yell at me, a lot left unsaid, but I wasn't sticking around for that. With Jae gone, my last good excuse for not going back home was spent. I was pushing my luck by staying away this long in the first place. I'd risked making a mockery of my family's good name, an offense my mom would never let me live down.

It didn't take me long to pack up my stuff. Like most dragonriders, I traveled light. Necessities only, for the most part. I didn't have a lot of sentimental crap to lug around with me. The only people who wrote me letters were extended relatives and old girlfriends trying to suck up and get on my good side. That tends to happen when you're destined for any seat of power—everyone wants a slice of the pie. So I didn't hang onto any of those letters.

Sure, maybe some of them had actually liked me—girlfriends, not relatives. The rules are different for nobles of my standing, though. Heck, the whole game is different. You have to keep one eye on your pocket at all times because you never know who's going to try sticking their greedy paws in and swiping whatever they can. I'd already learned that once, the hard way, and I wasn't about to be the moron who fell for the same trick twice.

Don't get me wrong; girls were good fun—especially drunk,

pretty ones. But I didn't trust them. I didn't even trust my own family members. The only person I had ever really trusted was dead now. Jae had never gone after my money or anything else I might have been able to give him. Money and social standing had never mattered to him. He always acted like he didn't understand any of it, and every time I'd ever bought him anything, it seemed to embarrass him.

I stuffed what was left of his belongings into my bag. I still wasn't sure what to do with all that stuff. I'd think of something later. For now, I just wanted to get out of here as fast as humanly possible.

With everything else ready to go, I left my gear stacked by my bed and made my way to the highest level of the tower, where the dragons were stabled. I wasn't leaving until the next morning, but I didn't want to chance running into anyone who might want to lecture me or try to change my mind again.

The stables were quiet and dim, with only a few torches lighting the corridor that ran down the center of the long, circular level. On either side, dragons were snoozing away inside their stalls. It was late and I was confident no one else would be up here at this time of night.

I rolled open the door to my dragon's stable. Nova raised her head, blinking at me sleepily with her bright, sea-green eyes. She yawned, showing off all her teeth.

She must have been able to tell that I was not all right because when I came over to check her tack, I felt a blast of hot breath on the back of my head. And when I turned around, she was right there—inches from my nose—looking at me inquisitively.

"You ready to get outta here, baby doll?" I rubbed her snout and scratched under her chin.

She just puffed another hot, smelly breath in my face.

I didn't know if she could understand me the same way she seemed to have understood Jae. I didn't have the freaky powers he did. But just having her there was a comfort. As of now, she was the only real friend I had left.

I dragged all our saddlery to the middle of the stall and began polishing and checking over every inch of it. It was habit, I guess. Habit and frustration.

Meanwhile, Nova curled around me like a huge wall of bronze, brown, and black scales. I'd always liked her coloring, even though it probably seemed drab to everyone else. Her patterning reminded me of a snake, or the striping on a cat. It was unique.

She plopped her big head down on the floor next to me and watched me work for a long time. I listened to the rhythmic sound of her breathing and tried not to wonder where Jae's dragon was. Mavrik had been caught in the wild, not bred and hatched like Nova. I hoped, for his sake, that he could find his way back to the cliffs he'd come from. I had a feeling that's what Jae would have wanted—for him to go back home and be with the rest of his kind again.

Nova and I both looked up when the stall door creaked. Someone was rolling it open again.

I wasn't expecting any visitors. I didn't want any. And Prax was probably one of the last people I wanted to see right now.

He stepped into my stall and shut the door behind him. He didn't look as angry as before, although I could detect some lingering frustration in the way his brow was furrowed. Some of the other riders in our flight had started teasing us about how much they thought we looked alike. I didn't see it. Sure, we both had dark blonde hair. And maybe we did favor each other a little, but they were blowing it out of proportion. That's the way it is with dragonriders. They're going to find something to tease you about, even if they have to make it up. It only had to be ten percent true. That was the rule.

"I guess you're all packed, then?" he asked as he ambled over and leaned against the wall nearby.

"Yep."

"I'm sure Duchess Farrow will be glad to hand the reins back over to you, eh?" He'd yet to make eye contact with me, which made me wonder what he'd actually come here to say.

"I'm sure she will." I kept my answers brief, hoping an uncomfortable silence would get him to cut to the chase.

Prax cleared his throat. Then he finally looked right at me. "I came here to say that I understand. Maybe you think I'm being hard or callous about this. Or maybe you just think I'm an ignorant old man with a bird's nest for brains."

I smirked. "Getting warmer."

That made him grin too, but it didn't last long. He rubbed the graying beard on his chin and sighed. He was acting fidgety, like there was something important he wanted to say.

"You know, I lost someone too. A long time ago. So I know it hurts. And you don't just get over it or forget. Time doesn't heal that kind of wound, you just learn to cope with it. Losing someone you love is a pain the heart never forgets."

"Careful. Don't get too mushy on me there, old man."

He gave a dismissive shrug. "I can't change your mind. I know that. Just be sure you're doing this for the right reasons, otherwise you'll regret it. And I'd hate to see another kid grow up to be an old man filled with regret."

It was hard to pop an attitude or even be sarcastic when I could plainly see that he was baring a little bit of his soul to me. I wondered what he regretted, whom he had lost. I knew better than to ask, though. Some things were better left alone.

"So what's the plan? You gonna hang around this dump and be a lieutenant forever?" I changed the subject.

"Unless someone kills me first," he replied. "I'm an old dog and we don't do so well with change. This is the only thing I know. And unlike the rest of you lot, I don't have anything or anyone waiting for me behind friendly lines."

"So there's no Mrs. Prax?" I don't know why that surprised me, but it did. I guess I figured an old guy like that, who had even one ounce of charm, would have a lady waiting on him back home, sitting by a window knitting him ugly scarves or something.

He just laughed. "No. Definitely not."

"And no kids?"

Prax shook his head. "Not a one."

I felt bad for him. Must be hard to be alone at his age with nothing to look forward to but the next battle. "It's not too late, you know. Maybe you could find some lady with a thing for old war dogs. Or, you know, a blind girl and we'll all just lie and tell her you're good looking. Either way."

He laughed again and came over to sit down across from me. Grabbing up a piece of my riding tack, he started to help me work. "Nah, I'm afraid it is too late. Especially for stubborn old soldiers who don't care to settle."

I admit, I was a little nervous when I presented myself to Colonel Bragg early the next morning and handed him my letter of resignation. He didn't seem all that surprised by it, though. I wondered if someone had tipped him off, or if he was getting a lot of these kinds of letters from the noblemen in his forces now that the war was essentially over.

"I wish there was some way to change your mind about this," were his only words, as he put his signature and seal at the bottom of my letter and handed it back to me.

I folded the letter and put it back in my pocket. "Sorry, sir. With greatest respect, I'm needed much more at home than I am here."

He nodded as though he understood and dismissed me.

That was it. With a signature and a few drops of red wax, I wasn't a dragonrider anymore. At least, not in the military sense. Now I was just Duke Farrow, like my mom had always wanted.

I'd expected to feel relieved. Instead, I was anxious and uncertain as I left Colonel Bragg's office. Prax's words were getting to me, pricking at my brain like a splinter. I wondered if I really was making a mistake.

I decided not to give myself the chance to go down that road. I hurried to get my bags and made a break for the dragon stables. It was barely after daybreak, and there were already a few men at work mucking out the dragon stalls. I was looking to make a clean escape, to get out without having to make any awkward farewells. Of course, that didn't happen.

I rounded the corner, headed for Nova's stall, and came face-to-face with everyone that was left of Emerald Flight—the guys I'd been fighting alongside. Prax was with them, and at first I was half-expecting to get jumped and beaten within an inch of my life for committing what they most likely saw as desertion.

There were no traces of malice in any of their eyes, however. I prided myself on being fairly intuitive about that kinda thing. As far as I could tell, these guys hadn't come here looking for a fight.

I hesitated and looked around, waiting for someone to explain what was going on.

"We know you're anxious to put this place behind you," Prax announced. "But we were hoping to convince you to come out with us one last time so we can give you a proper farewell."

A few of the others were nodding in agreement.

"To the Laughing Fox?" I asked.

Prax began to smile. "It is a tradition to give a toast to our retirees and drink to our dead."

I wasn't sure how to say no to something like that. I knew better than to try. "Sure."

Prax helped me put my gear down inside Nova's stall before we all began the downward trek out of the fifty-storey tower. The streets beyond were just barely waking. It was late spring, although that didn't mean much here. It was always chilly at night in Northwatch.

We walked together through the mostly deserted city streets, most of the guys laughing and heckling each other as usual. As for Prax and myself, well, I guess neither one of us was in a joking mood. The atmosphere was still heavy. By the time we arrived at the front door of the tavern, I was wondering if he would try to talk me out of leaving again.

He didn't, though.

He didn't say much of anything until we were all settled at our usual table, gripping mugs of warm ale, and reminiscing about the friends we had lost. That's something I'd venture to say all dragonriders love—telling stories, the more outrageous or hilarious, the better. And if your story was good enough, it might even earn you a nickname, but not necessarily one you're proud of.

"Tell us one about Jaevid," Prax insisted suddenly.

That caught me totally off guard. I dared to stare him down from across the table. His expression was steely and impossible to read. I couldn't tell if he was putting me on the spot out of sheer curiosity or if he had an ulterior motive. Was this supposed to expedite the healing process or something?

"Yes," someone else chimed in. "One we haven't already heard."

It wasn't totally justified, but something about being pinned down like this set me off. I put my mug down, crossed my arms, and let my elbows rest on the table.

They wanted to know a story about my dead best friend? Fine. I'd tell them one, all right.

All of a sudden, I had everyone's undivided attention.

"When we were fledgling students, you wouldn't have given him a second glance. He wasn't dragonrider material, and I think we all knew that. A stiff wind could've about snapped him in half. I spent a good portion of my spare time making sure he didn't get the life beat out of him. I wondered how he was ever going to survive in our world, let alone make it to graduation," I recalled. "But then I saw him work magic. I saw him speak to animals. I saw him heal people with his bare hands and bend the elements of nature to his will."

Total silence. I didn't look up to see anyone's expression. I wasn't interested in whether or not any of them believed me.

"Jace saw it, too. So did several others when we were nearly killed during our avian training on the Canrack Islands. They all witnessed what he could do. I should have died there, along with everyone else. But he saved my life. He saved all of us."

"I heard a rumor about this—that there was some sort of elven witchery about him," Prax murmured.

I flashed him a heated glare. "Not witchery. Power. The likes of which I never knew could exist in this world outside of legends and myths."

"Could he really be dead, then? Perhaps he swapped sides."

I didn't see who said it, but the mere suggestion infuriated me. I slammed my fists down on the tabletop. "Jae was many things, but don't you dare smear his name by calling him a traitor. He was a dragonrider—through and through. He never would have forsaken his oath."

"Relax, boy," Prax said gruffly. "No one's slandering your friend. I agree; I didn't take him to be a traitor. And I doubt he would have abandoned his dragon unless death itself pried him from the saddle."

I swallowed hard. I didn't want to sit here for another second. I was already behind on my own schedule.

Prax must have been able to sense that I was on the verge of losing it because he picked up his mug again and raised it to make a toast. "Let us remember him for who he was, for the good he did, for his loyalty and service, and his honorable sacrifice. We honor him and the rest of our dead, good men all. May they find peace on the white shores of paradise."

It was a good change of subject and everyone joined in. I raised my glass, too. But my heart wasn't in it. I was angry. There was a bitter taste in my mouth that the ale couldn't wash away.

The others seemed content to waste the day there, drinking and eating while they told more stories. If my head had been clearer, I might've enjoyed it. It might have been a relief to voice some of the memories haunting my mind.

After only an hour, I got up and put on my cloak again.

"It's not even midday," Prax pointed out. "You could stay a bit longer."

I shook my head. It wasn't open for debate. I was finished here. I knew what he was trying to do, anyway. I wouldn't be persuaded to stay. If anything, I wanted to leave now more than ever.

I kept my goodbyes brief and made a clean break for the door. Pulling the hood of my cloak over my head, I took a breath and stepped out into the pale, hazy light of Northwatch's dreary sky. The air was heavy and it smelled like it was going to rain again soon.

I'd only just left the Laughing Fox behind me. I was headed straight for the citadel, making my way through the streets alone. That's when I started to get the weird feeling that I was being watched—watched and followed.

Whoever it was, they were good. Better than most. I'd only catch a glimpse of a familiar combination of colors and clothing out of the corner of my eye, but just as soon as I'd turn to look they were gone, as quick as a shadow. It had my heart pounding away in my ears.

I decided to alter my route. I took the long way, crossing through the tangled alleyways behind some of the old shops. I thought I might lose them that way.

All I did was make myself an easier target. After all, I didn't know anyone who would have been a match for *her* speed.

I rounded a corner quickly and walked right into the point of a slender dagger. Just like that, she could have run me through. Thankfully, she didn't. Beckah was on our side.

Her big green eyes were wide and desperate as she stared up at me, her hand gripping the dagger with white knuckles

Slowly, I raised my hands up in surrender.

"Why isn't Jae with you?" she rasped. "Where is he?"

I could see she was at her wit's end. Her voice was hoarse and thick and her chin was trembling. Tears were beginning to pool in her eyes.

After staying up all night sorting through my thoughts and writing a letter to her family explaining what had happened, I had hoped I would know what to say when I finally came face-to-face with her. But I didn't. I couldn't remember anything I'd written.

"Gone," I managed. "Dead."

"No!" She pushed the point of that dagger against my neck until it started to hurt. "I saw the roster they posted on the fort gates. I read every name. His wasn't there!"

"Because they never found his body. They only post the names of the ones with a body left to bury, so the families can come retrieve it if they wish."

She took a few deep, frantic breaths. Her eyes widened and her chin trembled. "No … no, you're lying!"

"I'm not."

"He talked about going to Luntharda. He said he felt that—"

"He talked to me about that too, Beckah. But do you honestly think he'd go without telling us? And during the middle of a battle when he was supposed to be watching someone else's back? I think we both know … Jae wouldn't have done anything like that."

"Then it's your fault!" She started to scream. "You were supposed to protect him!"

The look of betrayal and raw agony on her face was more than I could take. I let my arms drop to my sides. If she was going to lash out and ram that dagger through my neck, I wasn't going to try to stop her.

"Tell me the truth, Felix Farrow," she railed. "Where is he?"

I couldn't look at her. It hurt, like nothing else ever had. I was a man. I wasn't supposed to show emotion. I had to swallow it, bite it, do anything to keep it from surfacing. But I nearly broke down when she slapped me across the face.

"I hate you. I'll never forgive you. Ever." Her voice was broken by sobs. "You abandoned him. You let my Jae die. You selfish, miserable coward!"

I didn't say anything. She wasn't telling me anything I didn't already know.

Beckah slapped me again, harder this time. "I hope you rot in that castle of yours."

Those words hung in the air, beating down on my head, long after she'd stormed away. I lost track of time as I stood there, staring at the tops of my boots. I was jealous of her. She could let it out. She could say what I was too afraid to admit to myself—that I had let him down. That my best friend was dead because of me.

three

Once I made my way back to the citadel, I found I couldn't get out of there fast enough. I didn't want to see or talk to anyone else. I'd had enough with the stalling games, the painful farewells, and the horrible way this place made me feel. After my dragon was outfitted and loaded down with all my gear, I strapped on my armor and clipped my sword on my belt. I pulled my helmet down over my face and climbed onto Nova's back.

The infantrymen manning the platform waved me out as they rolled the gate open so we could pass. Outside, the sky looked heavy. Dull gray clouds were gathering. It was bound to start raining any second.

Nova spread her wings wide, embracing the stormy winds and diving into the air. My stomach fluttered at the sensation of falling.

Then we were up, soaring higher, shooting through the clouds, and breaking free to the clear skies beyond. We left Northwatch behind, and I never looked back.

It took well into the night to make it to my family's estate on the eastern coast. As we started our final approach, I could see the winking lights of Solhelm—the city that my family was responsible for as part of our estate's duties. We were the local authoritative figures, answering only to the king himself.

Solhelm was nestled in a shallow valley, between a few small mountain peaks. I'd probably spent more time there as a kid, getting into varying amounts of trouble, than I had at my own house. My family's ancestral house was lit up like a beacon. Mom had really outdone herself this time. There was a candelabra burning in every window, and the paved courtyard for dragon-traffic to land was blazing like she was afraid I'd miss it or something. How embarrassing.

Servants were waiting on me when we finally touched down. They bowed or curtsied as they came to help me bring in my gear. Normally, I would've insisted on carrying it myself. But I wasn't in the mood to argue with anyone else right now.

I handed Nova's care off to one of the stable hands that'd also come to meet us. They would take good care of her; I had no doubt about that. She was in for a good meal of fresh meat, a soft bed of clean hay, and space enough to stretch out if she felt like it. After all, any lady of mine was going to get pampered. And as it happened, she was my queen.

"Welcome home, sir." One of the white-gloved butlers manning the front door addressed me with a stiff bow as he let me inside.

I didn't answer, mostly because of who was standing on the other side waiting for me.

My mom looked older every time I saw her—and not in a good way. It was as though she was withering away, drying up under the searing heat of her own scowl. Her eyes had once only regarded me with apathetic coldness were now brimming with what I could only guess was subdued fear. Why she'd ever be afraid of me, I didn't know. I'd never raised a hand to her, and neither had dad. But she looked thin and timid standing there, looking me over like she wasn't sure it was really me.

I couldn't remember her ever looking at me for that long before. It was unnerving. "Something wrong?"

Mom opened her mouth, but closed it again just as quickly. She shook her head, making the light catch in her jewel-encrusted earrings and hairpins. Her hair was slowly turning gray and her skin was beginning to wrinkle. She still dressed like she was going to a party all the time, decked out from head-to-toe in the finest adornments our estate could afford. It was like a barrier she'd built up around herself, although I wasn't sure what or who she was trying to keep out. Poor people, maybe?

"Send word to the groundskeeper. I want to see him in my study first thing in the morning," I told her as I walked past.

"Whatever for?" She sounded suspicious.

I didn't stop to explain. Did it matter? It's not like she cared. "Don't worry over it, mom. I'm not doing anything to your precious tea garden."

I heard her puff an annoyed sigh as I walked away.

And that was it—my welcome home. That was about as warm as things had ever been between my mother and I. It hadn't ended in a shouting match, which was actually some form of progress for us. When I was growing up, we never agreed on anything.

Actually, I'd never gotten on well with either of my parents. I was an enormous disappointment to them, which they both let me know several times. I was reckless, foolish, wasteful, and unappreciative. I didn't take my role as duke seriously enough to suit them.

Well, that much was about to change. I was lord of this manor now, and I already had my first task in mind. Boy, was she going to be furious when she found out what it was—even if it didn't involve her stupid tea garden.

After they took away all the pieces of my armor and drew up a bath, I dismissed all the servants from my quarters. There was a spread of food set out for me, since I was way too late for dinner, but I wasn't hungry. Instead, I poured myself a tall glass of the strongest liquor I could find in my wine cabinet and went to sit in the bath. I sat, sipping in silence and going over plans in my head, until the water had grown cold. Then I got to work.

I sat hunched over the writing desk in my private parlor, scribbling on sheets of paper until dawn broke. My nightshirt and hands were dotted with ink and there was a stack of completed order forms spread out all around me. It was finished. Or at least, it was ready to begin.

The chimes outside my private quarters sounded, warning me that servants were coming in. They brought in breakfast on shining silver platters, clearing away the meal left from the night before. The housekeeper, Miss Harriet, was the only one bold enough to ask about it, though. She'd been in charge of running the household for as long as I could remember. She was a plump, elderly woman with a blunt way about her, which I'd always liked. She took her job seriously, too. She managed all the other servants and made sure everything ran smoothly, just the way my parents wanted.

Only now, things were going to be done the way *I* wanted, for a change.

"It's not like you to turn down a meal, Master Felix," she pointed out as she poured a cup of tea and sat it down on the desk before me. "Was it not to your liking?"

"I'm sure it was fine. I'm just not in the mood."

I could hear disapproval in her tone. "Not in the mood for poached eggs and bacon over toast? That's not the man I know."

I shrugged as I stacked up all my papers. "Is the groundskeeper in to see me?"

She nodded. "Aye. Waiting in your study. I told him you'd be in shortly, once you'd had breakfast."

"Tell him I'm coming now," I commanded as I stood up and

went to get dressed.

"Master Felix?" She called after me. "May I ask what's going on? Are you all right?"

"Fine," I answered curtly. "Planning a funeral just doesn't leave me with much of an appetite."

I guess she got the message—I was not in the mood to be interrogated by the hired help. She left me alone with a few other servants who helped me dress. It was stupid. I knew how to put on my own clothes. But I figured this was one of those "duke-ish" things my mom had always nagged about. When I was ready, I took my papers and headed for my study.

The groundskeeper was waiting, wringing his cap and looking uneasy as I entered. He bowed low and eyed the papers in my hands like he was afraid to know what I was up to.

"Have a seat." I gestured to the chair across from the broad, mahogany desk that stood in the middle of the room. "We have a lot to discuss."

"Sir?" he asked with a tremor of anxiety. "Can I ask what this is about?"

I sat the stack of papers down in front of him. "Absolutely. There's going to be a funeral held here in a month. I'm commissioning a headstone be made and I want everything to be perfect, down to the last detail."

He looked confused. "A funeral, sir?"

"Yes," I clarified. "For a friend of mine. A dragonrider named Jaevid Broadfeather."

Big surprise, mom was furious. Well, furious was putting it mildly. She wasn't exactly enamored with the idea of having someone who wasn't family buried on our estate grounds in the first place. And when she found out he was a halfbreed? I'd never seen her face turn that shade of red before. She started gripping her dinner fork like she might use it as a weapon.

"Is it your intention to scandalize what's left of our good reputation?" she hissed. "To bring this family and all its proud history to the very brink of social disaster?"

I swirled my fifth glass of wine and admired how the liquid shone like liquid rubies in the light. "It's my intention to make sure a close friend of mine receives the honorable burial he deserves. Why is that so hard for you to grasp?"

"They tell me he was out of Mithangol, the product of a scandalous affair," she continued in a hushed voice, like she was afraid someone might overhear.

"His parentage doesn't matter to me."

She balked and made a frantic choking sound. "You don't even have his body! What are you planning on putting in the coffin?"

"Does it really matter?" I polished off my glass with one long swig and sat it back on the dinner table. "This is happening whether you approve or not. So put on a few more gaudy necklaces and get over it."

My mom sat up stiffly, pressing her lips together like she'd bitten into something sour. Her eyes flashed with wrath and I could tell she was choosing her next words carefully. This was going to be a well-aimed threat.

"Your father would be ashamed," she said at last.

I rolled my eyes. Like I hadn't heard that line before.

Getting up from my seat, I pressed my palms down against the table and looked her squarely in the eye. "Yep. I'm sure he would. But he's dead and I'm in charge, so things are going to be done my way. Am I clear? You are no longer in a position to be giving me orders."

Her mouth fell open. I could read the silent horror on her face as she gaped up at me.

I should have stopped there. I'd won. She had no more leverage over me; that should have been the end of it. But I couldn't stop myself. Words just started boiling out of me—words I'd never dared to say before. "Who are you to tell me what's best for this family? Who are you to tell me anything at all? You don't know me. I might as well be a stranger for all the time we've spent together. The only times you ever seemed aware I was alive was when I did something to piss you off. But you see me now, don't you? I am Felix Farrow, Duke and lord of this estate, just like you always wanted."

I didn't know what was happening to me. I'd coexisted with my mother for years, and I'd never spoken to her like that before. I'd been a lot of things—rebellious, defiant, sarcastic, and even rude at times. But I'd never been … cruel.

My hands shook and I felt flushed as I stormed out of the dining room. What I felt was as confusing as it was overwhelming. Rage, guilt, shame, fear—all of it rushed over me like a boiling tidal wave. All I wanted was to get away from everyone and everything.

What was I thinking? Was I totally losing my mind? Prax had been right all along. Of course coming back here was an awful idea. The only time I ever felt free or at all like myself was when I was in a dragon saddle. Being here was like being in a prison- trapped with all my memories of a miserable childhood spent alone- and shoved onto a pedestal I'd never wanted in the first place.

But where else could I go? Staying at Northwatch hadn't felt much different. There, I was haunted by a different set of memories. There was nowhere for me to go and no one I could turn to. I was alone, spiraling into a hell I didn't know how to escape from.

I was out of breath when I made it back to my chambers. A few servants were there, cleaning and preparing the bath and my bed for tonight. I yelled at them to get out, and they quickly obeyed.

Save for one.

Miss Harriet hesitated when she passed me.

I buried my face in my hands so I didn't have to see the look on her face. I knew she was worried. I'd never raised my voice to the staff before.

"This came for you this afternoon, Master Felix," she said softly, taking a letter out of her apron and handing it to me discreetly. "I took care to make sure no one else saw it."

I glanced down at an envelope made of crisp, gold parchment. There was no address. No name. But I recognized the seal stamped onto the back right away. Just the sight of it made my raging thoughts go quiet for a moment. It was like a break in the storm.

"It's been quite some time, hasn't it? Since she last wrote to you?" Miss Harriet kept her voice hushed.

It had. We didn't speak like this anymore. That was a rule of my own making, and one I swore never to break.

I wondered what had possessed her to write to me after all this time.

I tossed the letter onto the writing desk in my private parlor and immediately forgot about it. It's not like I was going to answer it. Nothing written in there was anything I wanted joining the rat's nest of thoughts tangled up in my brain. I poured another glass of strong liquor and went out onto the balcony. My room overlooked the sea, so the wind that blew in always smelled richly of salt. Once, I'd found that comforting. Now it just made my chest ache to be somewhere—anywhere—else.

"Master Felix?" Harriet's voice startled me. I'd forgotten she was even there. When I turned around, I was even more surprised to find her standing right behind me, anxiously wringing her hands in her apron.

"Yes?"

She cleared her throat. "I know you're having a difficult time right now. I just wanted to tell you something, something my grandmother used to tell me when I was a girl."

I kept quiet while she seemed to gather her courage.

"She used to tell me that souls were funny things. We think we own them, but they aren't altogether ours. Everyone we love gets a tiny piece of our soul and we get a bit of theirs, too. Those bits stay with us even after we part ways or pass on. So in that way, we get the smallest taste of eternity," she explained. "Through those tiny pieces of our soul, we are all immortal. If that's true, and I believe it is, then no one who dies is ever really gone. We carry them with us always."

four

I broke through the doors of my private chambers with servants hovering all around me like gulls following a fishing boat. Some were arranging my clothes and doing last minute tweaks to my hair. Another was waving a few sheets of paper in my face, which I gathered were the notes for my speech. About five seconds before I completely lost my cool, Miss Harriet appeared and chased them all away.

"Are you ready?" she asked, as she folded the notes up and tucked them into my breast pocket.

I didn't have an answer for that. Not a good one, anyway. So I just took a breath and nodded.

"Everyone's come. Even the king himself just arrived. His masked guards are making the staff terribly nervous. They insisted on checking the perimeter of the house themselves." She sounded concerned. "The last time I saw such attendance to a funeral was when the king's dear family passed. It's unbelievable."

"And my mom?" I already knew the answer to that question. I just wanted to hear it validated out loud.

Miss Harriet cast me a sympathetic glance. "She refuses to leave her bedroom."

"Good," I snapped. "I don't want her ruining this for me."

She didn't respond to that. Instead, she followed behind me quietly as I descended to the grand foyer that led out to the back portion of the manor. That was where I'd arranged for the reception to be held, so everything was decorated with white lilies—a flower associated with grief in Maldobar. A month of preparing for an event of this magnitude had stretched everyone thin. I'd been colder to and harder on the staff than any noble at Farrow Estate ever was. But I was determined that no one was going to screw this up.

The headstone I'd commissioned had cost a small fortune all on its own. It was made of solid jade, stood over eight feet, and was carved into the shape of a knight standing at the feet of his dragon, with his hand across his breastplate in formal salute. My mom had been horrified to see it being placed in such close proximity to her favorite tea garden, but I wasn't about to move it.

Today, it would be adorned in wreaths of lilies and olive branches. So would the coffin, which I commissioned to be every bit as fine and ornate as the one I would be buried in someday. Of course, I didn't have a body to put in it. I'd settled with burying what I had of his belongings and letters, along with a rolled-up scroll of parchment sealed with my family's crest. That was what had really set my mom off. She'd lost it when she got wind of what was written on that scroll. She immediately locked herself in her room and refused to come out again.

Not that I cared. If she wanted to act a fool in front of everyone, so be it. I wasn't going to coddle her.

At last, I stood before the closed double doors that led out into the garden. Beyond them, I could hear the murmur of the crowd that had gathered. They were here to pay their respects, to watch me make my speech, and then join me in lowering the coffin into the ground. My heart was pounding frantically. I felt flushed and panicked. I locked up, paralyzed with fear.

A hand touched my shoulder. Beside me, Miss Harriet smiled gently. "It's going to be all right."

I desperately wanted to believe that. Regardless, I had to pull myself together. I had to get this done. I owed Jaevid that much. Brushing off her hand, I opened the doors and entered the garden.

It was a bleak day. The dark sky seemed threaten rain at any moment. The wind blowing in off the sea was colder than usual, so most everyone was wearing a cloak and the ladies hadn't removed their gloves or scarves.

The crowd was gathered around the headstone. As I approached, I noticed that a few new items had appeared in the coffin. It looked like mostly letters, flowers, and a few ladies' handkerchiefs.

I recognized a few faces—fellow dragonriders from Northwatch, peers and instructors from our days training at Blybrig Academy, Jaevid's older brother Roland, and some of my extended relatives who had probably just turned up to see what kind of spectacle this was going to end up being.

I spotted Sile and his wife standing close together, but Beckah wasn't with them. Sile's face looked ashen and haunted. There were dark circles under his eyes, like he hadn't slept in weeks. When he met my gaze it put a hard knot in my gut, like someone had punched me square in the stomach.

Everyone else was staring at me, too. I could feel their eyes on me, intensifying my anxiety. But I couldn't bring myself to look back at any of them as I stood in front of the headstone and fumbled my speech notes out of my pocket. I almost dropped them because my hands were shaking. When I tried reading them, my eyes crossed. I couldn't focus.

A gust of wind caught them suddenly, sending all the pieces of paper scattering across the courtyard. I didn't even try to catch them. They hadn't been doing me much good, anyway.

Instead, I just started to talk.

"When someone you care about dies, the first thing you think about is all the stuff you should've done or said when you had the chance. You wonder if it would have made any difference. There was a lot I should have told Jaevid. And even though people keep telling me his death wasn't my fault, I'll always feel like there was something I could have done. That I let him down." My voice caught and I let my gaze fall to the empty, open coffin in front of me.

I took a deep breath. "I have parents. I have aunts, uncles, and cousins. But Jaevid was the closest thing to family I've ever had. And it's strange, because I always kinda thought I was the one letting him use me as a surrogate big brother, to keep him from getting beaten to a pulp. As it turns out … I guess I was the one who was using him. He accepted me regardless of what I had, who I was, or what my social rank or wealth could have done for him. I don't have to tell most of you what that kind of friendship means to someone who always has to take every relationship with the expectation that anyone trying to be close just wants something from me. But Jaevid never asked me for anything. And the only thing he ever expected was that I'd show him the same loyalty he showed me."

It was getting harder and harder to talk. My throat was growing thick. My vision was becoming blurry and I couldn't stop my eyes from watering. I took a second or two to clench my teeth, swallow, and collect myself. Then I stepped forward and took the scroll out of the coffin. I raised it for the rest of the crowd to see.

"That's why by my order as Duke of Farrow Estate, High Noble under the Crown of Maldobar and successor to the royal line, I hereby decree that Jaevid Broadfeather is my adopted brother. He shall henceforth be known as a member of my family, protected and marked by all the power that such a rank entitles him. May you all bear witness."

There was a collective gasp—mostly from my relatives.

I placed the scroll back in the coffin and closed it. I stood back with the others and watched as the king's own guards stepped in to lower it into the ground. Then I turned to Miss Harriet. "See that the burial is completed according to my instructions."

She nodded worriedly. "Aren't you staying for the reception?"

"No."

I couldn't bear being there for one more second. As I turned and made a break for the doors, I heard the sky open up. Thunder bellowed deeply and the pouring rain made a hissing sound over the cobblestone pathways. It chased everyone else out of the courtyard right behind me.

Well—all except for one.

I caught a glimpse of a man still standing over the deep burial plot while the elite royal guards stacked white alabaster stones over it. Through the rain and people clamoring to get inside, I couldn't identify who it was at first. Then he looked at me.

Sile looked at me square in the eye with a look of terror, like the world was going to come to an end.

I sat behind my desk, my drenched clothes dripping rainwater onto my office floor. I'd bypassed the reception. I didn't care to talk to anyone down there right now. Rage and shame boiled up in me until I couldn't take it any more. I picked up a glass paperweight off my desk and hurled it at the wall. It shattered into a million pieces onto the floor.

Miss Harriet immediately rushed inside. "Master Felix? What happened?"

I was doubled over my desk with my face buried in my hands. "Nothing! Get out!"

"But Master—" she tried to continue.

"I said GET OUT!" I roared and swung my arm across my whole desk, clearing everything off it onto the floor with one sweep.

She shied back against the door as though she were afraid of me. "S-sir. The King of Maldobar is right outside. He's asked for a private audience. You cannot refuse him."

It took a few moments for me to understand what she'd said. I had to close my eyes and breathe. When I felt like I could think clearly again, I answered, "Fine. Let him in. But I don't want to speak to anyone else. Am I clear?"

Miss Harriet curtsied. "Yes, Master Felix."

She hurried out the door and I could hear some commotion in the hallway outside. Voices murmured quietly until at last the door to my office opened again. This time four of the king's elite guards entered, all dressed in sleek, black leather armor, save for the white, expressionless masks over their faces. Two remained by the doorway while the other two stood behind me. I didn't like having them out of eyesight. Something about them looming right at my back felt like a subtle threat.

The King of Maldobar stepped into my office. I'd seen him before, and he didn't look any different now than he had then—a small-framed, downright pitiful looking old man. His dark crimson robes hung off his bones like wet laundry on a drying rack. He was bent at the back and walked with a gimp to his step. As always, a fur-lined hood was pulled over his head and his face was covered with a gilded mask. I could just barely see his eyes peering out at me as he shuffled over to sit down in the chair across from my desk.

I should have stood, saluted him, or showed him some gesture of respect. But if he'd already spoken with Miss Harriet, then he must have known I was in no mood for this. I was only entertaining him because I couldn't send him away. He outranked me.

That was the only thing that kept my butt in my chair, watching him take his sweet time examining every inch of the room. He glanced down at all the stuff I'd raked onto the floor in my fit of rage, at the decent-sized dent I'd put in the wall, and at all the shattered glass on the floor. Then he let out a deep sigh.

"I know what you must be feeling." His thin voice rasped. "Rage. Regret. Pain. I could feel it all in your words. It reminded me of that day."

I sat back in my chair and waited for him to explain.

"The day my family was murdered before my eyes," he added. Then he stared straight at me with those eerie bloodshot eyes peeking through the holes in his mask. "I know there are those who have begun to question my motives. They wonder if I have lost myself to my need for vengeance. I'm curious to hear what you think. So tell me, Duke Farrow. What do you think of your king?"

"I haven't much, to be honest. As a dragonrider, you were my supreme commanding officer. As a duke, the situation isn't much different. In either case, thinking is generally not in my job description."

The sound of his laughter made me downright uncomfortable. It was a hacking, dry sound. "Well, I see you haven't lost your frankness. My sources tell me you're quite the big-talker. Apparently you were able to make yourself something of a ring-leader amongst your dragonrider peers, regardless of your social rank. They respect you. Some of them might even be more loyal to you than to me."

"Is that so? Checking up on me then?"

I could hear a smile in his voice, even if I couldn't see it past that creepy mask. "You could say that. And I was very surprised to hear that you were so closely associated with a halfbreed."

"You wouldn't be the first." I was beginning to wonder when he would get to the point. He'd obviously come here for a reason. He never tried to make small talk with me like this before. As far as I knew, he seldom said much to anyone at all. So there had to be a motive for him to be singling me out.

"I despise rumors. They're so inconsistent. As king, I want to be sure I always hear the truth." He straightened in his seat, leaning forward with his gloved hands clasped and resting on the edge of my desk. "My sources told me something else—something I wanted to come and hear validated in person."

I frowned. "And what is that?"

"This halfbreed dragonrider, Lieutenant Jaevid Broadfeather, is it true that you witnessed him heal people with some sort of magic?"

I hesitated. This was obviously the question he'd come here to ask. I didn't see how it mattered now, though. Jae was dead. What difference did it make what he had done before?

"Yes," I answered.

"And what else do you know of him? His parentage? Did he ever mention anything about his mother? Her name, perhaps?" The king's voice took on a much more serious tone. It was unsettling. This was beginning to feel a lot like an interrogation.

I didn't like it one bit.

"You think he was a traitor? Or a spy?" I countered. "Is there some lowlife out there slandering my brother?"

He didn't reply.

"Because if that's the case I can assure you that Jaevid was never anything but dedicated to our cause. He gave his life for it. And I won't stand for anyone coming into my home and defaming his name." I stood up suddenly. Behind me, I could hear the elite guards move like they might try to restrain me.

The king sighed heavily.

I'd overstepped my boundaries. I knew it. He undoubtedly knew it, too. So now the question was: how would he respond? Duke or not, I'd just mouthed off to the King of Maldobar. People had been killed for lesser crimes against the crown. But honestly, he could have sent me straight to the hangman's noose and I wouldn't have cared.

"I suppose it was insensitive of me to ask such a thing on this particular day," he said calmly, as he stood up as well. From across my desk, he offered one of his gloved hands to shake. "Perhaps we can discuss it further some other time. I wish you well, Duke Farrow."

I could feel the bones of his hand through the satin glove he wore. More importantly, however, I could feel a surprising amount of strength in his grip. It made me wonder if maybe he wasn't as feeble as he wanted everyone to believe.

five

Things started to become hazy after the funeral was over. Well, I suppose you could say that they took a quick downhill slide. That's a little more accurate. I was losing myself, but I didn't have the energy or the desire to do anything about it. I could see him in my reflection, a ghost of what was staring back at me. But beyond that, I couldn't see much in myself that was still worth saving.

The days were muddied, each passing without any marked significance. At first, I avoided leaving my family's manor at all costs. I hated the way the citizens living in Solhelm looked at me. They stared like they suspected I was going mad—as though any sudden move from me might send them all scattering like rabbits.

Then, I couldn't even bring myself to go outside at all anymore. Every time I did, I inevitably found myself standing before Jae's gravesite, staring up at the headstone. I never knew how long I'd stood there, waiting for some miracle to happen, before Miss Harriet or another one of the servants would eventually come out and ask me if I was all right.

It was a stupid question.

I quit leaving my own quarters altogether. I kept all the drapes drawn to block out the sun during the day. But at night, I would sit out on the balcony sipping the strongest liquor I could find until I fell asleep or the sun began to rise—whichever came first.

Sleeping became its own version of torture. Whenever I tried, my dreams were invaded by visions of battlefields and the mutilated bodies of my comrades. And then there was Jae. A dream of him haunted me just about every night. Usually, it involved me finding him, wounded and dying, amidst the broken bodies of our dragonrider brothers. I'd reach out to help him, to try to take him away from there, but I was never able to reach him in time. I could only watch while his eyes grew distant and cold, his spirit slipping away right in front of me.

"Perhaps you'd rest easier in your own bed again, Master Felix?" Miss Harriet suggested, as she took away yet another platter of uneaten dinner from the night before.

I was propped up on the sofa in my private parlor, watching the flames crackle in the hearth. "No. I don't like being in there anymore."

She didn't push the issue. She'd already made that mistake a few times now. There were a few more dings in my walls to show for it.

I'd yet to actually hit her or anyone else, but I'd come close enough times to get my point across.

"What is that smell?" She wrinkled up her nose as she walked past, pausing and glancing at me.

I shot her a scalding glare. We both knew what it was. I stank. I hadn't bathed or changed out of my bedclothes in a week or longer.

"Your mother has asked about having dinner with you," she rambled on. "I think she misses you."

"If you're going to lie, do a better job." I grumbled and pulled my wool blanket up around my head. I stretched out on my side facing the back of the sofa, so I didn't have to see any more of the pitying looks she kept giving me.

"Sir, how much longer are you going to torture yourself this way? Is this what your friend would have wanted? For you to waste away to nothing in this room?"

I clenched my teeth.

"Come now, at least eat something," she pleaded.

I was about to shout at her again. I wasn't in the mood for any more of this insistent, pointless nagging.

Then I heard my chamber doors open. Another servant called to us from the doorway. "A Lieutenant Darion Prax has arrived. He requests an audience."

I sat up immediately.

Prax was here?

"What does he want?" I demanded.

The servant girl shook her head nervously. "H-he didn't say, sir.

He only asked to speak with you."

"Where is he?"

"Downstairs. Waiting in the front foyer," she answered shakily. She kept looking at Miss Harriet, as though she hoped the head housekeeper would save her in the event I lost my cool again.

I threw off the blanket and stood up. It made both of them jump. "Tell him I'll be down in a minute."

Miss Harriet was obviously stunned. She followed me into my bedroom while I pulled on a housecoat. I didn't bother with anything else.

Leaving the familiar dreariness of my room behind, I squinted into the sunlight pouring through the windows of the manor. It was early morning, so everything looked bright and pleasant outside my chamber doors.

I found Prax lounging on a sofa in the downstairs study, dressed from head-to-toe in his dragonrider's battle armor. Apparently, he'd asked for somewhere private that we could talk. The servants had brought in trays of breakfast with tea, coffee, and sweet-smelling pastries. Prax was helping himself. Typical. I'd never seen him pass up a meal.

He stood and gave a formal salute when I entered, which really caught me off guard. It made me feel awkward. Then I remembered that not only was I no longer a dragonrider—I was a high noble. Social custom required him to salute me.

"Knock that off, please." I waved a hand dismissively and went to sit down in a chair across from him.

Tension rose in the air as I watched him study me from head to toe, soaking in every detail. I knew I probably looked like death warmed-over. I definitely smelled like it. So I was just waiting for another one of those infuriating, pitying looks like all the servants and staff gave me.

I didn't get that from him, though. More like the opposite. As Prax looked me over, his eyes grew colder and colder. His brow hardened and he frowned disapprovingly, like he was repulsed by what he saw.

"Are you sick?" he asked.

"No."

"Dying?"

I frowned back at him. "What kind of a question is that?"

"Well I was going to give you the benefit of the doubt, rather than just assuming you're lying around this place, moping in your own filth by choice."

I smirked darkly. "Sorry to disappoint you yet again."

He gave an annoyed sigh and started pouring himself a cup of coffee. My eyes were instinctively drawn to his riding gauntlets and helmet sitting on the table. Just the sight of them brought back memories, stirring a part of me that had been lying dormant. It was like gravity, a pull on my soul I couldn't control.

I missed being in the saddle.

"I didn't come here to squabble over your lifestyle choices," he said sharply, after taking a long swig of coffee. "I came to invite you to come back."

His words hit me like a swift kick to the gut. "Come back?"

Prax nodded. "Mind you, I didn't come here to beg for it. Consider it a modest, hopeful invitation from your former brother-at-arms."

"But ... why? Why now?" I was confused.

He drained his coffee cup and took his time refilling it again before he answered, "Because something is coming. Orders have just come down from the throne—orders that are going to change the face of this world. And the rest of Emerald Flight and I want you with us. We'd all feel a lot better with you watching our wing."

I could tell he was being intentionally cryptic. He was trying to make me curious. It was annoying—but also effective. Now I was interested. "What are you talking about? What's coming?"

Prax carefully put his cup down on the table between us. "The end."

The force of those words made my insides wrench up painfully. I wasn't even sure what he meant, exactly. But it terrified me.

"The king has ordered a final strike. All the remaining forces of Maldobar are mustering, moving towards the northern border. He means to burn every last trace of the gray elves from the earth, down to the last infant," he explained. "This will end the war, once and for all. His vengeance will be complete."

Horror choked the breath out of my lungs. "That's insanity," I managed to rasp.

Prax gave a small shrug. "Call it what you will. We are all tired, Felix. Tired of fighting. Tired of blood and flames. We're ready for this to be over, and if this will finally appease the king's wrath, then so be it."

"You can't be serious!" I stood up and shook a fist at him. "It's madness! He's completely lost his mind; surely you can see that? What right do we have to wipe out an entire race of people? What about their women? Their children? Their elderly? You'd burn them to ash, too?"

Prax looked up at me as though he were on the brink of losing his temper. His eyes were smoldering and his teeth were clenched. "I follow orders, just as you once did. I didn't choose my king. But I swore to obey his commands—even the ones I despise. This is war."

"No, this is genocide," I shouted back at him. "The people you'd be butchering are innocent civilians. You should have known better than to come here and ask me to take part in that. I won't. I refuse."

"Then what will you do?" Prax shouted back. He snapped up out of his seat with his eyes ablaze with anger. If not for the coffee table between us, it might have come to blows. "Keep cowering in your castle like a frightened child? You think hiding here, doing nothing, makes you any less guilty than the ones who will burn those elven cities to the ground? No. Your soul will be marked with the same blame as if you'd murdered them all yourself, because you sat here on your rear and did nothing."

I froze. "What are you saying? You're not going to join the fight?"

Prax's expression became ominous. "I said I would fight. But I never said whose side I'd be fighting for."

"Then why make it sound like—"

He cut me off, "I had to be sure you that you'd agree; this is indeed madness. It's not war. It's murder. But I don't have to tell you what could happen to someone plotting conspiracy against a king willing to commit an act like this. So will you help us? Things are progressing quickly and there isn't much time. Our hope is to give the elves some measure of warning. Perhaps buy them some time so they can at least evacuate their women and children before the hammer falls."

I was seething. I didn't like being toyed with like some bratty kid. "You don't need my help."

"But we'd like to have it, regardless," he insisted.

I shook my head. "No, Prax. I'm done. I've already spelled this out for you. Do I have to do it again?"

Prax scowled darkly. "Then you're right."

"Right about what?"

"You have disappointed me." He bent down and picked up his gauntlets and helmet. He wouldn't even look me in the eye as he saluted me again, probably just to piss me off, and started to leave the parlor.

He'd almost made it to the door when it suddenly burst open in front of him. I heard my mom's voice calling my name from outside. I could tell by her tone that she was already worked up—upset or angry about something that was more than likely my fault.

The very second she flung the parlor door open and saw Prax standing on the other side of it, neither of them moved an inch.

They stood stock-still, like they were frozen in time, staring at one another with the strangest expressions on their faces. Mom started to get pale. Her eyes widened and she seemed to shrink, drawing back as though in fear.

She knew him.

And judging by Prax's strained, almost wounded expression, he knew her, too.

"Hello again, Maria," he said quietly. He gave her the same formal salute he'd given to me, clasping a fist across his chest and bowing slightly.

My mom didn't reciprocate. She didn't even speak. Her face was pasty and her mouth hung open as though she might scream at any moment.

When he stood up straight again, he shot me one last meaningful glance. "I suppose I understand now, although I'm not sure I can ever forgive you for denying me that right to which I was undoubtedly entitled. You robbed me. You robbed both of us."

Was he talking to me? I thought so. He was looking right at me, after all. But what he said didn't make any sense. Not right then, anyways.

Seeing Prax didn't put my mom in a very sharing mood, not that either of us had ever been very good at communicating our feelings to one another. But there was definitely something wrong with her now. Something had brought emotions to the surface of her usually apathetic face I'd never witnessed before. I'd seen her get angry—usually with me—plenty of times.

But she was absolutely hysterical now.

I followed her out of the parlor as she practically ran back to her wing of the manor, shoving servants out of her way as she went. I finally caught up to her right before her chamber doors. By then, she was gasping back frantic sobs.

"Mom! Stop! What the heck is going on?" I demanded. "How do you know him?"

"Leave me alone! Just go away," she screamed, and tried to slam the door.

I stuck my foot in the way to stop her. "Not until you tell me what's going on."

Mom glared at me through her tears. Makeup was running all down her face and she kept trying desperately to shut the door. "Get away from me!"

"What was he talking about?" I started pushing the door open further and further, muscling my way into the room. "I'm serious, Mom. What did you take from him?"

Until that moment, I assumed it was literal robbery. Maybe she'd actually stolen something from him. Or maybe she'd been party to some kind of embezzlement that had left him out to dry. I wasn't considering anything like …

Then it hit me.

All the teasing from my peers at the citadel, the weird looks Prax had given me sometimes when he thought I wasn't paying attention, and the uncomfortable knot that formed in my gut every time he gave me that disapproving glare. Man, I really hated it when he did that.

I felt like a total idiot.

Stepping into her private chambers, I shut the door behind us and locked it to keep anyone else from interrupting. "It's true, isn't it? What everyone's been saying about him. They weren't just teasing me."

Mom was sobbing frenziedly. She backed away from me with her hands raised like she thought I was going to attack her. "F-Felix! Please!"

"Just answer the question," I ordered. "Is Prax my father?"

She stood before me with her lips trembling, streaks of mascara running down her cheeks, looking more small and fragile than I'd ever seen her before. She didn't have to answer out loud. I could read the truth in her eyes. But that wasn't enough, not for me. I wanted to hear the truth finally leave her lying, deceitful lips.

"Say it!" I roared.

She cringed away. "Yes!"

I didn't expect hearing it to hurt so much, but it did. It hurt like hell. It made my eyes water like I'd been smacked upside the head.

"Darion Prax is your father."

All the wind was sucked out me. I took an unsteady step backwards and leaned against the door. It was too much to process. I wasn't sure how I felt, or even what I should be feeling to begin with. Was I supposed to be happy? Relieved? Angry? Sad?

All I knew was that my father—my *real* father—wasn't a duke. He was a dragonrider. He wasn't anyone famous. He certainly wasn't a noble. He was just a commoner. He didn't even have a profession outside of being a dragonrider, as far as I knew. Come to think of it, I knew next to nothing about him.

And myself?

I was a bastard child. My entire claim to the birthright of being Duke Farrow was a total fraud. All of a sudden, I was an imposter in my own home.

six

I wish I could say we shared a mother-son moment of reconciliation, hugged it out, and moved on with our lives having learned from our rocky past. But we'd never been a hugging family. And after that, nothing was the same.

I didn't know whom I could trust, or who knew the truth about me. And my mom … well, if we'd had a bad relationship before, now we were like two feral wolves trapped in the same house.

She refused to see me and wouldn't even leave her private chambers. She shut me out completely and no matter what I did, I couldn't get her to look me in the eyes, let alone tell me what the heck had happened between her and Prax. I tried reasoning with her. I tried shouting. I tried begging. Nothing worked. I might as well have been a piece of lint on the carpet in her eyes. She'd never made me feel so insignificant.

And it was really starting to piss me off.

Finally, something inside me snapped. It was only a matter of time, I suppose. You could say I'm not the kind of guy who handles loss well. And now I'd lost everything—right down to my own identity.

I threw mom out. Well, not literally; I didn't actually touch her. But I invited her to leave without the option of saying no. If she wasn't going to see me and come clean about her relationship with Prax, then she wasn't welcome in my world anymore. So I sent her packing and didn't bother telling her goodbye. I didn't know where she went. I didn't care. She was good at deception and manipulation, obviously. She'd survive. Otherwise, I wouldn't have ended up the duke of an estate I had no legitimate claim to.

The staff, including Miss Harriet, were understandably distressed. They walked on eggshells around me, which was exactly what I wanted. It made them obedient and cautious. And I had an agenda now, so there was plenty to be done.

My days of moping in my room were over. I shook off the chains of guilt and grief. Was Jaevid's death my fault? Yes, definitely. But was there anything I could do about it now? Nope. So I had to do whatever it took to make those feelings go away, to forget about him and everything that was happening around me. I was going to bury myself so deeply in all the rot and ruin nobles loved wallowing in, that no one would be able to find me.

I would be beyond saving. I'd be every ounce the whopping

disappointment all my parental figures took me for.

I did what I'd always done best. I threw parties. At first it was just one every weekend with a few local nobles from the surrounding area. Then, it was two a week. Then three. At some point, it was as though no one ever left. People were coming from all over the kingdom—people I didn't even know. The party never stopped and I always had more than enough guests willing to revel in whatever riches I decided to toss around that day.

The kitchens worked overtime to turn out course after course of extravagant morsels for my guests. Wine and ale flowed like ocean currents. I spared nothing on unceasing music, entertainment and extravagance. Naturally, it didn't take long for things to start getting sloppy. With hundreds of people filing through my family's estate daily, the staff couldn't keep up with the mess.

But my already intoxicated guests didn't seem to mind the smashed wine bottles and goblets on the floor, or vomit in the hallways.

So neither did I.

"You should have quit being a dragonrider a long time ago." A girl I didn't recognize was leaning against my shoulder. She'd been there a while, and she'd had so much wine she couldn't even keep both eyes open at the same time. "You're a lot more fun now."

"I'm just getting started, sweetie." I smirked and looked across the ballroom from where we were sitting on a long silk sofa—one of the ones my mother had picked out. She'd always had an expensive appetite whenever it came to spending other people's money.

It was early in the morning, barely dawn, and the guests were beginning to tire. The dancing had stopped, although the musicians were still sawing away at some jolly waltz. Some of the men were crowded around a pair of infantrymen who were attempting to brawl. They were so drunk that neither of them could get a good punch in, though it was hilarious to watch them try. Some of the guests had even passed out on the floor. Others were draped over various pieces of furniture taken in from the adjoining rooms. I wasn't interested in napping in the filth either, so I had my servants drag a sofa in from a parlor.

"What's next, hm?" The girl started playing with my ear.

I glanced sideways at her, sizing her up. Judging by her tacky dress, she was the daughter of some low-ranking noble who had come here fishing, hoping to snag herself a husband. She was young, a lot younger than I was, maybe sixteen at the most. Pretty, I guess. It was hard to tell with her makeup smeared all down her face. And she was drunk out of her mind.

"Want to go upstairs?" I suggested.

She licked her lips and nodded.

I stood up, surprised to find myself a little woozier than I'd anticipated, and dragged her up with me. She nearly fainted right then, but erupted into slurred laughter instead. She couldn't put one foot in front of the other, so I basically had to carry her out of the room.

Out in the hallway, the girl slumped against me suddenly. I had to catch her to keep her from collapsing into a heap on the marble floor. She was passed out cold.

It wasn't surprising, really. I'd watched her drink more than anyone her size should have been able to handle in one sitting. Young girls like her always thought they had to put on a show, doing anything they could to get me to notice them and hopefully score the spot right next to me as my duchess. Watching them get so drunk they couldn't keep their drool in was supposed to impress me somehow. It was entertaining, I'd grant them that.

That is, until they passed out or threw up everywhere.

I was looking for a convenient place to put her down so she could sleep it off and sober up, when a familiar voice stopped me dead in my tracks.

"Felix Farrow."

I stiffened. Turning around slowly, I narrowed my eyes at the last person in the world I wanted to see here.

She was standing in the front doorway to my estate, just down the hall. The doorman who had let her in knew he'd screwed up. He stared at the floor, the ceiling, and anything to avoid the blazing wrath of my glare. I'd deal with him later. Every member of the staff knew how I felt about *her*.

"Get out," I snarled.

She didn't obey. Instead, she took a step inside and brushed back the hood of her long, gray traveling cloak. Crap. She was even prettier than the last time I saw her. Why did that piss me off so much? It wasn't fair.

She was quiet while her eyes traced around the room at all the damage and garbage lying everywhere. When she looked back at me, it was like she didn't even see the girl I was holding in my arms. She only saw me—just like always.

"She told me it was bad," she spoke quietly. "But I didn't realize it was this bad. I would have come sooner."

"Who?" I demanded. "Who told you?"

"Your mother."

My temper caught fire with explosive force, blazing right through the haze of every drink I'd had that night. "You're not welcome here! I want you out! NOW!"

"That isn't your decision to make." She began taking off her cloak and handing it to the doorman, smiling at him graciously as though this was completely normal.

"Not my decision? Are you insane? This is my house! I'm duke!"

She glanced at me again. Her light brown eyes shimmered like amber glass in the dim glow of morning light. She had her ginger-colored hair wound into a long, intricate braid over one shoulder. Her skin caught the light like porcelain. It just wasn't fair at all.

"And I'm your fiancée. Unbeknownst to you, your father had it added to his dying will that so long as our engagement remains intact, I have shared ownership of this estate. Your mother was the only one who knew about it, and she kept it to herself in case something just like this were to happen." She calmly took her velvet gloves off one-by-one. "So you're wrong. This is *our* house. And I'm here to tell everyone that the party is over."

She called over one of the servant girls and began giving quick instructions for the staff to stop serving everyone, begin calling around carriages, and dismissing my guests.

"You may start with that young lady there." She pointed to the girl who was still sagging, totally unconscious, in my arms. "It seems the party is long past over for her. See to it that she's taken back to her family's home safely."

"I won't stand for this," I started to yell, but neither she nor any of my staff was listening anymore.

She smiled so graciously at everyone, using her presence like a soothing balm on the staff's nerves while giving them careful instructions about how to begin shutting down my party. I might as well have been invisible. Servants and footmen shuffled by without so much as a glance in my direction.

My blood pressure skyrocketed so high it felt like my eyeballs might pop out of their sockets.

"You're all doing a wonderful job. See to it that the kitchen has plenty of help restocking and cleaning up. It's a lot to manage, I know. But we'll get through this together." She patted the doorman reassuringly and sent him on his way. "And would someone call for Miss Harriet? Please tell her that Julianna Lacroix has arrived."

***

By morning everyone was gone. Even the hired musicians had left and the house was finally quiet. My servants were still toiling away, cleaning up the mess that had built up over the past several weeks. It was going to take them a while. But the atmosphere was calm— too calm—as though the whole estate was breathing a sigh of relief.

It was driving me mad.

Sitting in my study, I pondered the best way to destroy it while swirling my half-empty glass of wine.

The door opened without any knock of warning. Julianna came in with Miss Harriet right on her heels. Neither one of them looked happy to see me. Big surprise there.

"I suppose I should greet you properly." Julianna eyed the hole in my wall leftover from when I'd thrown the paperweight. "After all, it has been quite a while since we met like this."

I made a point not to look up at her.

"Hello again, Felix."

Those words stung. I licked the front of my teeth behind my lips, savoring all the angry things I wanted to say.

"I've asked Miss Harriet to open the guest room next door for me. I'll be staying here until things are put back in order," she continued, without missing a beat.

"Back in order?" I shouted. "What is that supposed to mean?"

Julianna didn't flinch. I couldn't scare her with my temper—I already knew that. She knew me well enough to be confident I wouldn't actually lay a hand on her. "I understand that you're grieving. I can't imagine how much pain you must be feeling right now. But this is no way to honor Jaevid's memory."

"What do you think you know about Jaevid?" I growled, slamming my wine glass down onto the desktop.

"Not as much as you do, I'm sure. I don't claim to have known him well at all. But I do know how much he meant to you. And I don't believe he would approve of the way you've been handling things."

I cut a threatening glare at Miss Harriet. That was her cue to go. She took the hint right away and left us, closing the door behind her without a word.

"And how is it any of your business?" I growled again, once we were alone. "Since when is any aspect of my life your business?"

She crossed her arms stubbornly. "You're drunk, and judging by the way you reek of soured vomit, I'd guess you've been that way for quite some time. You evicted your own mother and are now wrecking your family home."

"Right," I fired back immediately. "This is my family home. Mine. It has nothing to do with you. I don't know what screwed-up dream world you think you're living in, but just because our parents signed away my right to choose my bride doesn't give you any authority over me or anything I own. You really think you deserve to be my wife? I didn't choose you. I'll never choose you."

Julianna's expression skewed. I saw anger flash in her eyes. She snatched up my wine glass and emptied the contents over my head before I could get out of the way.

"I didn't choose you either, you selfish idiot," she muttered bitterly. "And I can't think of anyone who deserves a fate like being your bride. Such a thing would be the worst kind of torture."

I hadn't expected that. In all our years of knowing one another, I'd never seen her get this upset. Before I could come up with a good retort, she stormed out of the room and slammed the door so hard it actually made me cringe.

I was immediately confused—confused and furious. Hadn't she been the one who insisted on our marriage? Hadn't she begged her parents to make the arrangements?

We'd only been children when they'd announced it, and yet I remembered that day so clearly that it made me sick to my stomach. My parents and hers had sent out a public decree and announced it before a ballroom full of friends and family; she and I were to be wed as soon as I took my official post as duke. Julianna Lacroix would be my wife, whether I liked it or not. I had been completely humiliated and emasculated, which was pretty traumatic for a kid just beginning to come into manhood. My parents had decided without even asking me how I felt about it. I was already fighting tooth and nail to convince them to let me have a dragon of my own. And now they weren't even going to let me choose my own bride.

I guess I never considered that she hadn't wanted it, either. After all, that was usually what other girls wanted whenever they came around me. It wasn't exactly a mystery why. I was the highest-ranking noble in Maldobar. The most eligible bachelor in the kingdom. My family bloodline was shared with princes and kings going back generations. Marrying me would bring power, prestige, wealth, and security—everything a woman wanted.

Every woman except for Julianna, apparently.

I didn't know what game she was playing at, but I didn't want any part of it. I'd spent years driving as big a wedge as I possibly could between the two of us, hoping she would take the hint and get out of my life. According to the contract, she was the only one who could break off the engagement. Those were the terms. And I'd tried everything. I'd sabotaged her social standing amongst the other nobles, disgraced her at parties, and pretended not to know her at all. Nothing worked. She wouldn't call off the marriage.

Was it cruel? Yes. But the fact that she grew up to be beautiful, and smart, and … unfortunately, one of the nicest people I'd ever known didn't matter. She had betrayed our friendship in the worst way. I'd trusted her more than anyone, even my own parents. Going behind my back to plot this forced marriage to me was not something I could just forgive.

Maybe she'd been able to chain me down as her fiancée, but Julianna wasn't going to win this time. This was my last shot at freedom. She thought she could just swagger in here and run my life?

She was in for a rude awakening.

seven

"Give it to me now!" I yelled at the top of my lungs, flinging a tray of dishes leftover from my uneaten dinner across the room. Plates and cups shattered, raining porcelain splinters all over the carpet.

Miss Harriet had to duck to get out of the way. "Master Felix, the mistress has forbidden it. She had all the alcohol in the estate poured out. Even the wine!"

"Are you deaf or just stupid? How many times do I have to repeat myself? This is not her house. You don't follow her instructions. I am the master of this estate!"

I was so out of breath that I had to catch myself against the back of the sofa. My skin felt clammy and my head was swimming. I could barely put one foot in front of the other. All I wanted was a drink. It had been two days since my last one. Just one strong glass of wine and I knew I'd feel better.

"Sir, I can't—" Miss Harriet started to protest again. I picked up another object, which happened to be a sterling silver water pitcher, and reared back to throw it.

My chamber doors opened.

"That'll be all, Miss Harriet. I'll handle it from here." Julianna came striding in with her sleeves rolled up and an apron tied around her waist, looking as cool and collected as ever. She carried a tray full of supplies.

My housekeeper didn't argue. No doubt she'd been looking for an excuse to leave this whole time. She was the only member of my staff who was still brave enough to try coming in to bring me food. Everyone else was too scared of me, I guess.

As soon as she was gone, Julianna gave me a scolding glare. "You shouldn't be so unkind to her. That woman loves you like her own son."

"Hah!" I tried to steady myself. My hands shook so badly I couldn't grip the pitcher any longer. It clattered noisily to the floor and sent water splashing everywhere. "Come to watch me suffer?"

She frowned. "I came to help, since you've driven away everyone else. You've been drinking too much for too long. You're going through withdrawal sickness."

"I'm acutely aware of that, genius." I glared at both blurry images of her, since I couldn't tell which one was real. My vision wasn't so good and my head was pounding.

"Go lie down." She bent down and started picking up the debris I'd smashed on the floor.

I stood over her and watched for a few minutes. I was trying to understand why she was here to begin with. Because my mother had asked her to come? To fix the damage I'd done to the estate? Neither were good enough reasons, in my opinion. They both sounded made up. She hadn't come clean with me yet.

I grumbled a few more curses under my breath as I shuffled away back to my bedroom. My bed was a mess of wrinkled, sweaty blankets that I'd been tossing and turning in for two nights now. I couldn't get comfortable, no matter how hard I tried. Every part of my body felt sore, like I'd been run over by a horse.

I stretched out on my back and draped an arm over my face, trying to block out the light. Even with the drapes closed and the entire room basically pitch black, my head was still throbbing. Any hint of light made it feel that much worse. My insides felt like they were on fire. My throat burned. My body shook. And one drop of liquor, any kind at all, was all I could think about.

Julianna came in carrying her tray. I immediately sat up in bed. I was geared up for another argument, waiting to see what she was up to this time. But Julianna didn't look at me. She placed the tray on the nightstand and lit a candle.

The light stung my eyes. I cursed at her again.

"Hush," she said softly, as she pulled up a chair and sat down beside my bed. I heard liquid sloshing, but I didn't dare open my eyes to see. The light only made my head hurt worse.

I flinched away as she touched my face with something cold and wet—a rag, I guessed.

"I don't like you," I reminded her.

"I know," she answered, wiping the sweat from my face and finally placing the rag over my forehead. "You need to eat something. I brought some rice pudding. It's very bland, so it shouldn't upset your stomach."

I laughed hoarsely. "I already threw up everything I tried to eat before. It's pointless. Just bring me some wine."

Julianna stayed silent.

I cracked open an eye to steal a glance at her.

The warm candlelight made her already beautiful face shine like a star in the dark. My vision was hazy, especially with the bright light making my head pound, but I could see that she looked tired. Two days of this had to be wearing her down. Two days and two nights of me yelling and cursing at her, throwing things, and vomiting every time I tried to eat. Yet here she was, avoiding eye contact with me as she stirred a bowl of what must be the rice pudding.

"Why are you doing this?" she asked suddenly.

I scowled because I had been wondering the exact same thing at that moment. "You think I like throwing up?"

Our eyes met. Her expression was firm, even if there were sleepy circles under her eyes.

"You know that wasn't what I meant, Felix."

I stayed quiet.

"Is it because you want to die, too? Because there are easier ways than drinking yourself to death," she said. "Or is it because you don't know what to do with your grief?"

I had to clench my teeth to keep from yelling at her again. "Blow out the stupid candle and I'll tell you."

"What? Why?"

"The light … it's killing me. It's making my head hurt even worse," I answered.

With a puff of breath the room went dark again.

I breathed a sigh of relief.

"Are you really going to tell me why you've been acting this way?" I couldn't see her anymore, but I could hear the suspicion in her tone.

"Why does this matter to you so much?" I countered.

She didn't answer, and for several awkward minutes we just sat in darkness without saying anything.

I caved first, probably because I was in pain from the withdrawals. Or it might have been because the truth had been rotting away inside me for so long that I couldn't stand it anymore.

"You have no idea what it's like … to have no one you can trust. That's who he was for me. Jaevid was someone I knew I could trust. Without him, I have no one. I'm alone. And I'll always be alone." Dang, that had sounded a lot more whiny and melodramatic coming out than it had in my head. It was embarrassing to admit it.

"That's not a very good reason to be acting this way, you know."

I glared in her direction since I couldn't see her anymore.

"And you're wrong." Her voice became so quiet and small that I barely heard her.

"What?"

"You're wrong—I do know what it's like," she repeated. "You were my closest friend before, Felix. I thought I could trust you. You were always so kind to me, and always so understanding. We were only children, but I sincerely thought I would always be able to confide in you."

"Yeah, well, that was before you decided to plant your marital hooks in my back," I sneered.

I heard a scraping sound, like metal on metal. There was a spark, and the candle blazed back to life just in time for me to see the harrowing glare she was giving me. She was holding a flint striker like it was a weapon.

"I'm so sick of hearing you say that," she fumed. "That had nothing to do with me! I was just as surprised as you were when our parents announced their decision. They never mentioned it to me or asked how I felt. They just did it. And before I could explain that you shut me out."

"Well you certainly didn't protest it, did you?" I tried to sound snarky and clever, but actually … she'd just cut the legs out from under me. I always assumed that she was the instigator behind our arranged marriage.

"Of course I didn't." She began angrily stirring the rice pudding again. I wasn't sure because of how blurry my vision was, but it almost looked like she was trying not to cry.

"So? Why didn't you?" I pressed. "If you didn't want it, then why haven't you said anything all this time? Why didn't you try to stop it?"

She stopped stirring. Her chin was trembling and she wouldn't look at me. I watched her put the bowl down on the tray and stand.

"I think Miss Harriet should be the one to feed you tonight," she said stiffly, as she turned and started to leave.

"Julianna!" I yelled after her, trying to get her to come back so we could clear the air.

But she didn't stop. Instead, she started running. She darted out of my bedroom without ever answering.

Things were going to get worse before they got better. I knew that. I just didn't know how much worse. I was paying dearly for every drink I'd taken and, believe me, it wasn't even close to worth it.

The next day I started to get sick—beyond sick, really. I thought I was dying. From that point on, each day was worse than the one before it.

I didn't sleep. Even when I tried to sleep, I couldn't because I was hurting so much. My mind raced and my body ached like someone poured hot sand into all my joints. I was sweating like crazy, and even though I'd puked up everything in my stomach, my insides still constricted like I might vomit again.

It hurt. I was exhausted and for the next several days all I could do was lie in my bed and groan. Julianna and Miss Harriet took turns force-feeding me mild soups and water, not that anything ever stayed down for long. They tried to help me bathe, but had to revisit that plan when I collapsed halfway to the washroom and fell on top of Julianna, basically crushing her into the carpet.

I did feel bad about that.

But even when my strength was spent and my stomach was empty of everything including bile, the worst was yet to come.

It was bedtime, or so Julianna had ordered. She was keeping me on a strict schedule. The only time she really left my side was to look after her own needs or to give me some privacy while the servants helped me bathe. She'd forfeited that job after being squished.

I was actually starting to turn a corner—or so I thought. I wasn't feeling quite as awful. My head wasn't pounding as horribly and I could even walk to the bed myself. I'd just reached the bed and was preparing to put a clean nightshirt on when it happened. I started to feel strange. My body began trembling again. My tongue felt chill and I tasted copper. My fingers tingled and began to feel numb.

I barely had time to sit down on the edge of the bed when it hit. It was like being struck by lightning. Every muscle in my body went rigid. I couldn't think. I couldn't breathe. There was only pain and a sense of impending doom as my body shook violently out of my control.

Darkness started to close in around me and I knew I must be dying. But through the haze, I caught glimpses of what was happening around me. Julianna rushed in at the sound of the servants' distress. She held my head in her lap and forced something into my mouth. It was a leather belt.

"Open your mouth, Felix! You have to work with me or you'll bite off your own tongue," she pleaded. I could see tears streaming down her face.

It took everything I had, but I managed to do it.

"You stay with me now. Just keep looking in my eyes. We'll get through this." I could vaguely feel her taking my hand and squeezing it firmly. "You hear me? I'm right here. I'm not going anywhere. I'll always be right here …"

Then everything went dark.

I didn't know what had happened when I finally woke up. My body still felt strange and tingly, like my arms and legs had gone to sleep. I tried to sit up, but every muscle protested. I couldn't do it. It hurt too much.

"Just rest," a familiar voice whispered.

Julianna sat at my bedside, wearing nothing but a dainty, pale blue nightgown and a long white robe. Her hair was loosely braided over her shoulder with a few stray locks falling perfectly over her cheeks. I didn't have to wonder how long she'd been watching over me. The weary lines on her face and circles under her eyes told that story plainly enough.

She was still holding my hand just as tightly as before, like she hadn't let go of it since I passed out. "How do you feel?"

I tried to speak, but my throat was so dry I couldn't even swallow.

"Here, drink this." She pulled her hand away and poured the contents of a small porcelain teapot into a cup. It smelled good and tasted faintly of honey.

"W-what happened?" I finally managed to ask.

She refilled the cup again and insisted I drink more. "You had a seizure. For a moment there, we weren't sure if you were going to make it or not."

"I wasn't sure, either," I admitted.

Things started to get awkward as we both fell silent. My hand—the one she'd been holding—was still warm from her touch. It stirred things in my mind, emotions I'd tried my best to bury or destroy. For the first time in a long while, I felt clear. I could hear myself think. And all I thought about was her.

"Julianna," I started to talk.

"You need to rest." She cut me off. It was as though she sensed that I wanted to have a serious talk about how I had been a humongous jerk to her for the past ten or so years.

"I can't. Not until I know why." I was the one reaching for her hand this time. "Please tell me. If you didn't agree with the engagement our parents agreed on, then why didn't you say something sooner?"

I saw her stiffen. She looked right at me, like a doe caught out in the open. Her eyes widened and her face started to flush. For a second or two, I thought she might actually tell me.

Carefully, Julianna withdrew her hand and stood. She dragged the blankets up over me and tucked me in, all while doing an excellent job of not making eye contact. Then she started to leave, just like before.

"I'm glad you're all right," she said, as she hesitated in the doorway. "I think things might start to get better for you now. Tomorrow you should try going for a walk."

"Wait! Please. Just talk to me about this." I was beginning to get desperate.

"Just rest. This doesn't have to happen now."

"What doesn't have to happen? Why won't you talk to me?" I didn't know what she meant by that, but it didn't sound good. For whatever reason, it felt like she was slipping away—like she was frantically putting up walls to keep me at a distance. I was losing her. And it scared the heck out of me.

I watched her smile sadly back at me. "Goodnight, Felix."

The door closed and I was left alone. That's when things started to click into place in my brain. Without the booze and misdirected hatred blurring my thoughts, I could see what was happening now was completely my fault.

After everything I'd done to her, I really was an idiot for thinking she'd ever want to be friends with me again. Things couldn't be the way they had been when we were children. I'd destroyed our relationship in every way I possibly could, in the hopes that it would drive her to break up our engagement.

But all I'd done was hurt her over and over. I'd used everything I knew about her from when we were friends, every secret insecurity and fear she'd ever confided in me, to do as much damage as possible. I'd used every bit of my social influence and power to make her suffer.

And now she'd never trust me again.

eight

I would have to start over. Julianna didn't trust me anymore. I'd intentionally killed our friendship and every good opinion of me she'd ever had. So if I wanted her back, I was going to have to start from scratch and prove that I wasn't the evil son-of-a-dog she probably thought I was now.

I decided this while sitting next to her on a marble bench, tucked away in one of my mom's favorite tea gardens. It was peaceful there; I could see why mom liked it so much. She'd gone through a lot of trouble to have this place be as private and tranquil as possible. There were flowering fruit trees and perfectly manicured pathways winding off through tall hedges. Bubbling fountains hid amidst the foliage like secret paradises you'd only find by pure accident. The backdrop of deep green ivy and brightly colored flowers made Julianna seem even more beautiful than usual.

She sat next to me, close by but definitely not touching me, flipping through the pages of a book. She insisted I take these walks every day, to breathe in the fresh air and meditate. It was supposed to help calm my grief and give me time to reflect. I guess it did, to a degree, but I couldn't do much reflecting when all I could think about was how cruel I'd been to her.

"You know, I think I've about got my strength back now," I tried to start a conversation, yet again.

She didn't look up from her book. "Just don't overdo it."

I wasn't about to give up that easily. I'd been trying for days to get her to open up, to get a smile or a laugh or anything from her. But she was using that stupid book like a shield, pretending to be too distracted to notice me. Time to bring out my secret weapon.

"I was thinking of going for a ride this afternoon." I tried to sound indifferent, as I stood up and stretched my arms over my head. "Maybe you'd want to go with me? It'd be nice to get out for a while."

She took the bait hook, line, and sinker. Her eyes flicked up, peeking at me over the top of her book. "Through the countryside?"

I shrugged. "Sure. It's a nice day. Might as well make the most of it, right?"

Julianna raised the book higher to block her face from my view. "Okay. That sounds fine."

I smirked. Score one for me. This was my chance—I wasn't going to blow it this time. "All right. Meet me at the stables later then?"

I saw the top of her head move as she nodded. She was still

determined to hide behind her book for now, but that wasn't going to work so well for her later. I had a plan.

The expression on her face was priceless as she walked up to the front of the stables where my estate's horses were housed. Only— we weren't riding on horses.

Julianna stared at Nova like she was seeing something straight out of a dream. Or maybe a nightmare, I couldn't quite tell. She might have been terrified. Her eyes were wide and her mouth hung open like a fish gasping for air.

Nova was restless. I hadn't ridden her in a couple of months now, so she was itching for a ride. She nipped at me, giving me dragon love-bites while I fixed her saddle straps and checked all the buckles. When she spotted Julianna, though, she started to get even more anxious. I'd never let anyone else ride Nova with me before.

"I-I thought we were going horseback riding!" Julianna stopped about twenty feet away from us and wouldn't come any closer.

I grinned at her. "Where's the fun in that?"

"Felix, I can't do thi—"

"Don't even say it, Jules. You really think I would ask you to do this if I thought it was the least bit dangerous?" I arched a brow at her.

She didn't trust me, or so I'd thought. But as she started to take tiny, cautious steps to me, my hopes grew by leaps and bounds. Maybe, somewhere deep down, she still believed that I wouldn't let anything happen to her.

I held a hand out to coax her in. "Come on."

She gripped my hand like she wanted to pop it off my wrist. "I'm not dressed properly for this," she whimpered.

Nova swung her huge, horned head around and put her big snout mere inches from Julianna's face.

I thought Julianna was going to pop right out of her skin. She bounded behind me and clung to the back of my shirt. "I-is she friendly?"

"Sometimes." I laughed. "She's not gonna hurt you, I promise."

Julianna didn't appear convinced. She was chewing fiercely on her bottom lip as I basically shoved her back in front of me. I took one of her hands and brought it to Nova's snout, showing her that it really was all right.

The more she touched, exploring Nova's scaly hide, the more I saw Julianna's apprehension and fear become excitement. She started to smile, a smile that grew wider and wider by the second. Nova closed her big green eyes and made a deep, purring sound.

"She's incredible," Julianna whispered. She giggled when Nova started sniffing her over, blasting her with hot dragon breaths.

I was smiling now, too. "Ready to ride?"

When she looked back at me again, I saw nothing but pure exhilaration. She was finally seeing me again, without remembering all the terrible things I'd done to her.

She hadn't looked at me like that since we were children.

I had some casual riding gear leftover from my youth—before my training at Blybrig Academy—that I was able to loan her. It was huge on her, of course. But it would do for now. I helped her strap the helmet down over her head and pull the gauntlets up over her arms. She was light, so it was nothing for me to pick her up and get her situated in the saddle. I gave her a quick walkthrough about where on the saddle she could hang on, even though I knew she would probably freak out once we actually started flying. First-timers always did.

Then I put on my own equipment and climbed into the saddle behind her.

It was weird being so close to her. Her back was pressed up against my chest as I reached around her to grip the saddle handles on either side of Nova's neck. I gave Julianna a warning pat on the shoulder.

We took off in a whirlwind. Nova was eager to leave the ground behind, so she wasted no time climbing skyward. Over the rush of air, I could hear Julianna screaming her head off.

Once we leveled off and started soaring, dipping through the clouds like we were skating over fields of white cotton, her screaming stopped. Though I couldn't see her face, I could feel her body beginning to relax. The landscape below us slipped by sluggishly—rolling hills of green that stretched all the way to the eastern cliffs. Then, there was nothing but ocean as far as the eye could see.

I sat back in the saddle, relaxing to take everything in, and I was shocked when Julianna did the same. She actually let go of the saddle and spread her arms wide, her long red braid and frilly ends of her skirts whipping around in the cold air. It made me smile again because I knew what she was feeling.

There really is no comparison to the rush of freedom you get when you're sitting in a dragon's saddle.

We flew for hours until I finally had Nova land in one of the grassy, rolling meadows north of my estate. There, amidst the soft grass, I unpacked phase two of my plan in the form of a picnic. I had a blanket and a few snacks stowed away in my saddlebags.

Julianna wobbled around like a newborn fawn when she got her feet back on the ground again. I guess the rush and excitement still had her shaking. She didn't say anything as she helped me spread out the blanket and unpack the food. We sat together while Nova rolled in the grass, basking in the warm afternoon sunshine like a fat housecat.

"I remember you promising to do this when we were little." Julianna spoke up in a quiet voice as she fidgeted with the strap on my water canteen. "Riding dragons was all you ever talked about."

I remembered that, too. "I guess not much has changed in that regard."

She gave a small, guarded smile. "No. But everything else has."

The atmosphere between us was starting to get awkward again. Only this time, she didn't have a book to hide behind. Now was my chance.

"You're never going to tell me, are you?" I asked.

She glanced at me warily.

"I wish you would. I want to understand. I've turned it over and over in my mind, and it just doesn't make sense. If I'd known—"

"It wouldn't have mattered, Felix. I didn't say anything or try to stop the engagement because …"

She hesitated to continue. I held my breath and hoped she would.

"Because I was already in love with you. But everything you did, everything you said, made me believe that you definitely didn't feel the same way. And like a fool I kept hoping you'd eventually calm down, think about things, remember how close we'd been before. I hoped that maybe you would change your mind. You were my first love, and I wanted you to be my last."

I swallowed hard.

"I clung to those memories of our childhood for so long. You were my best friend, and I wanted that Felix back. Without him … I had no one." She turned away so that I couldn't see the expression on her face.

"Julianna, I—"

"It's okay. You don't have to say anything. I understand now how you must have felt. You'd always expressed to me how your parents didn't try to see things from your perspective. They didn't consider any of your opinions or wishes when they made decisions about your life. When they announced our engagement, you must have thought I was trying to do the same thing."

"That doesn't make it right," I said. "I shouldn't have treated you that way. And I'll spend a lifetime regretting it. You have to know how sorry I am."

She looked at me then, and I saw everything I'd been afraid I would see. The betrayal and pain on her face, the tears in her eyes, and the overwhelming sense that I'd succeeded in driving her away.

"I lied to you, Felix," she admitted.

"About what?"

She took a trembling breath. "I didn't come here because your mother asked me to. She did write to me to tell me what was happening, apologizing for your behavior, but I was already planning to come to the estate long before that. I wanted to make it official in person."

I didn't know what she was talking about. "Make what official?"

"I'm terminating our engagement," she said in a quiet voice. "Actually, I already did several months ago. I should apologize for that, too. I never had the authority to take over your estate, but I suppose you weren't aware of that. You never opened the letter I sent, did you?"

The letter in the golden envelope. I'd completely forgotten about it. It was probably still sitting unopened on my desk at home.

Now I was the one who was afraid. I was losing her—no, I'd already lost her. I just hadn't been aware of it until now.

"I wasn't even sure if I could help you or not, but I would have never been able to forgive myself if I didn't at least try. And now you're free of me, just like you always wanted." She smiled at me but it wasn't sincere. I saw the sadness in her eyes. It was like someone was driving a red-hot spike into my soul.

"That isn't what I want anymore," I tried to protest. "I was just being stupid, Jules. I was acting like a dumb kid. And I'm sorry—I really am. If I could take it all back, I would."

She shook her head and started to withdraw. "Please don't say that now. I can't bear it. I've worked so hard to put my feelings aside. It's time for me to let go of those childish things and move on."

"But—"

"No!" She shouted suddenly and got up.

Julianna started to walk away, although I wasn't sure where she thought she was going. It was miles back to my estate—too far for her to walk by herself. Besides, it's not like I couldn't catch up to her. I wasn't the fastest guy in the world on foot, but I wouldn't have been much of a dragonrider if I couldn't outrun her.

I caught up to her and grabbed her arm to make her stop and face me again. She was crying and she wouldn't look me in the eyes. But that didn't matter. I just needed her to hear me.

"I love you, Julianna."

She squirmed in my grip, trying to pry herself away from me.

"I love you, and I'll never deserve you," I repeated it because it was true. Every word.

At last, her teary eyes raised to stare back at me. It didn't look like she believed me at all. She seemed angry, like maybe she wanted to hit me.

So I kissed her.

She fought me. She beat her hands on my chest and tried to

shove away. I didn't let her. If this was goodbye, then I was going to savor this one little taste for as long as I could. She could hate me for it if she wanted; just add it to the stack of awful things I'd done to her already.

Then I felt her stop struggling.

All of a sudden, she wrapped her arms around my neck and squeezed me so tightly I could barely breathe. She kissed me back, and I'd never felt anything so sublime.

"Marry me," I begged, when I felt her start to pull her lips away from mine.

"Have you lost your mind?" She eyed me like she suspected I might be drunk again.

I dropped to my knees in front of her. I didn't know what else to do. "Please, Julianna. I know I don't deserve it. But I'll try every day to be worthy of you—to be the man you'd always hoped I would be."

She was hesitating. I could see her eyes darting back and forth like she was scrambling to think it over.

Then she smiled. "Even though you think I have big teeth?"

"I'll pull all my teeth out and gum my food for the rest of my life," I promised.

"And even if I'm a terrible dancer?"

"If I can teach Jaevid to dance, then I can teach you."

Julianna laughed. She put her soft hands on both sides of my face and bent down to kiss me again. "All right then, Felix. I'll marry you, if that's really what you want."

I couldn't hold back my relief. "It's the only thing I want."

nine

A nd then I lived happily ever after, right?

Yeah. I wish. But there was still a problem I had to take care of—one last demon to face, if you will.

I felt better about talking to mom this time, though, because I wasn't doing it alone. Julianna was with me, holding my hand as tightly as ever, as I climbed the steps of the small summer home where she'd taken up residence since I evicted her. And by small, I mean it had only fifty bedrooms rather than two hundred and fifty.

Mom was sitting on a balcony overlooking the sea, sipping tea like she was alone in her own private universe. When we entered, she didn't even look up at us.

"Mom?" I tried to get her attention, which was basically the story of my entire relationship with her.

She just went on sipping her tea.

Julianna leaned in to whisper in my ear, "Maybe I should just let you two have some time alone?"

"No, it's okay. You're going to be my wife. I don't want to go another step into our relationship without being honest with you." I tried to show her a reassuring smile, but I just couldn't quite get there. Julianna didn't know about me—that I was an illegitimate child. I was nervous and a little afraid she might change her mind about marrying me once she found out.

"That's quite a change you've made." My mom spoke up so suddenly it made me jump. Her tone had a strong flavor of sarcasm to it. Typical. "I suppose you've come to ask about Darion again, is that so?"

"Yes. But I also didn't come here to fight with you. Either you're ready to tell me what happened or you're not. Regardless, we can't go on like this, mom." I pulled up a chair for Julianna and then for myself. "So what's it gonna be?"

Mom put down her teacup and looked at me, then at Julianna, then back to me again. "You really want to discuss this in front of her?"

I nodded. "She might as well find out straight from the source."

"Very well, then." Mom sat up straight and folded her hands in her lap. "You were right. Duke Farrow was not your father. Darion Prax is."

I already knew that. She was just saying it again for Julianna's benefit, maybe even in an attempt to scare her. A hard knot of emotion formed in my throat. I didn't dare look at Julianna because I was honestly afraid to see her expression. Shock? Horror? Disgust? When I finally got the nerve to look, I didn't see any of those. She looked upset.

"You had an affair?" she asked, before I could say anything.

My mom smiled at her scornfully. "No. I was already pregnant when the Duke and I were married. Now tell me, is that better than an affair? Or worse?"

Julianna's expression tightened, as did her grip on my hand. "If the duke didn't know about it, then about the same."

"Darion and I had been lovers in secret for quite some time. He was just a merchant's son. No money that amounted to anything, and no prospects of improvement. At the time, that didn't matter to me. I was just a stupid, lovesick child. He'd been saving up what he could of his earnings working on the docks, I believed, so that we could be married and live on our own. But then he went off and spent it all on a dragon hatchling. I didn't even find out about it until the next solstice holiday when I had hoped he would propose. That was when he told me of his intentions to join the king's ranks as a dragonrider."

Mom's tone was venomous, as though the memories still burned in her heart. I could hear anger and resentment in every word. "Darion had never intended on marrying me. I was just something for him to toy with. And it was only after he'd left for training and we had severed all contact that I realized I was pregnant with you,

Felix. In an effort to save my reputation, I took the first offer for marriage I received—which happened to be from the duke. My parents were elated at the news. No one questioned my acceptance because a marriage to the duke would mean a comfortable life for me indefinitely. Only a fool would have refused a proposal like that."

"And you were able to cover up the pregnancy," I finished for her.

Mom shrugged like it was nothing. "Not so much cover up, as replace the one responsible for it. We were married quickly and I announced my pregnancy shortly after. You were born a few weeks late, which only wound up strengthening my story about your parentage. No one else ever had to know. That is, until you started to grow."

I shifted in my seat because I had a bad feeling I knew where this was going.

"You didn't look anything like me or the duke. You've always favored him. And every day since your birth I've been forced to look at the reminder of how Darion abandoned me. He treated me like dirt—as though I were disposable. Soon I found it was easier to simply not look at you at all." She managed to say that, too, without ever glancing my way. "So there you have it. Are you satisfied?"

Sitting back in my chair, I tried to decide whether I was or not. I had my answer. I just didn't feel like I had any closure.

"Don't you love him at all?" Julianna spoke up again, and this time she sounded really annoyed. "He's your son. He can't help whom he looks like or who his father is. How can you treat him this way?"

Mom didn't reply.

Julianna didn't back down. "Do you hate him?"

"Yes. Sometimes, I think I do." My mom's answer hung in the air like a foul stench. "Does that surprise you?"

Julianna did seem shocked; I'm sure we both did. I hadn't expected my mom to be so forthcoming. And while hearing that hurt me like you wouldn't believe, it also made me feel strangely calm. It gave me the closure I wanted, even if it sucked. She was a scorned woman. And she was determined to stay scorned and angry. I couldn't change that.

"No, it doesn't surprise me," I answered as I stood up. Julianna stood with me and clung to my arm as though she were afraid my mom might attack her. "I'll let you continue living here. Consider this house and everything in it yours. But I don't think your presence at our family estate is a good idea. You're not the sort of grandmother figure I'd want to subject my future children to. I trust you understand."

Honestly, I didn't care if she did. If she ever had a change of heart, maybe we could revisit the idea of letting her come back. But until then, she could stay here and stew in her bitterness.

"Goodbye, mom." I bowed formally, and then I took my fiancée's hand and left.

That was it. It was done. As I walked out of the chateau, I felt renewed. It was as though a weight had been lifted off my shoulders and I could breathe easily for the first time in my life.

Julianna, however, was still visibly tense. Her brow was furrowed and her eyes were fixed on the ground ahead of us as we walked hand in hand. I didn't know what she was thinking, and it made me nervous about how she was going to react to all this. I waited for her to speak first, though.

She stayed silent until we were alone inside our carriage, headed back to my family estate. "Are you all right?"

I grinned at her. "Never been better, actually."

Julianna's eyes widened. She probably thought I was off my rocker. "But Felix, she just said—"

"She told me the truth. For us, that's a first." I shrugged. "I guess I've always known she didn't love me. I just needed to hear her say it."

"Well, I'd still like to smack her. Someone should." I felt her squeeze my hand. "What if she tells everyone else?"

I squeezed hers back gently. "She won't. And even if she does, it doesn't matter now."

"What do you mean? If you aren't the duke's real son, then couldn't someone try to take away your title and inheritance?"

I smirked and waggled an eyebrow at her. "Why? Worried you're about to marry a regular old poor guy?"

Julianna shot me a dirty look. "That's an awful thing to say. You know I don't care about your money. I just don't want to see you get hurt again. What if she tries to publically humiliate you? I don't think I could refrain from wringing her neck."

I laughed. I couldn't imagine Julianna wringing anyone's neck. Except for mine, maybe. "Don't worry, Jules. Everything will be fine. When Duke Farrow signed over the estate to me, I became his chosen, rightful heir the second he put his seal on it. Who my father is doesn't have any effect on that. For better or worse, Farrow Estate is stuck with me."

She still didn't seem altogether satisfied. "And what about your real father, Darion Prax? Are you going to speak with him? Does he know who you are or even that you exist?"

Leaning over, I planted a kiss on her cheek. It made her blush. "Yeah, he does. We didn't exactly part on good terms the last time we spoke, though. I suppose I'll have to find him and apologize."

"Please do. I'd like for you to have a decent relationship with at least one of your parents. Otherwise holidays are going to be so lonely." Julianna put her head on my shoulder and out a small sigh. "Is it true what she said? Are you really a lot like him?"

"I'm not sure. I don't know him that well personally. People say we look alike, though."

I could hear a smile in her voice. "I can't wait to meet him."

The king still hadn't mobilized his grand attack on Luntharda. Word in the court was that he was having a hard time gathering enough of his forces to accomplish it. So I wasn't concerned about finding Prax. As far as I knew, he had no life outside of being a dragonrider. Actually getting up the nerve to talk to him? That was going to be a lot harder.

I must have looked just as nervous as I felt, because while I checked over my saddle, Julianna hovered right over me. When I kissed her goodbye, she squeezed me extra hard.

"Are you sure you don't want me to go with you?" she asked, as she fretfully straightened the buckle of my cloak.

"I'll be fine," I assured her. "It's just for a day. I'll be back tomorrow night."

She put on an unconvincing smile and stood on her toes to kiss my cheek. "All right, then. Just please be safe."

I had plenty of time in the air to think about what I was going to say. And yet when I touched down in Northwatch and set my eyes upon the citadel, everything got scrambled around in my brain. I didn't know how Prax would receive me or if he'd even want to talk to me at all. Our last meeting hadn't gone well—and that was putting it mildly. His last words to me still burned in my mind.

"You have disappointed me."

That hurt. It hurt a lot more now that I knew he was my dad. I'd never made anyone proud in my life—although it was sort of an intentional effort on my part. The duke, who'd raised me like his own because he didn't know better, had been unhappy with my behavior as a child, and the way I fought him tooth and nail over every little thing. I hadn't done much to deserve his good opinion. And my mother …

I put Nova up in the stable of one of the higher-end inns on the outskirts of the city, and then started for the citadel. On my way, I bumped into another member of Emerald Flight, standing on the corner just outside the Laughing Fox Tavern. He waved at me, and I strolled over to shake his hand.

"You look good," he said with a laugh. "Not at all how Prax described you. He made it sound like you were determined to drink yourself to death."

I tried not to let that faze me. "What can I say? I gave it my best shot. Speaking of Prax, do you know where he is?"

My former comrade pointed a thumb back in the direction of the Laughing Fox. "We all took the week off while we're waiting for rally orders. Most of the men went home for a few days. But you know Prax—he's got no one to go home to."

Well, that was about to change.

I thanked him and left, heading straight for the tavern. I hadn't been there in months. It felt strange to walk through those doors again. I spotted a few familiar faces around the dimly lit room.

And there, sitting by himself at the end of a long table, I saw my dad.

Prax was hunched over with his elbows resting on the tabletop. The light from the hearth put heavy shadows over his face, outlining every wrinkle and crease. It made him seem older and much more somber, as though he were lost in miserable memories.

I walked across the dining room, weaving around the tables until I was standing right beside him. "Hey, Dad."

He looked up in surprise. I saw him search me, examining every detail of my clothes and demeanor as though he were looking for evidence that I was still a wreck. Then he gave a small, almost bemused smile.

"I take it this means I was right," he said. "Maria finally admitted it?"

I spread my hands out wide and shrugged. "Yep. It's a boy. Sorry I didn't bring you any flowers."

Prax chuckled and nodded to the chair across from him, gesturing for me to take a seat. Things got awkward the second I settled in, though.

Neither of us seemed to be able to find a good place to start. We weren't even making eye contact, though whenever he wasn't looking at me, I took the opportunity to study his face. The face of my father— a face I supposedly shared.

By the time I came up with something semi-intelligent to say, Prax spoke up first. "I want you to know that I'm sorry, Felix."

I tensed. "Yeah. Me too. For a lot of stuff."

"You're not a disappointment to me," he continued like he hadn't even heard me. "And I should have been there for you when you were a child. As soon as I heard Maria had given birth, I was suspicious that you might be mine. The timing was too convenient to ignore. But you had a family and a father figure who I reasoned was much more stable than I would ever be. I had no evidence that you really were mine, and no desire to upset your life … or Maria's. Now I see I was wrong. I should have gone to Maria right away and insisted she tell me the truth. I'll never forgive myself for that. I've missed a lot. Now you're a grown adult and we might as well be perfect strangers."

He reached across the table and grabbed my hand. He gripped it hard as he stared directly into my eyes. "But I want you to know I am proud of you and the man you've become. You are my son. And I love you."

Suddenly, it was painful to swallow. I couldn't shrug this off or act like it wasn't a big deal to hear him say that. It meant absolutely everything to me.

"It's not all your fault." My voice was hoarse and broken. "I need to apologize, too, for everything I said before. For acting like a moron. And for leaving the ranks like that."

He let go of my hand and waved off my apology like he was dismissing the whole issue. "Don't worry about it. You have an estate to look after. And a young bride, too, I hear. I would never fault you for putting those priorities first."

If only my motives in leaving had been that pure. "We both want you to come to the wedding. Do you think you can manage it?"

He laughed that loud, booming laugh that filled the entire room. "You really think I'd miss my only son getting married?"

"Well, I told her I wasn't sure since we won't be serving any alcohol." I smirked. "I'm trying to keep this new leaf turned over."

Prax nodded like he understood. "Change is never easy, boy. If it were, most people wouldn't be so terrified of it. But the beautiful thing about it is that once the uncomfortable part is over, we get a chance to start again—fresh and unbound by the mistakes we made before."

"I've made a lot of them lately," I admitted. "And it almost cost me everything I've ever loved."

"Well, you seem to be better off now. At least you've bathed. That's an improvement over the last time I saw you." He winked, and we both had another good laugh.

Things got easier and much less awkward then. We talked for hours about absolutely nothing, but I needed that nothing more than anything. He wanted to hear about my life, and I wanted to know about his, as well. After telling him about my childhood, I asked how he'd wound up in a dragonrider's saddle. I saw his demeanor begin to change.

"I did it for Maria," he said quietly.

That was the exact opposite story I'd gotten from my mom, who insisted he'd abandoned her for the dragonriders' ranks. "What do you mean?"

"I asked her father for her hand, but he turned me away. He said I didn't make a good enough living to deserve her. We could have eloped, I suppose. She probably would have jumped at the idea. But your mother was a respectable girl from a good family. I didn't want to disgrace her like that, and I didn't want our life together to start out by driving a wedge between her and her family. So I had to find some other means of employment—some way to make myself worthy of her." He rested his chin in his palm and stared down at the table. "I was too proud to tell her that her father wouldn't give me his blessing. I was embarrassed. And I suppose that's how she got the impression I didn't want to marry her at all."

I sat back in my chair. I was completely blown away by how the whole situation had gotten misconstrued. Mom had taken it entirely the wrong way. She was bitter and filled with hatred over nothing.

"She said she hates me." I blurted without thinking. I guess I just needed him to know that.

Prax's expression was pained, but sympathetic. "It's not you she hates, son. It's me. Don't let her deceive you. I'm not there to face her anger, so she's directing it all at you instead."

"Regardless, I can't have her in my life when she's like this. It upsets Julianna. And frankly, it pisses me off."

"She's going to have to come to terms with what happened," he agreed. "But maybe I can lend a hand with that. It's long past time for her and I to have a talk."

I wasn't so sure. "You really think she'll sit and talk to you?"

"No, not willingly. But I don't intend on giving her a choice. Maria's always tended to be overly dramatic when she doesn't get her way. She was like that even when we were young. Now she's spent all these years taking out her hatred for me on her only child. It's time for both of us to move on with our lives. She can't go on blaming you for my mistakes, and I can't go on hiding here rather than returning to Solhelm and facing her."

I didn't think it would matter to Mom if he tried to reason with her or not. She was basically insane, as far as I could tell. Sitting around and stewing in hate tended to do that to people. But if he wanted to try, that was his business. I wasn't going to try to stop him.

"The wedding is next month. I suppose I can mark you down as attending?" I tried to change the subject. "We set the date for the engagement ball in a few days. I know it's short notice, but do you think you could make it to that, too?"

He smiled. "I'll be there with bells on. Awful quick though, isn't it?"

"Well, it's not like we're strangers. I've known Julianna since we were kids. She used to chase me with strawberries when we were little."

Prax cocked an eyebrow. He clearly didn't get it.

"I'm allergic to them," I clarified. "Anyway, we've technically been engaged for a long time already. I love her and I don't intend on changing my mind. And she's had a good, long while to reconsider it herself."

I decided not to tell him that I had almost lost her. I'd been downright awful to her. Luckily, Jules had a strength and resilience to her that any soldier would admire, even if she happened to be soft and delicate on the outside. It was one of the things I'd always found most beautiful about her.

"It'll be time to have a few tots of your own then, eh?" Prax teased.

I blushed. "L-let's not rush that."

He went on making playful jabs, questioning when he would be made a grandfather, passing the time while the tavern emptied of patrons and the barmaids began wiping down the tables and chairs. They'd be closing soon, but I didn't want this to end.

Prax had gone silent, and appeared lost in the same painful thoughts he'd been stewing in when I found him. His eyes were fixed on the mug of cider in front of him. He'd elected not to drink alcohol either, out of courtesy for me.

"They found the blue dragon," he said suddenly.

All the wind rushed out of me, like someone had punched me in the gut. He didn't have to explain which blue dragon he was talking about—I knew. He meant Jaevid's dragon, Mavrik.

"He never goes far from the edge of that forest. A few men tried to chase him down, but he's too quick. Only Jace's dragon could ever match pace with him. And as far as they could tell, he's still wearing all his saddle and gear. One even told me they saw him on the ground, roaring into the trees like he was calling for someone. Odd behavior for a dragon. Never heard of one acting like that before, even with a bonded rider."

I began to feel nauseous, and yet I hung on his every word. "So what does that mean?"

Prax met my eyes from across the table. I saw the intensity smoldering there. He had a theory, all right. "They never found his body on the battlefield. I, for one, don't believe they ever will because I don't think it's there at all. You told us before you'd seen him do things—strange works of power the likes of which this world had never seen. If that's true, then who's to say he isn't in Luntharda?"

I narrowed my eyes. "Are you calling him a traitor?"

"I never said that," he replied quickly. "But if something happened to Jace, if he was shot down, then you of all people should be able to tell me whether or not you think Jaevid would have gone down after him."

I had to stop and think about that. Yes, I'd been Jae's closest friend. I knew him well enough to make a guess about what he might do … and Prax was right. If Jae had seen Jace go down into the forest, he probably would have headed in after him. He'd done something similar for Sile when he was only a fledgling rider.

Not only that, Jae had mentioned to me once, not long before the battle, that Sile wanted him to go into Luntharda. It had something to do with a ritual—I couldn't quite remember the details. But maybe it was possible …

"So then you're suggesting he's still alive?" I demanded. I was beginning to get my hopes up.

Prax sat back from the table and gave a heavy sigh. "No, of course not. I'm not suggesting anything. Personally, I don't think he's still alive because if there was any way for him to come back to us, with or without Jace, I believe he would have done so by now. I'm saying that if he is as powerful as you believe, as you claim to have seen, then we have to accept that we may never know what really happened to him. There's been a lot of strangeness in the air lately—apart from the animals going madder than ever. Seraph has vanished, which many are taking to be either a sign that the war is finally over … or that something terrible is going to happen."

We were silent again for several minutes. I listened to the sound of the barmaids scratching at the stone floor with their brooms as they swept away the day's dirt and crumbs. My heart was aching. It was as though a heavy weight was settling over my shoulders.

"I miss him," I admitted.

Prax patted my shoulder from across the table. "I wish I could tell you that feeling goes away, son. But it doesn't. The important thing is to try to turn your focus to the living, to the ones who need your love and attention right now. That bride of yours, for instance. She needs you—all of you—and that is what should matter most. Take it from an old, lonely man who's spent a lifetime in the saddle and has nothing to show for it; family should always come first."

ten

I was dreaming.

I had to be; I'd never been in a place like this before in my life. It was cold and dark. The air smelled of a heavy musk, like damp soil. I walked forward slowly with my arms outstretched, feeling around for something. My fingertips brushed against what felt like the cold, moist walls of a cave.

Groping forward through the dark, I couldn't tell which way led up or down. I couldn't see anything and couldn't hear anything, except for my own frantic breathing. Then suddenly, there was a light in the distance. It was only a pale flicker, but it gave me hope and a direction to move in.

The nearer I got to the light, the more I could see of my surroundings. I was standing inside some sort of cavern with a ceiling so high you could have flown a dragon around inside it. It was bizarre. Soft, sterling light seemed to hang in the air without coming from any place in particular. It gave me the creeps.

I didn't feel any better when I noticed what stood in the very center of the chamber. It looked like some sort of altar made of a single slab of white stone. There were bones arranged on top of it, like someone had left an animal there to rot away, alone in the chilly silence.

When I reached the altar, I stretched out a hand to touch the antlers of the skull. They were long, sloping, and beautifully pointed, like they belonged to some species of elk. But the tips must have been sharp as razors, because as soon as I let my hand slide across them, I pricked my finger. It stung. Droplets of my blood peppered the altar and pooled in a place where the stone had a bowl-shaped indentation.

In the blink of an eye, everything went dark. It was as though something had sucked all the light out of the air in one breath. Noises began echoing all around me—the sound of footsteps, snorts of breath, chirps, screeches, and whispers.

I spun around. I could see spots of light winking in the darkness, a thousand eyes, all blinking and watching me. They were everywhere, slithering down from the ceiling and prowling just out of my reach.

A hot blast of breath rustled my hair.

I whirled around again and reached for my sword, but it wasn't there. Too late, I remembered that I'd stopped carrying it. I wasn't a dragonrider anymore.

"Something is coming." A soft voice spoke over the noise of the creatures lurking in the dark. Over my shoulder, I saw a pair of eyes that stood out from the rest. They were shining as brightly as stars.

"W-who's there?" I demanded.

He stepped forward, seeming to part the darkness around him like a curtain. Jaevid stood right in front of me, draped in a long, black cloak that covered everything except his face. His stare was piercing. It cut through me like he was inside my head, searching through my thoughts.

"Jaevid?" I rasped his name, hoping to see some semblance of my friend in that harrowing gaze.

But his expression never changed. "I have to return it," he said. "Everything depends on it."

"Return what? You're not making any sense."

"The stone. The balance must be restored. Otherwise Paligno's curse will ravage this world. All of nature will turn on itself. Everything we know and love will be destroyed."

My view of him was suddenly eclipsed, as something monstrous and scaly crawled by between us. When he reappeared, he was standing much closer. It startled me and I cringed away.

"Go to Mithangol, to my family home. Bring with you only those you can trust completely—those who are willing to fix what has been broken. I will be waiting for you there." He tilted his head back, raising his gaze up to the ceiling.

I looked up, too. Overhead, the ceiling had opened up—or

dissolved away, I really wasn't sure—to reveal the night sky. The moon hung above like a giant, lidless, silver eye.

"Meet me there on the night of the next full moon," he said.

I stared up into the sky, wondering what the heck was going on. And when I looked down again, Jaevid was gone. So were all the creepy shadow animals. I was completely alone, except for those gleaming white bones.

"Jae?" I called for him, turning in circles to search the whole chamber. But he wasn't anywhere to be found.

And then the ground fell out beneath me.

It gave way with a rumbling crack and I fell, down, away from the light, until I landed on the flat of my back on top of a huge pile of round, smooth stones. I clamored back to my feet, squinting up into the single shaft of light that filtered down from above.

That's when I realized they weren't stones under my feet—they were skulls. Human skulls crunched under my boots with every frantic step I took to try and get away. I sank down, and no matter how I fought I couldn't get free.

"*The balance must be restored,*" a whispering voice hissed in my mind, just as the sea of skulls swallowed me completely.

I wasn't sure how to tell Julianna what I had seen in my dream, or even if I should. I didn't know what to make of it, myself. Was it real? Had Jaevid actually been trying to contact me? Or was I just riding the emotional backslide from talking about him with Prax?

Sitting at the breakfast table across from her, I couldn't follow a word she said to me. She was going on about something wedding related. Colors of flowers, maybe. All I did was stare down into my teacup and twirl my spoon across my knuckles over and over again. My other hand was fidgeting underneath the table.

"Felix?"

I glanced up quickly when I heard my name. "Yes?"

"Is everything okay?" She was obviously concerned. Her soft eyes were brimming with worry.

I could lie to a lot of people and get away with it, but Jules knew me better than my own parents. I couldn't slip anything past her, so I didn't even bother trying. "I'm not sure."

She immediately shut the thick book where she'd been jotting down all our wedding plans and pushed it away. "Talk to me, then."

So I did. I told her about what Prax had said about Mavrik and that Jaevid's body still hadn't been recovered. Then I described my dream. When I was finished, I fixed my gaze back down into my teacup and chewed on the inside of my cheek.

"The next full moon is only a few days away, Felix." Her voice was quiet and thoughtful. "It's the night after our engagement ball. Remember? We moved the date so the two wouldn't coincide. It's bad luck."

I nodded. "I know."

Julianna sat quietly for a moment. I didn't dare look up to see the expression on her face. How could I go? No, I shouldn't. It was just a dream, nonsense, nothing more.

A small paper swan appeared next to my teacup along with Julianna's hand. The sight of it made me smile involuntarily.

"You have to go," she said suddenly.

"What?"

She was sitting up straight with a gentle, but stern look fixed on me. "If you don't, you'll always wonder. You need to go. It's the only way to be sure it wasn't anything more than a nightmare."

I picked up her paper swan and marveled at its clean creases. She'd made them all the time when we were kids. It was her favorite prank to leave them hidden around the estate in our favorite playtime places for me to find.

"What about our wedding plans?" I asked.

Julianna shook her head. "They can wait. Besides, you'll just keep agreeing to anything I choose, right?"

"I don't want you to think I'm putting this ahead of you," I muttered uncomfortably. "Our wedding is more important."

She smiled as she put her hand on top of mine to stop me from fidgeting with the swan. "You're a sweet man, you know, but sometimes you say really stupid things. You don't have to lie just to make me feel better. I know how much Jaevid meant to you. And I know you won't be satisfied until you know the truth. So go, please?"

I felt guilty because she was right. I wanted to go. I wasn't going to be able to think about anything else until I knew what that dream meant—if it even meant anything at all. Taking her hand, I felt myself begin to relax as she wound her fingers gently through mine.

"You sure you'll be okay here without me?"

Julianna rolled her eyes and gave me a teasing smirk. "Come on, Felix. How long have I gone without you before now? Besides, I've still got to pay a visit to my parents and explain what's happened. The last I spoke to them, I had just told them I was planning on breaking our engagement."

I groaned and slumped in my chair. "I should be the one telling them that. I'm sure they've wondered what the heck was wrong with me all these years."

She giggled, and made that cute expression where she nibbled on her bottom lip. I loved it when she did that. I think she must have known, because when our eyes met, she winked at me. "They're just going to be happy that everything is better now. So don't worry about a thing."

"Pfft. Right."

"You mentioned Jaevid told you to bring only people you could trust," she said, obviously trying to change the subject. "Who will you ask?"

The thought hadn't even crossed my mind. I'd been so caught up in trying to decide whether or not to go, I hadn't even considered taking anyone with me.

"Prax, I guess," I answered. "He's the only one who might actually believe I'm not out of my mind. I suppose I should write to him about it. Maybe he can convince a few of the others from Emerald Flight to come with him."

"And you trust those men?" Jules didn't seem so sure that was a good idea.

"They all knew Jaevid. The blood we shed in battle made us brothers. I trusted them with my life then, I see no reason not to now. There might even be a few other riders from our little excursion during our avian year who haven't forgotten what Jae did on that island."

"But do you trust them now?" she repeated earnestly.

I couldn't answer. It was a difficult question—one I was going to have to think about.

Julianna seemed unsettled as she sat across the table from me, still holding my hand. It looked like there was something else she wanted to say—something she wasn't sure she should.

"What is it?" I probed.

She dodged my stare. "What do you suppose he really was? Or still is, if that's the case."

"Who?"

"Jaevid. I mean, after everything you've told me about him … do you really think he's just a normal person?"

I didn't know what to think about Jae. I never had. Every time I thought I'd seen his last trick, he came out with some new, magical secret that saved our butts just in time. That was why I couldn't discount this dream as just a fiction of my twisted, stressed out imagination.

"He was my friend and that's really all that matters to me," I decided.

Julianna nodded. "Just be careful. My mother used to tell me stories. Old tales about the ancient gods who could shake the foundations of the earth until the mountains coughed fire, spin storms in the skies, and make oceans swell until they swallowed up the dry land. Those stories used to make me feel so terribly small and helpless. And when I hear you talk about what Jaevid could do, I get that same feeling."

I gave her hand a reassuring squeeze. "Trust me, Jules. Jae may have some strange powers, but he is definitely not some ancient god. I've never heard of a god who sucked at hand-to-hand combat as badly as he did."

"Someone told me he beat you once," she countered.

"That is such a load of crock. I let him win that match! Who told you about that? Was it Fredrick? That soft-handed little weasel always had it in for me. Next time I see him I'll …"

Julianna started laughing. I realized she'd just been baiting me into getting riled up over nothing. Crap. She'd really gotten me good that time.

I blushed and tried unsuccessfully to sulk.

Then she spoke again. "Just promise me one thing." Her voice became quiet and she sounded worried. "One way or another, swear you'll come back home."

I didn't know where all this insecurity was coming from. Maybe because I'd mentioned the skulls in my dream? "Jules, nothing's going to happen to—"

"You don't know that," she said. "So just promise me. I know better than to ask you not to do something dangerous. So instead, I'm just asking that you survive it. Please."

I guess I already knew that whatever might be waiting for me in Mithangol was probably dangerous. It usually was with Jae. But what could I say to that? If I was required to make the ultimate sacrifice, would I go through with it? It would mean leaving her alone, burdened with my family estate and—worst of all—my mother.

I shuddered. No, I couldn't do that to the woman I loved. Prax was right; I had to start thinking about more than just myself. Julianna depended on me now. After such a long time of being the biggest disappointment a fiancée could ever be, I wasn't about to repeat my mistakes as her husband.

I nodded and agreed, "I promise, Jules. I'll come back."

eleven

"I'm not asking you to do anything," I said, after I finished explaining everything to Prax. He'd come in a day early for our engagement party, at my request, just so I could have this little chat with him.

And in all honesty, I had absolutely no idea how he was going to react.

My story was bizarre. It sounded insane even to me. Dreams about ancient caverns and mountains of skulls? Just thinking of it made me shudder.

Sitting across from me in the privacy of my office, I could practically see the wheels turning behind his eyes as he studied me for several long, uncomfortable seconds. At last, he let out a heavy sigh and scratched anxiously at his chin.

"And you believe this was his way of trying to contact you?" He didn't sound convinced.

"I don't know what to believe. That's exactly why I'm going."

"Felix, I understand wanting to believe your friend is still alive. Truly, I do. And please hear me when I say that it was never my intention to give you any form of false hope about Jaevid's fate," he began to explain.

I cut him off, standing up from behind my desk. "No offense, but this had nothing to do with you. I've never understood why Jae could do the things he did. I may never understand. But I believe in him and if he needs me, I'm going to be there, sword in hand, ready to fight at his side until the bitter end. We are dragonriders—that's what we do."

Prax's expression was complex, a mix of confusion and concern. I guessed he was thinking I'd finally lost whatever marbles I still had rattling around between my ears.

And then he laughed. He laughed himself to the verge of tears and sat back, slapping his knee and trying to collect himself enough to speak.

I assumed he was making fun of me.

"I'm sorry, boy," he managed to rasp. "It's just that—Gods and Fates—I wish I could claim that courage and determination came from my side of your blood. But that was a speech straight out of your mother's mouth. When she was younger, she had that same fire in her blood. Seems there's more of her in you than she'd ever let anyone believe."

I stood a little straighter when he got to his feet.

"You're mad, of course. But it's good. Very good." He gave me a proud smile. "So give me the order."

"The order?"

His eyes glinted with mischief. "I can't just up and leave Northwatch of my own accord without being marked a deserter. You asked me to come here for your engagement ball, Your Grace, and of course I'm pleased to oblige. So if you'd like anything else from me, you're going to have to give me a direct order."

I hesitated, then stumbled over the words. "R-right. Lieutenant Prax, I request that you, and as many men from Emerald Flight as you deem worthy, accompany me to Mithangol."

"As you wish, Duke Farrow." Prax smirked and nodded approvingly. He stepped closer and began roughly adjusting the collar of my tunic and straightening the buckle on my formal cloak. "And let's just be clear—am I to tell them what you told me?"

"No," I answered quickly. "Just tell them to come and be ready. I hope I'm wrong, but we may be in for a fight."

He opened his mouth to add something, but Miss Harriet came flying into the office. She was flushed and her hair was wild.

"Master Felix, the king has just arrived!" She came at me armed with a golden collar that she draped over my shoulders before she started fussing with my hair.

"What?" I was stunned. Of course I'd sent him an invitation. It was a social obligation for someone of my standing, but I'd never expected him to show up.

"Yes! His carriage just pulled onto the drive. He brought his elite guard, thirty soldiers, and four dragonriders. No one has ever seen such a procession. They say he's brought an entire wagon filled with gifts."

I couldn't have cared less about the gifts. As if I didn't have enough stuff already. But I was having trouble understanding why he'd come and brought so many guards with him. It was beyond excessive. This wasn't a dangerous place. I had my own guards stationed around the house, watching the perimeter, and I knew every one of them was capable.

"Very good. You're dismissed." I shooed her away from trying to wipe smudges off my face with her thumb. She looked like she might faint with nervous excitement. I hoped Julianna was faring better.

As soon as she was gone, Prax and I exchanged a meaningful look. I knew we both had to be thinking the same thing.

"Sounds like he's brought a small army," Prax observed with a careful tone. He knew better than to speak out of turn—not that I would have cared.

I was already making a break for the door. "And to my doorstep, no less. How much you want to bet they aren't here just to dance and eat the free food?"

Prax fell in step beside me as I left my private chambers. His hand rested anxiously on the pommel of his sword. "I'm not a betting man, but even I like those odds."

We almost made it to the foyer when Miss Harriet caught up to me again. She seized me by the arm and practically dragged me into a parlor near the ballroom where all my guests were gathering. She went on about how it was nearly time and that I had to stay out of sight until the right moment. Julianna had gone to a lot of trouble planning everything. Blah, blah blah.

Prax just laughed and swaggered away to join the rest of the party. He didn't look very sorry for me at all. The big jerk.

I sat alone in the darkened parlor, listening to the noise of the gathering crowd and the swell of beautiful music. My mind was racing over everything—the wedding, the king and all his guards camping out on my lawn, and Jaevid. Things were getting more complicated by the second. And if there's anything I'd learned about myself it was that I don't handle complicated very well.

"Master Felix?" Miss Harriet appeared in the doorway, speaking softly as if she were afraid of disturbing me. "Are you ready?"

I snapped to my feet. "Always."

She led me back out into the hall. The sound of the crowd was louder, echoing off the ceilings. Two of my servants in their finest uniforms stood ready to open the doors to the largest ballroom.

And then I saw her.

Julianna was waiting for me. The soft light of the chandeliers made her hair shine and her fair skin glow. Her smile stopped me dead in my tracks. I'd seen her wear fancy ball gowns before, in all styles and colors, but I had never seen her look this beautiful.

I tried to tell her that when I finally got the courage to approach her. But like a total moron, I choked on everything I tried to say.

She smiled wider and threw her arms around my neck. I hugged her tightly, picked her up, and twirled her around. Girls like that kind of thing.

Behind us, I heard Miss Harriet sniffling.

"Are you sure about this?" Julianna whispered. "This is your last chance to escape, you know."

I slipped one of her gloved hands around my arm. "Tempting. But I think I'll pass."

One of the servants waiting to open the doors cleared his throat, so I gave him the signal. It was time. The doors opened before us and golden light spilled out. Julianna squeezed my arm nervously.

Good. At least I wasn't the only one.

After midnight, the party was in full swing and there were no signs of it slowing anytime soon. Couples continued twirling away on the dance floor, filling the ballroom with laughter and conversation. There was still plenty of food, and even though we weren't serving any wine or ale, everyone seemed to be in good spirits. I couldn't remember the last time I'd felt so relaxed and comfortable in a setting like this. It was a much different feel than the parties I'd thrown myself. This had Julianna's delicate fingerprints all over it. It was formal, refined, but comfortable—just like her. She looked happy, too. Happier than I'd seen her in a long time. That alone was enough for me to have a good time.

Besides the king, nobles and gentry had come from all over the kingdom. Everyone, of course, except my mother. I have to admit, I did look for her. I sort of expected she might show up, sour-faced, and skulk around like an old crow ready to badmouth me to anyone who might listen. But she didn't. For whatever reason, that disappointed me. I suppose as much as I wanted to believe I was completely done with her and it didn't matter what she said or how she treated me—none of that was true. I'd never be able to break the emotional tether that bound us together. Like it or not, she'd always be my mother. I'd always want her affection and approval.

The nobles that had come to wish us well on our marriage brought stories and rumors with them, some that I wished I hadn't heard. As much as Julianna tried diligently to change the subject, steering it away from those grim details, it just couldn't be done.

"Six hundred head of my finest cattle had to be butchered," Count Davron complained. "All because a few of them started showing symptoms of the madness. Such a waste."

"Well, didn't you hear? Baron Wingate's own hounds turned on his youngest boy. The poor dear is doomed to lose his arm, they say," another gentlewoman said in a hushed voice.

Julianna's face began to look pasty. "And they still can't find what's causing all this?"

"It must be the work of the elves. That's what everyone believes. How else can it be explained? It smacks of dark magic and witchery."

The Count's wife muttered from behind her feathered fan. "The king himself has declared it a national emergency. Just think of what would happen if the dragons took ill."

I saw Julianna take a deep breath, as though trying to steady herself. Definitely time for a distraction.

I slipped a hand around her waist and pulled her away towards the dance floor. "Come on. I haven't had enough of you just yet." My diversion didn't seem to convince her, though. She knew me too well.

As soon as we were alone, dancing to a slow waltz, she hit me with the full force of those worried, but lovely eyes. "Is that true? Could the dragons turn, too?"

"Dragons are smarter than cows and dogs, Jules," I assured her. "You really think Nova would try to hurt me?"

She didn't answer, but the troubled furrow in her brow told me she wasn't so sure.

Frankly, neither was I. I couldn't shake the feeling that something was about to happen—maybe something to do with the dream Jaevid had …

I stopped myself there. I couldn't let myself get caught up in that, not yet, not until I had some facts. I didn't know if my dream was real or not, but most importantly, I didn't know if Jae was alive.

"What is it?" Julianna was staring up at me pleadingly.

I almost didn't tell her, but then I thought better of it. "There was this time, when we were in training as dragonriders, I asked Jae to talk to Nova. When he did, he said that she was afraid; that she and the other dragons could tell something was coming—

something bad. I just wonder if this is what he meant."

She squeezed my hand tightly. "Felix, if the dragons turn … if they catch this madness."

"I know," I said. "There won't be anything we can do to stop them."

We finished our dance without saying another word, both of us imagining the horrors of what might be coming. The waltz ended and I escorted her to get a drink.

We never made it to the punch bowl.

One of the king's elite guards, wearing that eerie, expressionless, white mask over his face, stepped into our path. He bowed and gestured to the open doorway that led out into the candlelit gardens behind my estate.

"His majesty requests a private audience with you, my lord." His voice sounded young, but it was muffled behind the mask's thin mouth hole. Something about it was strangely familiar. "May I offer myself as a substitute escort for the lady until you return?"

Julianna was looking him over like she was trying to decide if she should run or not. The masks freaked her out—or so she'd told me. I had to agree with her. And after that encounter with the Lord General, I didn't trust any of them as far as I could throw them.

But what choice did I have? You didn't say no to the king.

"Right," I answered stiffly, and passed Julianna's hand over to him. "See that you take good care of her."

The guard bowed again, much lower this time, and Jules shot me a dirty look over her shoulder. Crap. I was definitely gonna hear about this later. I'd just have to make it quick.

I found the king standing alone before the burial site I'd erected for Jae. He looked small and fragile, hunched over a bejeweled cane as he eyed the large statue through the holes in his golden mask. He'd come dressed for the party, although I'd yet to see him talk to anyone. Come to think of it, I hadn't even seen him come inside.

"I hear you brought quite the entourage with you." I spoke loudly, giving away my approach as I went to stand next to him. "I didn't realize engagement parties warranted that kind of security."

"One can never be too careful," he rasped, not taking his gaze away from the statue.

"Were you expecting to meet an enemy here?" I decided to press my luck by not letting the subject drop without an answer.

He wobbled some as he turned to face me. "I wasn't sure who I would meet, based on what I've heard about your recent struggles. They say you went mad."

I stiffened. "Never mad enough to try assaulting a king."

He chuckled, which was an uncomfortably thin, dry sound. "Fair enough."

"You'll have to pardon my rudeness, but I have a bride waiting on my return. I was told there was something you wanted to talk to me about?"

He wasn't in a hurry to get on with it, which was beyond frustrating. I watched him sigh, nod his head a few times, and turn back to face the statue of Jae and Mavrik looming before us. "Do you know why no one speaks my name anymore?"

"No, your majesty."

"It was at my own request. All those years ago, as I buried what remained of my family—my progeny—I asked that no one in the kingdom ever speak my name again, because I buried myself with them that day. I had to, you see, in order to become someone terrible enough to carry out the vengeance they deserved."

I swallowed uncomfortably. "I see."

"I believe we must all do that, in some form, in order to be reborn. Names have unimaginable power—not just for the person bearing them. Just think of what power your own name, Duke Farrow, possesses now. It garners respect, fear, and admiration from your subordinates." He stopped there and peered at me through the holes in his golden mask. "What does the name Lord General mean to you?"

My heart took a swan dive into the pit of my stomach. Gods … did he know about what happened fledgling year? My mind raced, and in a matter of seconds I decided to play as dumb as I could. "I know you've yet to name a successor to the one that met with an unfortunate death a few years ago."

"Yes. I take the name of Lord General especially seriously. Such a person would be my right hand. It would have to be someone I felt I could trust unconditionally to be faithful to my every command. Someone who has sworn himself to me completely. Only then would they be granted all the power that name warrants," he said. "Surely you can see why it would take me some time to find an appropriate replacement."

"Of course." I dared to take a breath and let myself relax again.

"To be my right hand would give you power you cannot imagine. There would not be a single door in this kingdom that would not open for you. Nothing would be beyond your reach. Command of every dragonrider in my service would be yours."

"The way you're talking," I interrupted. "It almost sounds as though you're offering me the job."

"And if I was?"

His words hung in the air between us. Me become the next Lord General? The offer was tempting. Beyond tempting, really. Even if I hadn't given up the saddle, thinking of what it would be like to lead—to achieve the highest rank a dragonrider could ever have in his lifetime ... It had me star-struck for a moment.

"Of course, this would only be possible if you were to swear yourself to me eternally," he added. "It would be an oath far more significant than the one that put you in my service previously. But the rewards would be great. You would be privy to the ancient secrets of magic known only to royalty—knowledge I've never entrusted to anyone else."

"And that's all I have to do? Promise myself to you?" It sounded too good to be true.

"Yes. There would be a certain ritual, of course, to make sure that you kept your word. But since I have no doubt that a man like you would stand by his word until death, it would be purely a formality." His voice sounded different, as if he were smiling behind that mask. "What do you say, Duke Farrow? Are you the dragonrider destined for the title of Lord General?"

PART TWO

JAEVID

twelve

It's not an easy thing to do—asking people to betray their kingdom, put their lives and the safety of their families at stake, and murder the man they call king. So I wasn't surprised when I didn't get a standing ovation at the end of my long explanation as to why we had to do it. Everyone was gathered around me, mute and wide-eyed, in the light from the kitchen hearth in my home in Mithangol. One-by-one, they began drifting away without a word. At last, the only people left sitting beside me at the kitchen table were Kiran, Beckah, her father Sile, and Felix.

It was going to take some time for this news to sink in. It's not every day you learn that your king is actually a traitorous, murdering imposter who's been waging a genocidal war based on nothing but jealousy and bitterness. Unfortunately, time was not something we had a lot of.

"So that's why he always wears a mask," Beckah whispered, thinking aloud. "To hide the fact that he isn't human at all."

"It's to hide much more than that," I replied. "But yes, I suppose that's true as well."

"None of this makes any sense, Jae." Felix was shaking his head. "I want to believe you. I really do. But do you seriously want us to believe you're the embodiment of this pagan elf god?"

I sat back in my chair and let my hands drop into my lap. If only it was that simple. "I never said that. Paligno chose me to act in his place. That's the reason I have these abilities—the only reason I've ever been able to do these things. He's given me power and authority over the creatures of the earth with the understanding that I am to carry out his will."

"And now he's commanded you to kill the King of Maldobar?" Felix sounded more skeptical with each passing minute.

I frowned down at the tabletop. "He's asked me to restore the balance to nature—to put the stone back in its proper resting place. If you think you know a way to get Hovrid to surrender it peacefully, then by all means share it."

"There is no other way," Sile said suddenly.

Everyone looked at him. Even I was surprised.

"He can't be reasoned or bargained with. Either we do this, or we stand by and watch him wipe out all that remains of the gray elf race while Paligno's curse continues to spread and ravage this world and destroy everyone else left in it." Sile fixed me with a grim stare.

"I've spent a lot of time looking for some other means to put an end to this. Hovrid himself has tried to appease and manipulate the stone by using blood sacrifices. There is no alternative, either Hovrid dies or we all do. It's that simple."

A stifling silence settled over us. I didn't know what else to say to them. I couldn't do this without their help, and yet nearly everyone had wandered off without any indication as to whether or not they believed a word I'd said. Not even my half-brother, Roland, had hung around to ask any follow-up questions.

"You look tired. You know, some of us came a very long way to see you. I'm sure we could all do with a night's sleep to clear our thoughts." Under the table, Beckah took my hand. She must have been able to tell I was fighting that sinking feeling of failure. If she'd only known it was so much more than that.

I nodded. Next to me, Felix puffed a loud, exhausted sigh. Sile still looked deeply aggravated as he got up, rubbing the back of his neck, and headed for the stairs.

I watched him go and silently marveled at everything he'd seen and done. I believed I knew the majority of it now. He'd spent a large portion of his life trying to clean up the mess my father had made when he stole the god stone from the gray elves. So much of his sweat, blood, and time that could have been spent with his family had been invested in one thing—one chance at atonement for Ulric's mistake.

And I was that chance.

In some respects, I imagined that had been fairly disappointing for him. Especially when we first met, before I'd hit the gray elf version of puberty and started looking less like a sickly, child-sized skeleton. I wondered if he'd questioned his own sanity when he volunteered to take me on as my sponsor and instructor. Any other sane person would have.

It wasn't until that moment that I realized there was a lot more furniture in my house than there had been when I left. Rather, I'd left it nearly bare because Ulric and my stepmother had all but pried up the floorboards and took them along with them when they moved out. Now there were pictures on the freshly painted walls, parlor chairs perched near the fire, wool rugs on the floor, and new curtains on the windows.

Beckah had a knowing grin on her lips, like she'd been waiting for me to notice. "Well, you did say my parents could move in here if things got complicated. After your funeral, when we all thought you'd died, we moved here in secret."

"It looks good with a woman's touch," I said. "I'm not much of a decorator."

"My mother said it was the cleanest house she'd ever been in." Beckah giggled and nudged my shoulder with hers. "I told her about all the furniture you made. Now she's determined to pay you to make a crib for the baby."

I smiled. "I suppose when this is all over I could give it a try. I won't have her paying me for it, though."

"Well, you know, after this is over, you might find occasion to make lots of cribs," she mumbled and avoided my eyes. I could have sworn her cheeks looked a little red.

I started blushing, too.

"I think I might puke." Across the table, Felix smirked from ear to ear. "A whole flock of pointy-eared lady dragonriders running around. Just what we need."

I blushed harder. I'd forgotten he was still sitting there.

"Oh shut up. You're the one getting married in a month. To the girl you've been bullying all your life, no less. I'm tempted to ask if you held her down and threatened to spit in her eye if she didn't say yes." Beckah fired right back without hesitation.

"Wait, you're getting married?" I couldn't believe it. It had to be a joke. "To who?"

Beckah batted her eyes sarcastically in Felix's direction. "Julianna Lacroix."

My jaw dropped. "Wait—*that* Julianna? From the officer's ball?"

Felix's ears were beginning to turn red. "Yeah, yeah. Let's not make a big deal of it, okay?"

A big deal? Last time I'd checked, he absolutely hated Julianna. She was the only girl he'd ever taken special care to warn everyone away from. He'd almost single-handedly made sure no one would dance with her at any ball.

"You really think I'm just going to drop it after everything you—"

Beckah cut me off, "Oh, Jae, he's been holding out on you. He's been engaged to her for years. Since they were children, even."

Now Felix's whole head was red. He looked like a beet wearing a shaggy blonde wig. "I'm going to bed," he grumbled as he stormed away from the table.

"Humans," Kiran muttered under his breath. He didn't look amused.

"I should go help get the beds ready," Beckah announced, as she stood up as well. "It's going to be close quarters, housing so many. We'll have to put pallets out on the floor. My parents want you to have your room back, though."

I tugged at her wrist to stop her. "No, please tell them to keep it."

"Are you sure?"

"Yes. I don't sleep much these days, anyway."

Kiran cast me a meaningful look. "Paligno has a lot to say?"

"Always. Seems like my loyalty is in question—as though he's afraid I'll lose my nerve." It was strange to talk about my dreams so openly. I'd never been able to do that before. Not without worrying that people would think I was out of my mind.

Beckah brushed her fingers over my cheek. "You'll do what's right. You always do. Even when the courage of everyone around you is failing."

Across the table, Kiran cleared his throat noisily. Now he was the one grinning tauntingly at me. But before he could make a snide comment of his own, Beckah seized one of his pointed ears and pulled him to his feet.

"You best keep your thoughts to yourself," she warned him,

wagging a finger in his face. "I am not a woman to be crossed. Human or elf—it makes no difference to me. Now come, we need help making the beds."

Kiran dragged his feet as he followed her, grumbling complaints in the elven language under his breath. It made me smile. That is, until I realized I was now alone at the table.

I sat for a long time, listening to the strange, new sounds in my house. The fire in the kitchen and living room hearths crackled. Roland had disappeared upstairs, and I could hear Sile's wife barking orders on the proper way to make the pallets on the floor for everyone to sleep on. She was giving Sile and my older half-brother a hard time if they didn't make them to her satisfaction. Now and again I heard her baby let out an excited shriek or coo. Beckah laughed. Kiran argued in elvish. Quarters were going to be cramped, and I got the impression there weren't enough blankets.

But these were happy, warm, comforting sounds—sounds that hadn't echoed through this house maybe ever. Certainly not when I'd lived here with Ulric and his family.

For some reason, I just couldn't bear to listen. I felt bitter, frustrated, and estranged as I walked to the front door. My heart was heavy in my chest. I needed some space and a little time to sort things out before I tried to sleep myself.

Prax, Felix, and the other members of Emerald Flight were gathered on the porch, talking amongst themselves in low voices. A few of them were smoking long pipes, blowing smoke rings into the chilly night air. They all went silent and began watching me anxiously when I walked past.

"Everything all right?" Felix called out as I started out across the lawn. He sounded concerned.

"Fine. I just need to think." I tried to sound casual.

He still looked uncertain when I turned away, leaving him standing amidst our dragonrider comrades. But he didn't follow.

I walked without realizing where I was going. It wasn't until I found myself climbing the ladder to my old room in the loft above Ulric's abandoned workshop, that I even bothered to notice my surroundings. Up there, in that drafty place, I blew the dust off my childhood memories. Everything was just as I'd left it. Moonlight filtered through the gaps in the warped boards, casting strangely-shaped shadows on the floor.

I sat down beneath the window where I'd peeked out at Sile when I was just a kid. That same year, I was chosen by Mavrik. I became a fledgling dragonrider, and my life took a drastic turn in a direction I never would have expected.

It felt so far away now, a distant memory. I'd cowered here in this room, filled with so much fear and uncertainty. Now I sat in the same spot, as a man, warrior, and dragonrider, with those same feelings turning my insides to knots.

And yet, part of me felt like that frightened little boy again.

"So this is where you're hiding." Beckah's head popped up through the door in the loft floor, startling me. She carried a candle and wore her nightgown and robe. She shuffled over to plop down right beside me.

I couldn't think of a single thing to say to her. Rather, there was so much I wanted to say that I had no idea where to begin.

"Everyone's asleep." She placed the candle down on the floor in front of us. "Except for Felix. He's still sitting on the porch. Waiting for you to come back, I expect. He was a mess after you—well—after we all thought you'd been killed at Barrowton. I think he's worried you'll run off and leave him again."

I listened and watched the candle's flame dance before us.

"I was so awful to him." Her voice got quieter. "I want to tell him I'm sorry. I'm just not sure how."

"I'm sure he knows you didn't mean it."

"Even so, he was suffering, too. I was selfish— cruel even. But the thought of losing you ..." Her voice faded into silence. She turned to look at me, and I could see the pain in her eyes. "We don't have to teach ourselves how to fall in love, you know. We just do it without even trying. But no one ever warns us about how, if that love is damaged or destroyed, we have to teach ourselves how to go on without it. It just doesn't seem right, does it?"

"There's not much right in the world anymore," I replied. "At least, that's how it seems from where I'm sitting. This was my room, you know. When I was younger, before I became a dragonrider, this is where I slept every night. Ulric and his wife didn't want me in the house. To them it must have seemed like a punishment to put me out here. But ... I liked it. I liked being far away from them. It was the only time I wasn't afraid."

Beckah's touch was gentle as she took my hand. She gave me a small, hopeful smile. The warm candlelight bathing her face made her eyes shine like evergreen-colored stars.

"I slept right over there, and every day I looked out this window. That's where I got my first good look at your father. He came to get a saddle. Maybe that was just an excuse to spy on me." I laughed because the memory seemed so ridiculous now considering how far I'd come. "I was different, back then. I know I've changed a lot. I'm just not sure it's all been for the better."

I could feel her thumb rubbing against the back of my hand in a comforting way. "I don't think that's something we get to decide for ourselves, Jae," she said quietly. "We change because of what's around us. Little by little, the events of our lives chisel away at us until we're someone altogether different at the end."

I managed to smile back at her. I was determined to at least look like I had it all together, even if my heart felt so heavy. I suspected it was the weight of reality sinking in—the reality of the terrible thing I was about to do. It was going to change the world. It was going to make things better for everyone else. Or so I hoped.

But I wasn't stupid enough to think that change like that wouldn't come at a price.

She smiled and began tracing her fingertips lightly along the scar that ran from my brow down over my cheek. Then she brushed some of my hair away from my eyes and let her forehead rest against mine. "What happened to your hair?"

"It's a long story," I murmured as I stared at her, hypnotized by how close she was.

"I can't believe you're back," she said softly. "It's like I'm too afraid to let myself feel it. Did you miss me?"

Reaching under the leather vambrace strapped to my forearm, I took out a small, stained, tattered piece of cloth. It had once been a handkerchief—one she'd embroidered especially for me with the image of two dragons. I'd carried it with me into battle, into Luntharda, and now it was looking a little worse for wear.

Her eyes widened with amazement as she took it carefully and held it up to the candlelight.

"Sorry it doesn't look as nice as it did before," I started to apologize.

"Oh Jae," she whispered as she ran her fingers over the stitching. "I can't believe you still have it."

"I'm never giving it up," I assured her. "It was like carrying a piece of you with me."

Without saying a word, she folded the handkerchief up and placed it next to the candle.

Then she doused the light.

The sudden darkness blurred my vision and I was confused until I felt her hands on my neck and her warm lips press against mine.

Felix was still waiting on us when we returned to the house. He sat on the front step, hunched over with his elbows on his knees and a dejected expression pointed out into the darkness. He perked up a bit when he spotted us making our way back.

"I had a nice long chat with the others," he announced proudly as he got to his feet. "They're all in agreement. We're with you, Jae, to the bitter end."

Beckah gasped. "How did you manage that?"

He grinned and combed his fingers through his hair proudly. "Charm, of course."

"Right. Because that nonsense works on war-hardened soldiers." I rolled my eyes. I wasn't about to show it, but I was impressed. Felix had a way with people that I clearly lacked. It made me grateful that he didn't hate my guts for disappearing and making him believe I was dead. I was going to need him in order to pull this off.

For a few awkward seconds, none of us spoke. Felix was giving me a meaningful look out of the corner of his eye, and I got the feeling he still hadn't forgiven me for letting him think I was dead.

"Don't be too long, it's getting late. I can only imagine how interesting tomorrow is going to be," Beckah whispered. She gave me a wink before disappearing into the house.

And I was left alone, staring my best friend in the eye. The atmosphere between us was still tense and awkward. My face hurt where he'd punched me for not letting him know I was alive. I'd probably have a nice bruise there by morning.

"Figures," I heard him mutter under his breath as he sat back down on the steps.

I sat down next to him. "What does?"

"That you'd still be alive. That I went through all that hell for nothing." He made a point not to look my way. "I adopted you, you know. Signed the documents and everything."

"Adopted?"

"Yeah. So technically now you're my brother. That makes you a marquess, if you're interested. Also, it would be appropriate to change your last name to Farrow, you know, as a gesture of gratitude."

I gaped at him. "Why did you do that?"

"It's always the way I've felt. I just decided it was time to make it official. And since you were dead, you couldn't argue with me or give me that dumb look you're giving me right now."

"Sorry." I closed my mouth and tried to compose myself. "Thank you. That … well, it means a lot."

I was stunned. I'd almost shaken that heaviness in my chest, that feeling of anxiety and pain. But knowing he'd done something like that for me brought it all back with a crushing vengeance. I couldn't look him in the eye.

He shrugged. "I'm still pissed at you, for the record."

"I know. You have every right to be."

"See, that pisses me off even more. You could at least act like you were justified or something. Be a little self-righteous about it." He reared back and punched my arm hard. Bruise number two.

I winced. "Fine. I was doing what I thought was right. I couldn't allow myself to reflect on what was going on here because every time I did, it clouded my judgment."

"That's better." Felix smirked as though satisfied. "Now you're sounding more like a Farrow."

More time passed and we sat together without saying a word. I had a lot of questions for him—particularly about how he was apparently marrying a girl I had assumed he hated. I had a hard enough time imagining him getting married at all. He didn't strike me as the "till death do us part" sort. But what did I know? Besides, now didn't seem like the right time to get into all that. I had a bigger question in mind, one that had nagged at my brain for years.

"Why did you befriend me in the first place?"

His eyebrows went up and his mouth scrunched uncomfortably.

"When we were fledglings at the academy, you went out of your way to sit with me and get to know me. I've always wondered why."

"I'd heard about the halfbreed student who was joining our ranks. Everyone was talking about how puny you were and that they didn't expect you to last one day in real training," he recalled. "I suppose I just wanted to see for myself what you were really like—if you were actually that brave, or just dumb."

"And? What was the verdict?"

Felix grinned again. "I dunno. The jury's still out."

That wasn't exactly the answer I'd been hoping for.

Before I could come up with a good comeback, he draped an

arm over my shoulders and gave an over-embellished sigh. "We really are going to die this time, aren't we?"

I couldn't tell if he was serious or just being sarcastic by his tone. Knowing him, I decided to bet on sarcastic. "Probably."

"Well, it was bound to happen sooner or later," he chuckled. "You know, they'll write songs or tell tales about us. We'll be remembered as heroes."

"More likely, villains," I retorted. "Evil or not, you don't kill a king and expect to walk away with a clean reputation."

Felix shook his head. "Nah. I'm too good-looking to be a villain. Besides, anyone who's actually met you knows you're basically an overgrown fluff ball with pointy ears and a bleeding heart. Definitely not villain material."

"Gee, thanks."

My guard was down. I wasn't even thinking about how he'd positioned himself to put me in a perfect headlock. Before I could react, he squeezed my neck with his arm so hard I could barely breathe. I flailed and tried to get an elbow into his ribs without success.

"Seriously though," he growled threateningly. "If you ever do that to me again, I will kill you myself. And your headstone will say something like 'I was a total jerk and I really am dead this time.' Got it?"

I made a choking sound I hoped he would take as a yes.

"Good," he said as he let me go.

"That hurt, you know." I shot him a glare. Bruise number three.

He scowled back. "So did thinking you died in battle. We're even."

I cursed at him as I rubbed my neck.

"And now you just act like it's nothing," he rumbled.

"What's that supposed to mean?"

He looked frustrated as he kicked the toe of his boot into the dirt. "You're always like this. You keep everything inside, hiding it from everybody including me. You've always kept things from me because you think I can't handle it. And that really sucks, because it feels like no matter what we've been through, you've never really trusted me unless you had no other choice. You are my family. And I buried you. Do you have any idea what that was like?"

I didn't. And all I could do was hang my head in shame. "I should have let you know somehow that I wasn't dead. I realize that now. I'm sorry, Felix."

"Like I said, sorry doesn't cut it."

"Then how can I make it right?" I was beginning to wonder if he'd ever forgive me. "Tell me. Whatever it is, I'll do it."

"Don't let it happen again, for starters. The rest … I'll just have to think about." He was muttering under his breath. "From here on out, whatever happens—regardless of how weird or dangerous you think it is—you better tell me what's going on. I can't stand by you if I don't know where you are. That's what we do, you know. It's what we've always done. There's nothing you can do or say that's going to scare me bad enough that I won't be there, ready to fight to the death right beside you."

"Felix," I started. I wanted to tell him. Gods and Fates, I *needed* to.

He just looked at me and waited.

"I think I'm going to die. I think at the end of this, Paligno is going to take my life as compensation for what my father did. There's nothing I can do. I can't barter for it. It has to be Ulric's bloodline who pays the price and it has to be the lapiloque who puts the stone back—it has to be me."

Felix didn't reply.

I tried to hold it in. I tried swallowing, looking away, rubbing my forehead, and anything else that might help. Men weren't supposed to cry—dragonriders least of all—and definitely never in front of other men. It was an unspoken law of manhood. No one liked to see a man that way, vulnerable and broken. But suddenly the weight, the stress, the lies, the years of pain and fear bore down on me all at once. I couldn't take it. Something snapped.

I turned away so he wouldn't see.

Felix put a hand on my shoulder.

I bit down hard on my words, and yet I still couldn't keep from stammering. "D-don't tell Beckah. P-please."

"Not a word."

After a few deep breaths, I found I could talk without choking and stuttering. But despite my best efforts, my voice still sounded as broken as I felt. "I know I can't afford to second-guess myself. This has to be done," I confessed. "But I'm terrified. I'm angry. I want the assurance that this really will put an end to the war, that it's all going to be worth it. But whenever I ask Paligno for an answer or a sign, all I get is silence."

"We don't get to know that kind of stuff, dummy. Even if you are this god's 'chosen one,' we just have to go on faith." He shook my shoulder roughly. "Faith in the cause. Faith in the people we love. Faith that however this ends, we'll have done everything we possibly could to make things right."

I wiped my face on the sleeve of my shirt. "Are you still going to feel that way if we fail and Hovrid puts us all to death? Or if the curse spreads and devours every living thing on the earth?"

Felix wore that cocky, crooked, know-it-all smirk. "Sure. And now that we have that settled, let's go over this plan of yours. How do you intend to overthrow the King of Maldobar in his own throne room?"

thirteen

As much as I needed—and wanted—to sleep, it just wasn't in the cards for me. My brain was a tangled rat's nest of worries that I tried desperately to unravel as I lay on the floor in front of the living room hearth. I was stretched out on a woven wool rug that Mrs. Derrick had put down. I used a rolled-up blanket as a pillow and watched the dancing flames cast flickering shadows over the walls until dawn.

Beckah, Felix, and Kiran were the first to wake, bounding down the stairs like rowdy children. They made a lot of racket, enough to wake everyone else up, as they began clanging pots and pans together. Beckah handed out orders as efficiently as her mother, instructing them on how to properly light the kitchen fire, crack the eggs, and cut the vegetables for breakfast. Kiran was much better at taking her directions than Felix.

I lay still with my eyes closed, hoping that anyone who peered in at me would just assume I was asleep and let me have a few more minutes alone with my thoughts. Besides, it was interesting to hear them squabble back and forth. Beckah was in rare form.

"Congratulations on your wedding, by the way." She heckled Felix mercilessly. "It was good of you to finally make an honest woman out of Julianna."

"Yeah, yeah," Felix mumbled. He sounded embarrassed. "She had to make an honest man out of me first, though. Which wasn't so easily done, unfortunately. If there's one thing I do best, it's making a fool out of myself."

"No argument there." Beckah giggled. "Still, we were all glad to hear you two had resolved your differences. Especially since no one was even sure you were still engaged. And then when she kissed Jae at the officers' ball—"

Someone—probably Felix—dropped one of the metal pots on the floor. It made an awful racket. "She what?"

"Or maybe he kissed her. I don't remember which it was." I could tell Beckah was baiting him on with her dismissive tone. It was working beautifully.

Felix was practically beside himself. "Gods and Fates, woman. How could you not remember which?"

"What difference does it make?" Kiran grumbled as though the whole conversation were annoying to him. "A kiss is a kiss."

"What difference does it make?" Felix repeated his question in a mocking tone. "Well, either my fiancée kissed my best friend, or he kissed her. Makes a pretty big difference, if you ask me."

Beckah was laughing again. "Oh come on, Felix. We all know she just did it to make you jealous. And can you blame her? The way you fawned over every girl in the room right in front of her. Honestly, it was as disgusting as it was pathetic."

"So she kissed him?" Felix didn't even seem to notice that he'd been insulted.

"You really think Jae would force himself on a girl he just met?" Beckah countered.

"No. I suppose not."

Beckah huffed. "Of course he wouldn't. Like I said, I'm sure she only did it to get your attention."

"Yeah, well, it didn't work," Felix was the one grumbling now.

I could hear the smirk in Beckah's voice. "Seems like it's working now."

"I hear a lot more talking than I do breakfast-making," Sile barked from the top of the stairs. His heavy footsteps descended into the kitchen, which was a relief. I needed time to scramble and come up with a good excuse for not telling Felix that Julianna had kissed me. Of course, I hadn't known she was his fiancée. I hadn't told him because I thought he hated her and letting him know I'd locked lips with her would be the perfect invitation for more of his teasing.

And for the record—she was definitely the one who kissed me.

I listened to them banter and continue to taunt each other, as the house filled with the lively sounds of my friends and the smell of a delicious breakfast. The smell lured the rest of our guests down from upstairs and eventually I went to join them in the kitchen as well.

Leaning in the doorway, I watched everyone muscling around to get a bite to eat. Beckah had made biscuits from scratch, fried up two-dozen eggs, and roasted more links of sausage than I'd ever seen in my life. There was plenty to go around, which was good since the majority of our group were full-grown men with big appetites, but I couldn't bring myself to join in.

"Strange, isn't it?" Roland appeared next to me, seemingly out of nowhere. It startled me a little.

I glanced over him again, now from a much closer angle. He'd changed so much I barely recognized him, especially with a beard. It made him look older and less like our father. Too bad I couldn't grow one myself, if only for that reason.

Roland still had his arm bandaged up and cradled against his chest in a sling. I wondered if he would refuse if I offered to heal it for him.

"What is?" I finally remembered to ask.

"Seeing this many people here all smiling. Hearing laughter instead of screaming, crying, and cursing. I didn't think I would live to see the day when I witnessed this happening in this house."

"I've been thinking the same thing since I got here," I answered.

"If you're wondering whether or not I'll follow you into this insanity, the answer is yes." He still spoke in that same somber, serious tone I remembered from my childhood. He'd never been keen on self-expression or drawing unnecessary attention to himself.

"I'm glad to hear it."

Then he cut to the chase. "That girl with the long, dark hair. She's yours, isn't she?"

I tensed because I had no idea where he was going with this. "She might argue the reverse—that I'm hers, that is."

For a brief second, it almost looked like he cracked a smile. "I thought as much."

"Why do you ask?"

Roland was in no hurry to let me in on whatever it was he was thinking. And when he finally did explain, I wasn't sure how to respond. "I was afraid after the sampling of family life you'd had with us, you wouldn't want it for yourself. That you might never want to marry or have children of your own."

His tone, much quieter and reluctant than usual, made me wonder. "Is that how you feel?"

He gave a noncommittal shrug. "Sometimes I worry that one day I'll wake up and realize I've become someone I hate, someone like Ulric. I don't think I could stand that. And even worse, I don't think I could forgive myself for putting anyone else through it. I've never courted anyone for that reason. I'm not sure I ever will."

"I know what you mean," I replied. "But I don't think that would be the case, if you did decide to take a wife. We're not like that—we're not like him."

He didn't reply. He watched everyone as they went on eating and talking, oblivious to the irony of their company in this house.

My eyes were drawn to Beckah, as though by gravity. That's

when a new, harrowing realization reared its ugly head in my already frazzled brain. I made a radical decision.

"Can you promise me something, Roland?"

He stared straight at me with piercing eyes. "Yes."

"If anything should happen … to me. Something unfortunate. Look after her, would you? I don't want her to be alone. Felix already has someone. You'll be the only family I have left who could do it. She's a special person. She deserves to be happy. She deserves to be happy. She won't like it. She might even try to scare you away. But promise me you won't give up on her."

The noise from the kitchen filled the silence between us until, at last, he gave a small nod. "Very well, Jaevid. If that's what you want."

I hoped it wouldn't come to that. I was still clinging to a fleeting hope that Paligno had a greater plan, and that whatever happened next would mean an end to the war that everyone in this room got to witness—including me. But I didn't know that for sure. All I knew was that for the stone to be replaced and the balance restored, the blood of the traitor who had stolen it would have to be spilt.

I had to be prepared for the worst.

After breakfast had been cleaned up and the kitchen scrubbed to Beckah's satisfaction, we gathered at the table again. Only Mrs. Derrick and her baby were absent, banished upstairs until we were finished. Sile didn't want either of them involved.

I sat at the head of the table, looking around into the eyes of the only people in Maldobar I knew that I could trust. It was time to settle things. Felix and Beckah sat on either side of me wearing stoic expressions. Only Felix knew the details of what I intended to do. Maybe that was why he was sweating so much.

"Before we go any further, I need to know who is with me. I need to hear it from your own lips because what comes next will be dangerous. It will be treason, and it will very likely kill every last one of us. But if we are successful, then we may see the end of a war that has gone on for far too long." I chose my words more carefully than I ever had. "No one will blame you or think badly of you for walking away now. And I won't mince words; I want to be very clear. I have every intention of killing Hovrid—the man you've known as the King of Maldobar. So speak now, if you intend to stay and fight with me. If you choose to go, now is the time."

No one spoke at first.

Then Felix clasped a fist over his chest, giving the dragonrider salute. "I'm with you."

"So am I." On my other side, Beckah repeated his gesture. A few riders from Emerald Flight looked at one another as though confused. It seemed they still didn't know who she was.

"If Felix goes, then so do I," Prax chimed in.

"And if you go, then so do the rest of us," declared one of the dragonriders from my old flight, and the rest of them muttered their agreement. That put a decent number of strong, skilled swordsmen on my side.

From the corner of the room where he was lurking and watching, Roland raised two fingers. "I'll go."

"With that bum arm, you won't be much good in a fight," Prax reminded him.

I smiled down at the tabletop. "Never mind that. I'll take care of it. He'll be fit to fight."

From across the table, Kiran gave me one of his finest, cunning, gray elf grins. "I look forward to dying at your side, lapiloque."

Dying—his brand of a joke. Very funny.

"That just leaves you, then. Seems you've had quite a hand in all this. So are you going to see it to the end?" Prax pointed an interrogating stare in Sile's direction.

Normally, I would have jumped to his defense. But Sile could handle himself, and this was his choice to make. I wasn't going to add any pressure in either direction.

"Guard your tongue, Prax. I've raised more dragonriders than you." Sile's words were venomous, but somehow he managed to sound complacent. "I didn't come this far just to abandon my mission now."

Right. For him, this wasn't about me. It wasn't even about Hovrid or the war. It was about setting things right—about undoing the damage Ulric had done under his watch. It was about keeping his word to my mother.

"It's settled then." I closed my eyes and collected my thoughts. Then I began laying out my plan, detail by excruciating detail. Hours ticked past. They had a lot of questions, and I did my best to answer them. It wasn't going to be simple.

But we did have one factor that I thought might tilt things in our favor, and that was the element of surprise. Hovrid wouldn't be expecting any of this. His eyes were fixed on Luntharda, anticipating an attack from there and pouring all his efforts in that direction. His rage and desire for vengeance would be like blinders on a carriage horse. We were going to hit him from within his own borders with a weapon he didn't even know existed—me. He didn't know the stone had chosen a new lapiloque, and he certainly didn't know what I was planning. I felt confident about that much.

That is, until Felix sheepishly raised his hand. "Actually, that's not … completely accurate."

You could have heard a pin drop.

"What do you mean?" Sile's face had gone a pasty white.

Felix shrank back in his chair as though he knew this was going to be bad. "I may have let it slip to him that Jaevid could do things."

In an instant, Sile was in his face. He practically dove across the table and grabbed the front of his tunic to jerk him out of his chair. "What did you say? What exactly did you tell him?"

Felix stammered out the specifics, and when he'd finished, Sile basically threw him back into his chair. "You're a fool. A useless moron! Do you have any idea what this means?" He snarled as he thrust a finger directly at me. "If Hovrid knows he's coming, none of this is going to work. He'll put every dragonrider in Maldobar in our path!"

"Not every dragonrider," Prax countered.

Sile's eyes bulged and his nostrils flared. I sensed a fight was about to break out if I didn't do something to resolve it.

"Stop it, all of you." I stood up and shouted loudly enough to get their attention again. "This doesn't change anything except our timing. We'll have to act now, immediately, before Hovrid can call together any more of his forces. Our plan will still work."

"And if it doesn't?" Sile still had a challenging growl in his voice.

I narrowed my eyes at him, letting him feel a bit of pressure from my power, and making the floorboards and beams of the house groan. "Hovrid isn't the only one with reinforcements at his disposal."

For the first time, Sile backed down. He dropped his gaze, shoulders drawing in somewhat. I wasn't the shy, scrawny little boy he'd trained. I wasn't even a dragonrider anymore. I was something else—something even a battle-seasoned rider like him might fear.

"Very well, then." Beckah stood up and started whipping her hair into a braid. "Shake the lead out of it, boys. We've got work to do."

fourteen

Time was against us. Our key element was gone. And while I didn't necessarily blame Felix for it, he'd hardly said a word as he followed me around with his head down—literally.

As much as I wanted to console him, there wasn't time for it. We could only reasonably allow one day to prepare. Every hour could mean Hovrid gathering more and more soldiers to himself to defend the stone. That meant more swords, armor, and dragonflame would be standing between us and our goal. Felix was going to have to pull himself together on his own.

There was a lot to go over. Our gear had to be prepped, saddles checked, and swords sharpened. We reviewed the specifics of our plan over and over again, leaving no room for confusion.

That is, until it came to Beckah.

As far as I knew, the rest of the dragonriders from Emerald Flight, including Lieutenant Prax, still had absolutely no idea who she really was. I became certain of it when she marched out the front door of my house, down the steps, and straight towards us with her battle armor on and her helmet under her arm. Every bit of her gear had been polished until it shone like obsidian glass, and the golden wings painted onto the various pieces looked like they had been touched up as well. She walked with her head held high, confidence in every step. When she wore that armor, she wasn't Beckah anymore—she was Seraph.

Every one of the dragonriders around us, except for Felix who already knew who she was, stared at her like she'd spontaneously grown a second head.

"What's this? Some sort of joke?" One of the riders began to protest.

Prax eyed her up and down like he was experiencing a bad case of déjà vu. "That armor ... it resembles ..."

"A dragonrider's?" Beckah interrupted him. "Or Seraph's? In either case, you'd be right."

"But you're a woman." Prax scowled at her disapprovingly. "And a very small one at that. I doubt you can even heft a sword."

"You've seen Seraph do it plenty of times, haven't you?" Beckah scowled back at him fearlessly. "Or perhaps you'd rather draw your own sword and test me?"

It didn't take long for another rider to chime in. "You honestly expect us to believe this little girl is Seraph? The rider chosen by

Icarus? The one we've witnessed turn the tide of battle after battle?"

The rest of Emerald Flight muttered their agreement. A few of them were even laughing at her, as though the idea were totally ridiculous. To them, it must have seemed that way. No woman, big or small, had ever been a dragonrider. It was absolutely forbidden.

I was going to intervene, to speak up in her defense, but I never got the chance. Icarus put an end to the debate when he landed behind us with a thunderous boom. The monstrous black dragon flared his wings and spines, baring all his jagged teeth as he crawled closer and put his huge head right beside Beckah. She rewarded him with a scratch on the chin. "You'll have to excuse him. Since he chose me, he doesn't like it when it seems like someone's threatening me."

No one was laughing now.

A dragon had chosen Beckah, the same way I was chosen. By the most fundamental law of the dragonrider brotherhood, that meant she was one of them—regardless of who she was.

"Good. Now that we've got that settled, I'm sure none of you will argue with her leading the second group?" I couldn't resist a proud smirk as I waited for someone to dare to object.

Of course, no one did.

Prax chuckled suddenly. He slapped a hand on Felix's shoulder so hard it almost made him fall over. "Don't tell me you knew about this the whole time, son?"

Felix was wearing a coy little smirk, too.

It only made Prax laugh harder. "Sly devil. Got it from my side, I'd wager."

I'd missed it at first, but when Prax said that and looped an arm around Felix's neck to wrestle him into an aggressive, headlock-enforced hug … it hit me. He'd used the word "son," and not as a joke.

I stared at Felix, hoping for some kind of clue as to when this had come out.

Felix didn't give me one. He was grinning at Prax, seeming proud of himself, and looking disturbingly like a much younger version of the elder dragonrider. I'd been right all along, then. Prax really was his father.

Boy, did Felix owe me an explanation about that later. He had no idea how I'd wrestled with asking him about it. I was relieved, though, and glad I'd listened to Jace and kept my nose out of it.

"We should practice formations. None of us have ever fought against another dragonrider in anything but training. We've trained to kill shrikes, but never our own kind. It's my intention to get through this without ever having to take the life of another dragonrider, but in the event that you have to choose between your own life and someone else's, you'll need to be prepared. Even more challenging will be that some of you will have extra passengers," I said. "So let's use the time we've got left. Tonight at midnight, we decide the fate of this kingdom."

I sent up a request for the rest of the dragons to gather. At my command, our fleet of dragons dropped below the clouds and began landing, one-by-one, in a circle around us. They shook their heads, snorted, snapped, and growled with anticipation. Next to me, Kiran seemed very anxious.

"Beckah, you'll have to double-up so Roland can ride with you. Prax, you'll take Sile. Kiran, you'll have to ride piggyback with Felix. He'll probably need your archery skills to give him some defensive cover since he won't be able to match my speed. Remember, no one goes it alone. This only works if we stay together."

Together, all my comrades gave me the dragonrider salute— even Roland. Then we took to the air, keeping above the cloud cover as much as possible to avoid being spotted by anyone in the city below.

When it began to get dark, we landed and let the dragons loose to feed and rest before battle. The rest of us took the time to fix anything we'd found wrong with our gear, eat a last meal together, and sit down to rest. It probably would have helped to sleep, but everyone else was just as anxious and fidgety as I was. No one was sleeping tonight.

I set about healing Roland's arm, and everyone gathered around to watch curiously as I unwrapped it from the bandages and assessed the damage. His arm was broken in two places because it had been wrenched backwards while still buckled to his shield. It was already healing on its own, so all I had to do was finish the job. I brushed my fingers over his skin, leaving behind a faint, glowing trail of soft, green light. The pieces of bone knitted together. The irritated muscles relaxed. I took his pain and stiffness, and when I was finished, his arm was bound to feel as though it had never been broken.

"Told you," Felix said smugly to the rest of my captivated audience, who were stooping over to watch with wide eyes. "And this is nothing. You should see what he can do with vines."

Sile swatted him on the back of the head.

The crowd gathered around us began to disperse after that. With every passing hour, the atmosphere grew more tense. Some of the riders were pacing nervously. Felix spun a dagger over his hand, over and over, while he talked quietly with his father. Beckah was sticking close to her mother, holding her baby sister on her hip, and doing a great job of acting like nothing was wrong.

Everyone waited, doing whatever they could to keep themselves sane while the time ran down. Well, everyone except for me. I still had work to do.

The whispers of my predecessors, their memories and wisdom, buzzed around in my head like a swarm of bees. I'd learned how to use those memories in Luntharda. By channeling them and listening to them, I was able to tap into more of my abilities than ever before. I had powers that even I wasn't aware of yet, but the whispers were very good at guiding me.

Knowing Hovrid might be expecting our attack had me

worried—worried that our meager forces wouldn't be enough. We needed more people on our side. We needed assurance we could reach the temple where the stone was meant to rest.

Basically, we needed a miracle.

Roland and Sile were right on my heels as I left the house, following from a cautious distance as though afraid I might tell them to go back. It was dark, but instead of carrying a lantern or candle, I opened my palm and called my power into an acorn I picked up off the ground. It glowed brightly, filling the night air with a green aura. I walked into the forest almost half a mile, a safe distance from the house, and found a small clearing where the ground was open and flat. There, I started to prepare.

Roland cleared his throat to get my attention. "Can we help?"

"I need a small pile of brush just there, in the center. Use only green, freshly picked branches and leaves," I instructed.

"Green stuff won't burn," Sile was quick to point out.

I smiled. "I never said I was going to burn it."

While I cleared away the dry, dead brush from the clearing, Roland and Sile worked. They came back with their arms full of broken-off branches and leaves from all sorts of different trees. I picked the ones that were most perfect, and began arranging them on the ground in a circle.

I took a deep breath as I stepped into the center of the circle and sat down. I crossed my legs and let my palms rest on my knees. "All right. Stand back."

"Where did you learn to do this?" Roland asked.

"I didn't. Others learned it for me."

He arched a brow, looking unsure of what that meant.

"It's hard to explain. I'm not the first person Paligno has chosen, and the spirits of the others still exist within him. So they exist within me, too. It's like bits and pieces of their memories run over into mine. It used to only happen when I was asleep, through dreams, and I had no control over it. But now I can access those memories at will." I struggled to find the least insane-sounding way to describe it to him. "It's sort of like animal migration, I guess. The instincts of one generation are passed on to the next. I can hear them sometimes."

"So … you hear voices?"

"Yes."

He nodded like he understood and as if it didn't make me sound absolutely insane.

"I take it this is about those reinforcements you mentioned?" Sile had a challenging tone to his voice, like he was still waiting to be impressed.

"Yes." I closed my eyes and let my mind become still. "When they get here, don't move, don't speak, and don't look any of them in the eye. I can't control them like I can other animals."

"They?" Sile asked.

I didn't answer. I had pushed out all other sounds, voices, and thoughts from my mind. I was alone in the dark, feeling the thrumming energy of the world around me—the trees muttering to one another like shy children, the roots of the earth squirming far below my feet, and the spirits of the animals still untouched by Paligno's curse. Those spirits shone like stars to my mind's eye—pure and quietly powerful. But there were others, the ones the curse had touched. Though they weren't close to me, I could feel the heat of their presence like a foul breath on my neck. It was offensive and infuriating not only to me, but also to the other generations of lapiloque that had gone before me.

My eyes were closed, but I could sense the movement of the green branches and leaves around me. I felt them rise and fuse together, twisting and changing until they hung around me like a halo of brilliant, green light. Then, with one push of my will, the light burst and spread out in every direction like a ripple on still water.

It took a few minutes. After all, waking the ancient spirits of the earth isn't done every day. Many of them, like the paludix turtle, hadn't been roused for a great many centuries. I honestly wasn't sure how they would respond, or if they'd even come at all.

But they did.

I knew it when I heard Sile and Roland gasp and their footsteps retreated backwards a ways. Opening my eyes, I found myself face-to-face with a host of creatures I had no name for. Each one was stranger than the last, and they all seemed to materialize out of the dark forest around me, gathering to look at me with glowing eyes that flickered like bog fires.

"*Why have you have summoned us, my lord?*" one of them spoke. It resembled an enormous fox with black and silver fur. On its back were wings like a raven's, and its fur was covered in curling, swirling markings that shimmered in the moonlight. The creature loomed over me, bigger than a dragon, and with a presence that reminded me of a cold, dark winter's night.

Around him, the other spirits waited, gazing at me expectantly. I laid out my request.

"*Such a thing will cost us dearly, for even we cannot break the laws of our god that forbid us from murdering our children,*" the foxlike creature hissed. "*What you ask must be bought at a high price, lapiloque.*"

"I understand."

There was a tense silence. Though I couldn't hear them, I sensed the spirits communicating with one another. They had some sort of link, as though their minds were able to commune instantly without uttering a sound. Unfortunately, I wasn't invited to the debate.

"*We know the price Paligno has demanded to be paid for the sins of your father,*" the creature said at last. "*The blood of the traitor must be repaid. So we will ask for something else. Something far more precious than blood.*"

I was starting to get nervous. This wasn't something I'd anticipated, but it was far too late to turn back now. We needed their help. Without it, even if we had the stone, we might never make it back to the temple. I had no other choice.

"Name it," I said as I stood up. I offered a hand to the creature, pulling back the sleeve of my tunic to reveal the bare skin of my forearm.

In the blink of an eye, the ancient foxlike spirit dissolved into a cloud of black mist that swallowed me whole until I couldn't see anything around me.

"*The wisdom of the ages, the secrets of Paligno known only to lapiloque—all are contained within the memories of your ancestors. We will have it all.*" The spirit's voice cut through my mind like a cold wind ripping over a hillside.

"So be it," I agreed. "But only after you've held up your end of the bargain. No one touches them. If one life is lost, the deal is void."

I felt a sharp, scalding pain on my arm that made me double over. And just as quickly as they had appeared, the ancient spirits dissolved into their own curling clouds of mist and vanished—leaving me alone in the middle of the clearing.

My head spun and I could barely stand. Through the haze of my pain, I saw the black mark left on my arm. It was burned into my skin as though branded there. I could feel the power resonating from it; it was as wild and ageless as the spirits who had given me the mark.

Just as I felt my knees buckle, someone caught me and held me on my feet. Roland pulled my arm over his shoulder on one side and Sile did the same on the other. Together, they helped me stagger out of the forest.

"You want to tell us what just happened? We couldn't make out a word of it. All just snarls and hissing—sounded like a foreign language," Sile growled. He sounded frustrated and maybe even a little worried. I doubted it was about my welfare, though.

"I made a deal," I rasped. "They're going to help us."

Roland was as pale as if he'd seen a ghost. I could feel him shaking. "What did they do to you?"

I didn't want to tell him. I was used to keeping that sort of thing private because my friends couldn't handle it. Felix would have freaked out. Beckah would have been furious. But these two were possibly the only people who might understand.

"Everything has a price," I replied.

I felt better once they helped me back to the house. I sat down at the kitchen table and leaned over to let my arm rest where the mark wasn't touching anything. Touching it just made it worse.

"Yeah." Sile muttered as he turned away. "Too bad you're the only one footing the bill."

I watched him go, wondering if that fact really bothered him or not. He seemed fine enough to let me do it, although I was technically the only one who could. He knew about the god stone and what it would take to put it back. Not just anyone could do it. It had to be someone with the blood of the traitor—my father's blood—who put it back …

I froze. Across from me, Roland had sat down with a bowl of clean water, a rag, and some bandaging for my arm. I realized I wasn't the only one who could pay the blood price for Ulric's sin.

Roland had the traitor's blood, too.

I vowed to myself right then that he would never—*ever*—know that.

I couldn't risk that he might try to intervene and offer himself as an alternative. Whatever the past had been between us, I couldn't allow that to happen. Roland was my brother, my closest blood relation besides Hovrid. I loved him and I wouldn't let him take my place.

This rite was mine and mine alone. It was bad enough to have come here and asked my friends, the people I loved and cherished most in the world, to join me in this potentially suicidal endeavor.

"*So you finally see,*" Paligno's whispering voice trickled through my brain. It gave me chills.

I didn't dare answer out loud—not with Roland sitting there.

"*That love, the love of a family, is not so easily dissolved. It is a bond that is nearly impossible to destroy,*" Paligno continued. "*It transcends all other bonds of love and loyalty. Blood is the tie that binds beyond the grave.*"

I bowed my head slightly. So this was why the god questioned my ability to see it through to the end. Hovrid was my half-brother as well. I had the same familial bond with him that I had with Roland, only we shared a mother instead of a father. That bond might make me weak, might cause me to stumble or question the task that had been charged to me.

Paligno's whisper became louder and more insistent, "*You must not fail.*"

I clenched my teeth. Across the table, Roland was quietly tending to the wound on my arm. He mistook my reaction as pain and cast me an apologetic glance.

"Jaevid! Where have you been? What happened?" Beckah's voice interrupted my conversation with Paligno. The god fell silent and my focus was broken as she came flying down the stairs and across the kitchen to see what had happened to my arm.

"It's nothing. I'm fine. Just a little training accident. We were, uh, letting me practice using my power in combat," I tried to wave her off, but of course she wasn't having that.

Roland quickly covered the mark with a bandage before she could see it. I gave him a grateful nod and he went on wrapping my arm like nothing was wrong.

"Can't you heal it?" she asked worriedly, as she brought a chair up to sit beside me.

"I can't heal myself," I admitted. "But Roland's doing a pretty good job."

Beckah clearly wasn't buying what I was selling. She narrowed her eyes at me like she knew something was up. She didn't push the issue, though.

All of a sudden, Kiran came striding into the kitchen fully dressed in his gear. He'd had to improvise with a few human weapons, like a short sword and a collection of daggers, but he still brandished his elven bow and quiver proudly. "It's nearly time," he announced.

Roland tied off the bandage and jerked my sleeve back down over my arm just as everyone else began to gather around the table. Not everyone was completely dressed and ready to leave yet. We had a few minutes left, after all. Just a little time left to stand around before the coming storm and consider our fate together.

I took a deep breath.

"All right," I heard myself say. I was so numb, it was like an out of body experience. "Let's go."

fifteen

At midnight, our carefully organized plan was set into motion. I stepped off my front porch and into the darkness. There was no turning back. I knew that from now on, my name would either inspire hope or hatred in every heart across the kingdom. It was very likely I was going to be the most hated person in Maldobar's history. I might even be tortured or killed. But the slim chance of success, of ending this war, was more than worth it.

Gathered around me in the chilly night air, I looked across at the faces of my friends, comrades, and family. No one else knew what we knew—that the king was not really the king, or that the god stone was the reason all of nature was going mad. Not to mention that it was my own half-brother who had kept this genocidal war going for over twenty years, and unless we did something to stop it, the curse that was ravaging this land would spread and destroy the entire world. The stone had to be returned to its proper place in Luntharda, and the price of blood had to be paid for the sacrilege of removing it.

I called down our dragons, and they began descending one after the other through the moonlit clouds to land nearby. No one smiled or spoke. I saw their eyes fixed upon me, looking to me for guidance and assurance that this was the right thing to do.

I gave them a nod. It was time.

We split off into our groups to do our preflight check on all our gear. From across the lawn, I watched Beckah expertly examining her saddle while her huge king drake, Icarus, nuzzled at her shoulder. She was beautiful, strong, and confident in a way I only wished I could be. She always accused me of being the brave one—though she couldn't see herself and how her presence inspired things in the other dragonriders. She was the brave one, the real hero.

I just couldn't take it anymore.

Crossing the yard, I grabbed her in my arms, armor and all, and kissed her. It felt like the night had frozen, like time paused long enough for me to hold her close. I forgot anyone else was there, or that her father was one of the people watching us.

Slowly, I let her go.

Out of the corner of my eye, I saw Felix grinning like an idiot.

Sile's eyes narrowed and his jaw tightened. I saw him stiffen as his scorching gaze went from me, to Beckah, and back again.

Beckah wasn't paying them any attention, though. She seized

my hand and brought it up to her face. Under all that armor, her skin felt so soft and fragile. "Please be safe."

"You, too."

"When this is over, let's go back to the beach." When she smiled, I could see tears gathering in her eyes.

"We'll do anything you want." I kissed her again. Somehow, I was able to smile back. I prayed she wouldn't see the pain in my eyes or suspect the secret I was carrying. Even if I survived, I might not remember her. I already bargained away my ancestors' memories for a chance at saving her and the others. While I didn't know for sure how much those ancient spirits might take from me, or what they might leave intact, I had to accept the possibility that they might take everything—including my memories of her.

Guilt made my insides sour as I walked back to my dragon, Mavrik, and attempted to focus on checking my gear. That secret burned in my mind like a smoldering ember. It was going to hurt her. She might never forgive me, but someday, she might understand it.

There wasn't a price I wasn't willing to pay for her to live.

Next to him, Prax gave Sile a taunting jab in the ribs with his elbow. "Don't look so sulky. Surely the chosen servant of a god is good enough for your daughter?"

Sile kept on glaring daggers at me like he might throttle me the first chance he got. "No one is good enough for her." Somehow, he made that sound like a threat.

As soon as Beckah was in her saddle, Roland clinging to her

back with an expression of restrained panic, she gave me the signal. They were ready to go.

I waved them off, and in a burst of wind and snarling dragons, the first group departed. Then it was just Felix, Kiran, and I left standing there, staring up at the sky.

"She'll be fine, Jae." Felix punched me in the arm. He probably thought I was worried about her. "She's got more grit than any male dragonrider I've ever heard of. If anyone can handle this, it's her."

"I know." I turned away. Watching the silhouette of her great, black dragon sailing away across the night sky was too much. "But it's more than that. Destiny is with her. She cannot fail."

"Neither can we," Kiran said suddenly. He was standing next to me, holding his bow and wearing an especially resolved expression. "Not with you on our side, lapiloque."

I couldn't resist a grateful smile. It was nice to hear someone have complete faith in me. I nodded towards Felix and his dragon, Nova. "Time to saddle up. You'll like her better. She flies slower."

"It isn't the speed. Our shrikes fly much faster," Kiran scoffed, all the while keeping a wary eye on Mavrik. "It is the fire."

Felix studied our gray elf companion as he prepared to mount up. "You're not gonna puke, are you?"

"Relax. He's fine. And a much better shot than either of us, thankfully." I tried to sound confident. "Ready for this?"

Felix laughed. "No. Of course not. Who the heck would be? We're about to storm the king's castle, steal his most prized possession, and potentially murder him if he tries to stop us. Not exactly something I have any experience with."

I offered a hand out to him. "No. But it will be amazing—especially if we succeed."

He seized my palm and shook it, "Definitely. And unexpected, too. Your specialty."

"It's been an honor flying with you," I squeezed his hand firmly.

Felix made a face. "Don't say that. It sounds like goodbye, which makes me think we are definitely about to die."

"Not goodbye," I laughed. "But definitely good luck."

"Lucky." He reared back to give me one more solid punch in the arm. "That's practically my middle name, you know."

The royal city of Halfax rose up from the darkness before us, a pool of light against the dark landscape. Through the visor of my helmet, I saw the sun rising on the horizon, turning the ocean into a rippling pane of blood-red glass. I tried not to look at the prison camp that was throwing plumes of foul, black smoke high into the air, but my eyes were drawn to it.

I curled my lip in a snarl. Beneath me, Mavrik did the same. There was our first target. I had come to finally end my brother's war, and all the disgusting madness that went along with it.

"Get in close. We'll do one pass, focusing on the soldiers guarding the ramparts," I murmured, knowing that Mavrik would hear my thoughts even if he couldn't hear my words. "Let Nova know what we're up to. Let's make this quick."

Mavrik made a series of chirps and growls, and together our dragons moved as one, flying in perfect sync. Mavrik and Nova leaned into a spiraling dive, dipping down to begin a close-in assault of the prison camp. I leaned into Mavrik's speed, feeling his heart beating in harmony with mine. We were one being in that moment. Deadly, powerful, and as fast as a tongue of blue lightning in the night.

Flying two abreast, Mavrik and Nova stormed the prison camp walls with a cacophony of roars and a shower of burning venom. Their flames lit up the dark, focused on the prison camp walls and the guards keeping watch there. I saw our enemy scramble. Some managed to fire a few arrows at us, but not a single one hit its mark. As quickly as we'd come, we disappeared, leaving behind an inferno that was sure to keep our enemy busy.

More importantly, it was going to draw Hovrid's eye.

We touched down less than a mile outside the prison camp, taking refuge in the rolling hills that shielded us from plain view. Felix and I dismounted quickly and left Kiran clinging to Nova's back like a scared baby monkey. He wasn't wild about the fire.

It was eerie to be back here. Felix and I had come here once before under similar circumstances when we were just fledglings.

This time, however, we weren't here to deal with a mere Lord General.

I rubbed Mavrik's snout as I fed him my thoughts, careful to make sure he would wait for my signal. "Don't try to save me if things start to look bad," I told him as I scratched behind his scaly ears. "The last thing I want is for you and Nova to be caught the fray. Just stick to the plan. Wait for my signal."

His bright, yellow eyes focused on me, glittering with intelligence and concern. I could feel his thoughts and moods flowing through me. Images of myself, or rather, a much smaller, pitiful-looking version of myself from a few years ago, flashed through my mind. Regardless of what the dragonriders' academy or Paligno had made me, in his eyes, I was still that fragile, little kid. I was still his—and it was his duty to protect me.

He growled deeply and pushed his nose against my chest.

"I know, and you're right. It's dangerous." I gazed past him at the flames from the prison camp. They had the whole skyline glowing red. "But after this, we're both due a retirement, I think."

"We all will be," Felix agreed as he gave my arm a punch. "So let's just get this over with, shall we?"

I nodded. From my saddlebag, I pulled out two big, long, black cloaks—one for Felix and one for me. They were long and baggy enough to cover our armor. Well, Felix's anyway. I took off everything but my vambraces, the belt holing my scimitar, and greaves. I needed to be able to move freely and couldn't afford to be weighted down.

Leaving my dragonrider helmet on the grass, I donned the cloak and pulled the hood over my head. Once we were ready, Kiran gave us a gray elf salute and we started for the city. Behind me, I heard the thunderous pulse of dragon wingbeats and felt the wind as Mavrik and Nova took off again. I couldn't bring myself to look back and watch them leave.

Side-by-side, Felix and I walked up to the grand main gate that led into the prison camp. The complex boiled with chaos as soldiers tried to douse the flames. Dragonriders were coming from the royal city, only a few miles away. I could sense them and their mounts, but something about them was … off. It wasn't Paligno's curse. Or if it was, I'd never experienced it this way before.

I knew better than to let my guard down or to hesitate. The time had come. No more hiding. No more shame. It was time to become what I had been born to be.

Next to me, I saw the flames dancing in Felix's eyes as he looked at me, waiting for my cue. I gave him one second's worth of a smirk.

Then I let myself go.

Something rose up from deep inside me, tearing past every barrier like a tidal wave. It was primal rage—Paligno's rage. I couldn't control it and I didn't try to. Heat swelled inside my body, sizzling through my veins and stretching out to every fiber of my being.

My mind cleared. My doubts, fears, and inhibitions vanished. Every flicker of life—from soldiers, slaves, and everyone in between—twinkled before my sight like an ocean of stars. I could feel the pulse of their energy, the thrumming heat of their life force.

I sensed the soldiers gathering on the other side of the prison gates, preparing to rush us as soon as they were opened. They scrambled to douse the flames on the ramparts above so archers could get in position.

I stretched out a hand, calling forth a burst of power that pulsed through the earth under my feet. The ground began to shake. Next to me, Felix stumbled to keep his footing. His hand was on his sword hilt and his face was pale.

The golem shook itself free of the ground, as though it had been buried there since the dawn of time. An entity made of rock and root, clumped with soil, arose at my command and towered before us. It swung its arms wildly, pounding down the prison gates and bellowing with fury as it was met with a volley of arrows.

I sent the golem ahead to stir things up. It was like throwing a rock into a hornet's nest. With the prison gates now standing wide open, soldiers and gray elf slaves alike came pouring out. The slaves ran right past us, as though we were invisible. Some of the soldiers did, too. But others recognized that we were the source of the commotion.

It was time for another golem.

I raised a second golem much like the first and sent him lumbering into the compound to pound anything too slow to outrun him. With my two monstrosities keeping most of the soldiers distracted, the few that came rushing out were all we had to deal with for the moment. They encircled us, their swords and bows drawn.

Next to me, Felix had drawn his sword and was squared up for a fight. He bared his teeth like an animal, his nose wrinkled in a snarl as he shouted, daring one of them to make a move.

I moved before anyone else did.

With a flex of my hand, the wooden shafts of their arrows and the staves of their bows came to life. They sprouted new limbs and began growing—attacking the men holding them by entangling them in branches and vines that grew bigger each second. The soldiers screamed and some of them began to flee, however, others weren't so easily intimidated.

One of the soldiers lunged at Felix and the two crossed blades. Out of the corner of my eye, I spotted two more gathering the courage to rush me. I drew the scimitar from my belt and waved them in.

The soldiers came in waves. As soon as I had beaten one down, there were three more to take his place. Back-to-back with Felix, I knew we were outnumbered and running out of time.

Then I heard it—the cry of a dragon over the roar of combat. The cavalry had arrived.

Only, it wasn't our cavalry.

Hovrid's reinforcements were upon us, bathing the ground around us in flame so we couldn't retreat. They burned up several of their own soldiers in the process, but I got the feeling they weren't too worried with friendly casualties.

In fact, I couldn't feel anything from them at all. Not a pulse of energy, not a light of a soul. These dragonriders, and the beasts they rode, gave off no suggestion that they were living beings.

Ten of them landed, encircling us on the other side of their fire barrier. Beside me, Felix panted and growled as he eyed them. Suddenly, his expression became confused, then surprised. Then horrified.

"T-this can't be. These riders," he whispered. "I know them. They were supposed to have died at Barrowton."

"Drop your sword," I said.

"Are you insane?"

"Do it," I repeated and let my own scimitar clatter to the ground. I raised my hands in surrender.

Reluctantly, Felix followed suit.

The dragonriders came through the flames one-by-one, their helmets covering their faces. None of them said a word. They kicked our weapons out of reach and began to search us, taking away every other instrument we might use to fight back. Even without a blade, it took two of them to bring Felix down as they began shackling our hands.

I didn't resist. So far, everything was still going according to plan.

sixteen

Alarm bells tolled in every tower of the royal city. Halfax buzzed with activity, as the dragonriders who caught us outside the prison camp forced us through the streets at sword point. Citizens poured out of their shops and homes, filling every avenue and clamoring to see us. They took one look at me, the half-blooded traitor who laid siege to their beloved prison camp, and I could feel their hatred and anger building. It was like a disease, a madness that spread through them. They fed off one another, becoming a mob that the soldiers and city guards could hardly keep restrained.

They spat on me. They cursed at me. They slandered my parents, accused me of heinous things, and dared me to show them some of my pagan power.

"Why don't you free yourself, if you're some kind of great

sorcerer?" One man broke free of the guards and got right in my face, so close I could see the pores on his nose.

"Hah! I've killed and burned hundreds of filthy halfbreeds just like him. He's nothing special," a soldier sneered.

Someone threw something at me—a shoe it turned out. That began a shower of everything from pots and pans, rotten food, and … worse things, raining down on Felix and me from every side.

"Why did you come here? Did you really think you could defeat the power of the Maldobarian Army?" Another soldier laughed at my back.

"No." I looked back at him. "I came to save you."

His expression twitched. I saw fear and confusion for the briefest second. And then he laughed again and gave me a violent shove that made me stumble. I fell face down in the middle of the street. With my hands shackled, I couldn't catch myself to break the fall.

My head cracked off the stone surface of the street. For a minute or two, I was delirious. I could hear Felix shouting, calling my name. He was fighting them again.

One of the dragonriders grabbed me by the hair and dragged me back to my feet. He forced me to start walking again. My vision was still swimming from the fall. I caught glimpses of Felix as he kicked, fought, and wrenched against his chains.

My head had finally cleared when they brought us into the courtyard where I had sworn my oath to become an official dragonrider. Memories of that day snapped at my heels, mocking me for my ignorance, as I climbed the steps into the grand front foyer of the castle.

The doors were standing wide-open to receive us. The wave of raw power that seeped out through them hit me like a boulder to the forehead, which didn't exactly feel great considering what I'd been through. For a few seconds, I was dazed again and I staggered. I knew that power came from the god stone. It really was here, hidden somewhere behind these walls. And the closer I got, the stronger the pull of its presence on my soul became.

"Remember what I said. You mustn't touch it. Don't even look at it." I murmured to Felix, as we were taken down a long, cavernous hall into an even larger room, with ceilings so high you could barely make out the details of the sky that was painted there. Any other time, I would have been awed at the beauty of this place.

Before us, on a raised platform of alabaster, was a throne made in the shape of three dragons. Two made up the seat, with their heads fashioned into armrests and their clawed feet as the legs. The last had been carved into the back of the chair, rising up with wings spread and its head looking straight down at us. The light from the burning golden braziers made the rubies set into its eyes seem to flicker with life. There was a large, jagged black crystal set into the center of its head that shimmered like obsidian glass.

Seated in that grand chair, his face still covered by an intricate mask, was the King of Maldobar. He was slumped to the side, as though this whole ordeal bored him. The fingers on one of his gloved hands rolled as he drummed his fingers impatiently.

On either side of his throne stood ten of his elite guards. All of them were dressed in black, wearing their trademark white masks, and were armed to the teeth. I saw swords, scimitars, bows, spears, and all manner of weaponry strapped to them. One was even carrying a belt loaded with round canisters made of clay. I had a bad feeling about those.

Felix and I were brought forward and forced to our knees, with swords held to the backs of our necks in case we made a wrong move. Behind us were the ten dragonriders who's captured us at the prison camp, although I still couldn't sense even a hint of life from any of them. They stood between us and the only exit.

Thirty-one to two. Exquisitely bad odds, even for me. So much for being lucky.

I imagined that right about then, anyone would wonder how this was possibly a part of the plan. Hovrid could just have us killed without letting us say a word. But I was counting on something—that his pride wouldn't let him end this so quickly. He had an ego to feed.

"So, these are the traitors who have stepped forward to challenge my rule," Hovrid's voice dripped with sarcasm and amusement. He pointed to me. "That one, I want to see his face."

The dragonrider looming behind me grabbed a fistful of my hair and jerked my head up so that I was forced to meet Hovrid's seething glare.

The moment he was able to see my face clearly, Hovrid sprang out of his chair with surprising agility. He prowled towards me, dragging the length of his kingly robes behind him. He grabbed my chin and forced me to look up into his eyes. There, I could see something I hadn't expected:

Fear.

"You—you—*you!*" He hissed in a fit of rage. "Tell me your name, swine!"

"Jaevid Farrow."

Hovrid snatched the sword away from the dragonrider standing nearby and beat Felix over the face with it. It made an awful sound. I cringed and looked away.

"Care to try again?" Hovrid leaned down closer to my face. I could hear his furious breaths hissing through the holes in his mask.

"Jaevid," I snarled. "Jaevid Broadfeather."

I saw him hesitate. I wondered if he actually remembered my father's name. Then, slowly, Hovrid began to pace around me. I felt his gaze all over me, sizing me up from every angle. I heard blood dripping onto the marble floor next to me. Felix was hurt, but I couldn't see how badly. I didn't dare look at him; I was afraid I might do something reckless if I did. I couldn't lose it, not now. Not when we were this close.

"Why did you come here?" Hovrid demanded.

"To surrend—" Felix began to answer.

Hovrid hit him again, even harder than before.

"Your friend isn't very intelligent, is he? Humans seldom are, I've found. Don't think for a moment I don't know who and what you are. You may not look like her, but you are the son of that foul witch, Alowin. You are the chosen of Paligno. The stonespeaker. The one they call lapiloque. Why else would you be here? Why else would you be willing to risk your own life, however vain and pathetic a gesture it may be. Dying for these wretches? Honestly. They're like rats. Worse than rats, really, for even animals have a base sense of what's going on around them."

Hovrid kept pacing around me, his steps smooth and calculated. He spun the sword over his hand with expert ease, twirling it over and over again. I could see Felix's blood on the hilt.

"But then again, Paligno is the source of all life. And so you are duty bound to care about these pitiful creatures, too." He pointed an amused smirk at Felix. "You must know I have no intention of surrendering the stone. It is *mine*. So why would you come here? Or is this fool the only one who was willing to follow you on this futile crusade to save your mother's people?"

"They're your people, too," I reminded him. "You may have everyone else fooled, but you cannot hide from me. I see what others can't. With or without the mask, I know exactly who you are."

"Oh? And who is that?"

I clenched my fists, flexing against the heavy shackles on my wrists. "By name, Hovrid. By blood, my brother."

He stopped. Standing before me, I saw him sizing me up from behind that gilded mask. Slowly, he brought up a hand and took it off.

I heard Felix suck in a sharp breath.

I tried not to do the same.

It was heinous, what he had done to his face. It was gnarled, skeletal, and warped like a wax-carving that had been held close to an open flame. It didn't look like he should even be alive. I fought not to gag.

"A strange thing, shrike venom. At first, I feared I hadn't diluted it enough. I thought I might die. So much pain … I even prayed for death, before it was over," Hovrid mused as he dropped the mask on the floor between us. "But it was the necessary price for anonymity. You know, it was that stupid human boy who helped me do it. I believe you call him Father, don't you?"

I bit back a curse.

"Now you must tell me, Jaevid Broadfeather," he stepped in closer and put the point of his sword against my throat again. "Tell me why you came here, if only to satisfy my own curiosity. I should like to know before I cut off your head and use it as my footstool."

I reached into my belt and took out a seed—one about the size of a pumpkin seed. I'd been carrying it around for quite some time now, waiting for the right time to use it.

Now, while I stood at the epicenter of our enemy's stronghold, was that time.

I held it out to him in my open palm. "I came to give you this."

Hovrid laughed like a maniac and plucked it out of my hand. "Is this some sort of offering? Something you hope to bargain with?"

I didn't answer. I was waiting. Every muscle in my body was tense.

"You're every bit as stupid as your father before you," he hissed and crushed the seed in his fist.

The whole room burst into chaos.

Out of that tiny seed exploded a monstrous boar, who was every bit as enraged as he had been on the battlefield in Barrowton when I'd captured him. It broke free of my magical prison and sent Hovrid flying across the room before charging headlong for the elite guards. They drew their weapons and rose to attack the beast. Behind me, the dragonriders immediately rushed in to join the fray.

Arrows zipped through the air. Men shouted. The enormous boar bellowed with fury, using tusks, size, and speed to tear through Hovrid's ranks. The guard holding those strange clay spheres threw one against the floor. It smashed, and fire burst into the air along with an acrid smell I knew all too well—dragon venom.

"Felix," I shouted and leapt to my feet. "Now!"

He was already moving. He jumped up, sweeping his arms underneath him to get his shackles in the front. Then he took off running for the body of an elite guard that had already been mauled by the boar. He pried the sword out of the corpse's hand and reared back.

I dropped to my knees and held my arms out behind me, my wrists as far apart as the chain allowed. One stroke with the sword severed the chain.

I was free.

"Go!" Felix yelled over the noise. It looked like his nose was broken. Blood was pouring down the front of his shirt.

I hesitated, not wanting to leave him here in this mess.

"Idiot, I said go!" He pointed the sword across the room. "He's getting away!"

I spotted Hovrid and one of his elite guards fleeing. They made straight for a hidden doorway tucked into the corner of the throne room and vanished behind it.

I sprinted after them, seized the door, and flung it wide open. Beyond it, I could see only a few feet down a narrow corridor that led into utter darkness.

I had no weapon. I had no idea where I was going or what new terror might be waiting for me down that dark passage. I was outnumbered, and there was no telling what traps Hovrid had set for me. Once again, my odds were beyond terrible.

So naturally, I plunged straight into the gloom without looking back.

seventeen

The corridor ahead of me was so small that I had to stoop at an awkward angle as I ran. I heard nothing except my own shuffling footsteps and noisy, panting breaths. I felt like a rat running through a tiny maze, the walls shrinking around me with each step.

Then, suddenly, the tunnel opened into a small room. I made a fist and squeezed it as tight as I could. I brought it to my lips and breathed into my hand. Green light bloomed through my fingers. As I opened my palm, an orb of light formed and hovered above my hand, shining brilliantly against the darkness.

The air was colder here. Immediately before me was a staircase leading straight down into pitch darkness. Looking at it made my stomach swirl with anxiety.

But I could hear footsteps and voices echoing up the stairs, from within the catacombs beneath the castle. Who knew how far those passages went? Or where they went?

I swallowed. Step-by-step, I descended the staircase. I cursed myself for not thinking to grab some sort of weapon before charging after Hovrid. Stupid, stupid, stupid.

"*You are my weapon,*" Paligno's voice roared through my mind, startling me. It made me trip over my own feet and nearly fall face-first down the stairs. Some weapon I was.

"You've made a huge mistake," I muttered back under my breath. "You chose wrong. I'm not the right person for this task. I don't even know what I'm doing down here. Why didn't you pick someone braver, like Beckah? Or stronger, like Jace? I can barely beat my best friend in a sword fight and you expect me to go head-to-head with Hovrid and win?"

"*No,*" came the god's bellowing reply.

It was so loud it made me cover my ears—which didn't help. It's hard to block out something coming from inside your own head.

"*I expect you to have faith; faith that cannot be broken. Many candidates were considered, but you alone were found worthy. I am Paligno, and I do not make mistakes.*"

I curled my hands into fists. More than anything, I wanted to believe that.

The shining orb hovered next to me at my bidding, offering guiding light as I reached the bottom of the staircase. Before me was another long hall. I passed by open archways and tunnels on every side. My fingers twitched. I was sweating and nervous, but focused on keeping my pulse calm and steady.

My focus was breaking. The orb's light started to wane. But even when I could hardly see my hand in front of my face, I began to sense things around me with much more clarity. There wasn't anything visual to distract me, so I had to trust my ears and powers to discern where to go. It was bizarre. The further I went, the more aware I became of just how far underground these tunnels were. I sensed the weight of the earth pressing down from above. It thrummed with energy from the surface world like vibrations through a tuning fork.

I felt Hovrid's presence, along with that of the god stone. The stone, however, sent raw, unfettered power snapping through the air like tongues of lightning. Every step I took brought me closer, until I could practically feel the heat on my face as though I were walking towards an open furnace. But instead of wincing and turning away, I was drawn to it like a moth to a flame.

And then I saw it—light coming from one of the passages to my left. I headed straight for it. The intensity of the god stone's presence grew until I was pouring a cold sweat. I felt flushed and energized. That was it—the reason my senses were so enhanced. Its presence strengthened me, made me sharper.

My foot crossed through the doorway to the chamber. I glanced around, and a second later, a searing pain shot through me. I felt a ripping jerk as someone yanked a blade out of my back, right at my shoulder.

I crumpled to my knees. Pain made my vision go spotty and I could barely breathe. Someone had attacked me—someone whose life-energy I couldn't sense. They might as well have been invisible.

The elite guard who had followed Hovrid was on me in an explosion of speed and strength that reminded me of Jace. The light glinted off of the dagger he'd stabbed me with. It was as long as my forearm and dripping with my blood. Through the holes in his white mask, I could see his eyes flicker.

He lunged again, poised for a killing blow.

I spun and swept his legs out from under him. He hit the ground hard, and the impact sent his dagger skidding across the floor. I pinned him down and planted a hand on the wooden mask that covered his face. I pushed my power into it, awakening the dormant fibers of the wood. They sprang to life. Roots burst from it, wrapping around his head and spreading over his body.

The guardsman howled in fury and tried ripping the roots away, but they grew back as quickly as he tore them away. That was bound to keep him occupied for a bit, I hoped.

I staggered to my feet and scrambled to seize the dagger. It had pierced me through, and warm blood oozed from the open wound. It hurt to move my arm at all.

I looked for Hovrid. The air was tinged with a metallic, sour smell that made me want to retch. The chamber before me wasn't very big. It was like a vault of stone with a low ceiling and no other passages in or out—a secure place. The perfect place to hide something precious.

Every flat surface in the room was covered in rust-colored ink. Strange writing in a language I didn't recognize was scrawled in patterns that swirled from floor to ceiling and back again. It was like a strange, disheveled web.

And resting in the very center of it, on an intricate gold stand surrounded by small braziers, was the god stone.

It had been placed in some sort of silver bowl. From where I was standing, I could see that the bowl was filled with a liquid. I was standing too far from it to see exactly what it was. That is, until Hovrid stepped forward from the shadows and dipped his hand into it. It was thick and an unsettling shade of red.

Blood.

Hovrid drew his hand out of the blood-filled basin where he was letting the god stone soak. He began licking the blood from his fingertips.

"For the longest time, I tried to appease Paligno's curse with my own sacrifices. I thought I might win its approval and cooperation. But coincidently, I stumbled across an interesting fact that made all that fuss completely unnecessary. You see, when a divine artifact touches blood, the blood becomes infused with the power of that artifact. Partaking of that blood grants the drinker that same power, albeit temporarily. So more must be consumed. More, and more, and more. It becomes a need, an addiction. In ancient times they called it sanguimancy—blood magic."

"That's sick," I snarled at him.

"Indeed. The rest of the world deems this practice wicked, as well. It was banned from ever being used, stricken from all historical records in the hopes it would never be discovered again. But there is a legend older still about the one who discovered this art. One not unlike you. A god's mortal pet. The one they called God Bane. Legend has it he discovered this precious procedure and sought to use it to destroy the very god who'd enslaved him." Hovrid smiled as he wiped his chin of a few droplets and then slurped them into his skeletal mouth. "After a while, it becomes delicious. I've found that using the blood of the innocent yields more potent results. I wonder what it could do with your blood."

I glanced at my wounded shoulder. Then I raised the dagger, sinking into a defensive stance.

"Fortunately for me, you don't have to be alive in order for me to test it." He surged towards me suddenly, a hand outstretched. From it came a burst of light, an explosion of magical energy that overwhelmed my senses and sent me flying across the room.

I hit the wall on the other side. My head bounced off the stone, and once again I was seeing stars.

"Did you honestly believe you were the only one in this world who could do miraculous things with divine power?" Hovrid sneered. "Don't be so naïve. The stone is mine now. It answers to me alone. That Paligno sent a filthy little halfbreed to do his bidding it utterly pathetic … futile … Insulting!"

He zapped me again, and this time it felt like my skin was on fire. I flailed my arms to get away. My hands groped for anything to cling to while my soul felt like it was being stretched outside of my body. I couldn't get my breath long enough to even scream.

The burning stopped as suddenly as it had begun. I was left lying on my back, staring up at the stone ceiling while my ears rang. I was in shock. I couldn't move.

"Take his weapon," Hovrid commanded. "And cut his throat."

I heard footsteps coming closer. It had to be that elite guard. When he leaned down over me, I realized his mask was gone. I could see his face.

I knew him.

"L-Lyon?" I rasped.

His eyes were vacant and dark. His complexion was ashen. When he touched my hand to pry his dagger out of my fist, his skin was as cold as ice.

No matter how I searched, I couldn't sense anything living about him. No spirit. No pulse.

"You can only heal the living, and not even yourself. It's almost cruel, isn't it? For Paligno to cripple you so?" Hovrid's voice was filled with pleasure as he read the horror on my face. "But I can raise the dead, and they make such obedient soldiers. So do the living, as it turns out. One drop of cursed blood and their minds become as useless as mud."

It wasn't him. It couldn't be. The Lyon I knew was dead. I had watched him die with my own eyes. His body had been burned on a funeral pyre overseen by his entire family … hadn't it?

Suddenly, I was on my feet again. I grabbed Lyon's reanimated corpse, flung him across the room and turned on Hovrid.

He shrank before me. I saw panic in his eyes. But more importantly, I saw myself—my reflection. My eyes burned like green fire. My teeth flashed like fangs. From my head grew two white horns like those of a stag.

Hovrid flung his power at me again, screeching with fury.

I raised a hand, forcing outward with my will. When the two collided, it turned his wicked magic to nothing but mist.

"*You have no idea what divine power is*," I roared in Paligno's voice, a chorus of whispers from the melded souls of my predecessors.

Hovrid staggered backward, tripping over the stand and bowl where the god stone was placed. They clattered to the floor, sending blood spraying everywhere and the stone rolling away into a corner. He began screaming again, this time in the elven language. He called me every vulgar name he could think of. He cursed Paligno and all the gods.

When his back touched the opposite wall, Hovrid realized he had no more room to run. He kept looking behind me, as though he expected someone to come in and save him. Maybe he was hoping some of his undead dragonriders or his prized elite guard would find us just in time.

This time, he was the unlucky one.

I seized him by the throat and held him off the ground. He felt so fragile in my hand. With Paligno's power coursing through my body, I could have crushed him. I wanted to. I was supposed to.

"Pathetic! You want to kill me—you've been ordered to—and still you hesitate!" Hovrid choked as he clawed at my arm desperately. "Sentiment. Weakness. Just like your coward father!"

I bared my teeth. A growl ripped from my chest that sounded as monstrous as I felt.

A second too late, I saw the knife. He'd pulled it out of his robes. It was a wicked-looking knife made of white wood—a greevwood knife made by the gray elves.

He plunged it straight at my heart.

eighteen

I should have died.

That blade was made of the sharpest material in the entire world. It was supposed to be indestructible. A blade that never dulled, that could split iron like butter.

But the instant it touched my skin, the knife shattered into a million pieces, leaving Hovrid holding nothing but an empty hilt.

"*You swore upon my stone that no member of his household would be harmed by your hand. I hold you to your oath,*" Paligno's voice thundered around us. It shook the foundations of the castle. The earth quaked, making the stones of the room chatter like teeth.

A deep fissure split open beneath my feet, like the earth's gaping maw. Hovrid was dangling over it, suspended only by my hand.

"*Deliver him to me,*" Paligno commanded.

The fissure was growing wider by the second, devouring the entire room. Lyon's corpse was swallowed first. He didn't even scream. The dead can't beg for a life they don't have.

"No," Hovrid was pleading over the roaring of the shifting earth. "Don't do this, please."

I hesitated.

Questions and doubts blurred through my mind. Was this even his fault? He'd only looked at the stone and been driven mad by it. Could he be blamed for every terrible thing he'd done because of that one mistake? What right did I have to be his executioner?

I looked into what was left of Hovrid's face and saw what I'd been dreading. I saw my brother. I saw someone my mother had loved, a child she'd carried and raised. I saw how, in another life, we could have been close. We could have been friends rather than enemies.

But that wasn't this life.

And this wasn't my choice to make.

"I'm sorry," I said.

And I let him fall.

The fissure opened wider, a yawning mouth of the earth, hungry to feed. Far below, I saw a pinpoint of boiling red light. Then the ground began to cave in under my feet. The god stone rolled towards the abyss, teetering on the edge. I dove after it, seizing it in my bare hands. Then I ran—even thought I knew I couldn't possibly make it. The ground was falling away beneath me. I was too late. The pit was going to swallow the stone and me.

But it didn't.

One step became two, then three, then four. I couldn't fathom how I was making it to the exit, even as the earth crumbled around me. I glanced down and saw that beneath the places where my feet fell, fragments of rock and soil gathered like hovering stepping stones. They created a floating pathway.

This was new. None of the whispers had ever told me about anything like this.

Tucked away into the folds of my cloak, the god stone thrummed with energy and power. Just touching it made me feel like my bones were rattling. I wondered if I was able to draw more power from the stone when I was touching it. I stretched out a hand and decided to test it.

Instantly, a curved, hovering staircase materialized out of the debris, bringing me up out of the depths to safe ground. But the castle was collapsing, splitting at the foundations. Soon, it would be completely destroyed.

Unless I did something to stop it.

I willed the rocks to move around me. I brought forth more and more of them, gathering them around the weak points at the foundation and drawing them in tightly to hold the castle together. Then I willed thick and mighty roots to weave around them like a subterranean net.

My pulse raced. I was running, focused on the path ahead, but my mind was ablaze with power I'd never known. It was a thrill unlike any other. I didn't realize that I was pushing things too far.

I wasn't leaving without Felix. Even if I had to haul his dead body out of here over my shoulder, I wasn't going anywhere without him.

But when I found him standing, spattered with gore, amidst the carnage and smoldering pools of dragon venom in the throne room, I realized I might be the one who needed to be carried.

My head swam and my arms started to feel heavy. Something wasn't right; I was losing a *lot* of blood. It made my focus slip and I knew I wasn't synced with Paligno anymore. At least, not like I was before. The horns were gone when I touched the side of my head. I couldn't feel fangs in my mouth anymore, either.

I caught a glimpse of Felix as my knees began to weaken. He looked awful, but he was alive. Furious—but alive.

"You," he snapped and pointed the business end of his sword at my face as soon as he saw me. "You said it would only be a few guards. You said we'd fight them together. But more importantly, you failed to mention that stupid pig has a hide four inches thick!"

I glanced hazily at the beast's corpse lying before him. There were arrows sticking out of nearly every inch of it. It looked like a pincushion, and it wasn't moving. But he still rammed his blade into the boar's neck one more time. I got the impression that was just for spite.

"I was nearly trampled to death," he yelled, although he seemed satisfied now that the animal most definitely was dead. "Killed by an overgrown pig!"

For all the noise he was making, it didn't seem like he was

hurt any worse than when I'd left him. The most serious wound I saw was a deep gash across one of his palms that was bleeding everywhere. That was a relief.

"H-how did you beat so many of them?" I stammered in disbelief.

"I'm bloody Felix Farrow, that's how," he fumed and thumped his breastplate.

"We need to hurry. Kiran is waiting for our—"

The castle shuddered dangerously.

There was another low, droning sound that echoed off the cavernous ceilings. It sounded like a muffled roar.

Felix and I looked at one another.

"Please tell me that was you," he murmured.

I shook my head slowly. This wasn't anything Paligno was doing. I would have been able to sense that. And as far as I could tell, my mending of the castle's foundations was holding fast. No—this was something else.

I couldn't sense them, but I knew that sound all too well. There were more dragonriders mobilizing, no doubt heading straight for us.

"You got it, right?" Felix was looking up, his eyes tracking the sounds of angry dragon coming from outside.

I pressed a hand against the round lump tucked away under my cloak. I had to keep the stone hidden. No one could see it—not even by accident. Just one glimpse would plant a seed that could grow into madness the same way it had in Hovrid's mind. I was the only one who could look at it or touch it without risking those effects.

"Good. Give them the signal. It's time to go." Felix seized my arm and began dragging me behind him. Together, we ran out of the throne room through a side door and into the castle halls.

The entire royal castle was in shambles. The alarm was raised that someone had broken through the King of Maldobar's private guard and murdered him. Soldiers were storming every hall, searching for us. Servants ran around in a frenzy, terrified of the armed men pouring inside. It took everything we had to stay one step ahead of them.

I knew the courtyard was bound to be a veritable hornet's nest of people waiting to kill us, but our main concern was the dragonriders. Losing them wasn't going to be easy.

In fact, I seriously doubted we could.

As we darted through servant's passages and hallways, hiding and dodging soldiers at every turn, I sent out my signal to Mavrik. It was time to move. We'd be waiting at the top of the tallest tower for them.

At least, that was the plan. I had to trust Felix's judgment now.

Of the two of us, he was the only one who'd actually been here before. The perks of being a high noble.

There were just three little problems with our plan.

One: based on what I could sense mustering outside the castle, there were a lot more dragonriders waiting for us than I had anticipated.

Two: Hovrid had built himself a literal army of reanimated dragonriders using that foul blood magic that were all immune to my abilities. I couldn't communicate with any of their mounts like I'd intended, so I had no way to slow them down.

And three—which was actually something I hadn't even considered would be a problem—I was hurt, badly. And it was taking every ounce of my strength and concentration to keep myself moving.

It was worse than I'd initially thought. I couldn't see the wound because of my clothing, but I definitely felt it. I was also getting extremely lightheaded from blood loss. I didn't know how much time I had before my body gave out, but I had to hang on. None of this was going to matter if I died before we got to Luntharda.

Felix kicked in the door to the staircase leading up to the castle's tallest tower. By now we were definitely being followed, thanks in part to my leaving a very obvious trail of blood behind. I gawked at the staircase. It made me nauseous just looking at it.

I wasn't going to make it.

"Come on." Felix didn't give me the option to turn back. He started running up the steps.

I tried to keep up.

In my mind, I reached out to Mavrik. I told him I was hurt. I didn't know if I was going to have the strength to catch the saddle when I jumped. He filled my mind with worried, urgent hues of orange and yellow. They were coming as fast as they could.

My body began to give out halfway up the stairs. My knees buckled under me and I hit the wall. Everything was spinning. I fell backward, back towards all the steps we'd already climbed.

Suddenly, Felix caught me by the front of my shirt. He yanked me forward and draped one of my arms over his shoulder so he could basically drag me up the rest of the way.

"Hovrid did this to you?" he gasped between panting breaths. He had to lean over and wheeze for a minute when finally we reached the top of the stairs. Before us, a small door led out onto the turret.

I didn't answer. There were some things better left unsaid.

The wind was fierce so high up in the air. We looked down at the staggering drop and the castle grounds below. Dragons were circling, scouring the perimeter for us. They didn't know where we were and so far, they hadn't spotted us.

Not yet, anyway.

Felix squinted into the sunlight. "I don't see them. I don't understand, why can't you just get their mounts to rebel? Wasn't that the plan?"

"Hovrid did something to them, something I'd rather not go into right now. They can't hear me. They won't do anything I say."

Then I heard Mavrik's thundering cry. Not literally, of course. I heard him in my mind. He was close.

"We have to jump." I pushed away from Felix and staggered to the edge of the turret.

He tried to stop me as I climbed over the edge. "Are you insane? They aren't here. I don't see them anywhere."

There wasn't time to explain. Mavrik was insisting. His thoughts overwhelmed my own, telling me to jump *right now*.

I grabbed Felix and dragged him over the edge of the turret with me. I flung us both out into the open air.

He cursed me all the way down.

At least, until we both smacked into our dragon saddles.

Felix hit Nova spot on, catching his saddle at just the right angle.

Mavrik, on the other hand, barely snagged me. I hit his back hard and rolled off, frantically trying to get a good hold of the saddle as I felt myself beginning to fall again.

Then someone caught me. Someone strong.

I looked up to see Kiran sitting on Mavrik's back, gripping my arm. With his help, I was able to get back up into the saddle.

I didn't know how he'd gotten over to Mavrik's saddle, or how the dragons had ever convinced him to do it in the first place— since they couldn't talk to him the way they were able to talk to me. I wasn't all too worried about it right then. The dragonriders gathering below had seen us now. They gave chase, taking off by the dozens. Soon there were so many I lost count.

This wasn't good.

Prax, Beckah, and the rest of our friends were waiting for us at Solhelm. They were prepared for a fight, but not for one on this scale. We were vastly outnumbered, with only a few hours at most until we arrived. Worst of all, I had no way to warn them.

We were going to need help—and lots of it. So I closed my eyes. I gathered what I could of my scrambled, frantic thoughts, and sent out a desperate request that rippled across the kingdom.

I just hoped they'd be willing to assist.

I wasn't doing so great, and that's putting it lightly. I'd already lost a lot of blood. My body felt weak and sluggish, and I could barely keep my head up. I tried my best not to move any more than necessary; to conserve what was left of my strength.

Felix used the dragonrider's code of hand signals to communicate to me. While we were in flight, it was the only way to talk because of the noise from the wind.

Are you sure about this? He signed.

No, of course I wasn't sure. I was doing my best not to completely freak out. But in the limited time we had before we reached Felix's estate at Solhelm, I'd come up with a frantic, last-minute, more reckless than usual, Plan B. Now I just had to pray it would work and that my request might be granted.

You know what this will mean, Felix continued to gesture. *No turning back. No matter what happens, we can't stop.*

I didn't reply. I knew he was right. This was our one and only shot. Our only advantage now was a decent head start. If we hesitated, if we stuck around even one minute too late, we might not make it to Luntharda at all.

I tried not to look back because every time I did, it seemed like the dragonriders chasing us were getting closer … probably because they were. Nova couldn't keep pace with Mavrik, and even he wasn't making spectacular time while weighed down with two passengers. Even so, we pushed hard and managed to keep our lead up until I spotted Solhelm on the horizon.

Then I heard a dragon's roar that sounded like it was right behind us. I felt the heat from a blast of burning dragon venom.

They were close—really close.

I had about a second to loop an arm around Kiran so he didn't fall off before Mavrik whipped into an evasive dive. We whirled toward the ground, Nova following right behind us.

I struggled to suppress my panic as I clung to Mavrik's back. I trusted in his speed to save us. He shot through the air, weaving and rolling through erratic patterns to try to lose the dragonriders who were right on our tail.

I couldn't see Nova and Felix anymore. Kiran was hanging on for dear life. Every time I got a clear look at what was around us,

I saw more dragonriders than before coming straight for us. They seemed to come from every side.

Then, straight ahead, there it was—Felix's family estate.

"You can do it," I urged Mavrik with every ounce of my concentration. "We can make it."

Suddenly, there they were. The dragonriders of Emerald Flight were rising up from where they'd been lying in wait behind Felix's family home. Beckah and Icarus lead the surprise attack, headed straight for us.

Mavrik tucked into another whirling dive as the dragonriders of Emerald Flight clashed in combat with our pursuers. Immediately, the sky erupted into fiery chaos. Everywhere we turned, there were plumes of burning dragon venom. Dragons locked into aerial combat like eagles, clawing and snapping as they fell. It was a deadly game of chicken to see who would pull away first before they hit the ground.

I caught brief glimpses of my friends through the fray. Icarus was the only king drake, and the biggest dragon by far, so I found him easily. His size wasn't exactly an advantage for him, though. Since he was obviously the leader, it made him and his rider primary targets.

Beckah was like an avenging angel, wielding her bow while standing up in the stirrups of her saddle. The golden wings painted on her black flashed like fire in the sunlight. At her back, her father rode tandem and fired his bow with that same deadly accuracy.

Injured or not, I wanted to join the fight, to stand with the people I loved till my last breath. I could taste the flavor of bloodlust on my tongue. Judging by the way he was gripping his bow, Kiran wanted the same thing.

We were still outnumbered by a lot. They couldn't hold our enemy off for long. We were overwhelmed and flying for our lives.

Mavrik zipped through the sky— rolling, diving, climbing, and falling. My strength was nearly spent, and I was losing my grip on his saddle. Kiran had to put his arms around me to keep me from falling off. I was cold. My sight was growing dim and I couldn't comprehend anything going on around me.

Then I heard a chorus of roars louder than all the rage of combat. The sound cleared my head for an instant. Over my shoulder, I saw them, flying in from the cliffs, the sea wind under their wings. All the wild dragons of Maldobar had heard my request.

The cavalry had arrived. The odds were evened now, and the battle raged on with fire and steel, scales and claws, over Solhelm. People in the town below were running for cover as stray bursts of dragon flame scorched the rooftops.

Felix appeared next to me, frantically signaling that this was our chance. It was time to go, he was right.

But that meant leaving our friends behind to their fate—to victory or death.

My insides churned at the idea of turning my back on them now. I was faltering. There had to be something more I could do.

Felix made his dragon veer dangerously close to us. Mavrik had to swerve to avoid colliding with her. It got my attention and I saw him signaling.

We don't stop. We don't turn back. If we mess this up, then everything they've done will be for nothing.

I clutched the round lump in my robes where the god stone was hidden "Go," I told Mavrik, before I could think about it anymore. "Go now! And whatever I say, do not turn back!"

He aimed away from the battle and started for the north—for Luntharda.

I couldn't let it go that easily, though. Not when half my heart was in the thick of that battle. I reached back with my mind, scouring the thoughts of every dragon on that battlefield that would still let me in—the mounts of my friends. I searched until I found Icarus.

He was fighting hard. I felt his intensity, his rage—and that he was hurt. One of his wings had been wounded. It was slowing him down, making him vulnerable, and Beckah was being pressured that much more because of it.

I saw her and her father through Icarus's eyes, like peering through a looking glass. Sile was nearly out of arrows. Beckah had torn her helmet off. Her dark hair was wild about her face. Her expression revealed a level of intensity I'd never seen from her before. Over and over, she drew arrows from her quiver, firing them into the battle, hitting marks as effortlessly as she breathed.

I saw it coming only a fraction of a second before it happened.

One of Hovrid's riders swooped in from behind. Icarus's injury prevented him from rolling fast enough to evade the attack. The enemy dragon's wings flared, its hind legs outstretched.

Beckah's expression suddenly went blank. In an instant, those powerful, crushing claws ripped her from her saddle. Her father reached for her. Their fingers brushed.

Icarus and I cried out in unison.

But it was too late.

I commanded Mavrik to turn around. I screamed at him. I didn't believe it. There had to be some chance I was wrong, that she was still alive, and that I could still save her.

Mavrik knew otherwise. His thoughts were melded with mine. He'd seen everything I had—felt what I had felt. So he refused to turn around.

And little-by-little, the sounds of battle faded behind us.

PART THREE

FELIX

nineteen

Something had happened. Something bad. I'd heard Jae make a lot of strange sounds and do a lot of bizarre things before, but never anything like that. Now he was just slumped over in his saddle, with our weird, little, gray elf sidekick struggling to keep him upright. I couldn't see his face to tell if he was even conscious. It gave me a bad feeling. All I could think about was landing as soon as possible.

We couldn't stop, though. Not until we reached the edge of Luntharda's towering jungle on the northern border. By now, there were bound to be orders sent out by frantic messengers to every corner of the kingdom. We'd just given every soldier and dragonrider in Maldobar the perfect reason to grant Hovrid's final wish to launch an all-out attack on Luntharda and the wipe gray elves off the map once and for all.

Forces would be mustering now to take up the pursuit, to capture or kill us at any cost. And according to Jae, we would be essentially be leading them to the one place in the jungle that his people had left to hide. So, a lot was riding on this.

On, Jae, rather. A lot was riding on him.

I just hoped he was still up to the task.

When we touched down in the wreckage of Barrowton, I sprang out of my saddle and ripped off my helmet. I sprinted to Mavrik's side as the blue drake flattened himself against the ground. That's when I got my first look at Jaevid.

His face was ashen, with eyes wide and fixed. His shirt and cloak were drenched with blood coming from the wound on his shoulder. I called his name, but he didn't even look at me. Behind him, Kiran fumbled with the straps to get them out of the saddle. When the last buckle was undone, Jae keeled over sideways and started to fall.

I threw myself in the way, arms out to catch him before he hit the ground. My back creaked in protest. For a tall, lanky guy, Jae wasn't light.

"Grab the gear." I started to give out orders. "Empty the saddle bags, all of them. We have to take cover as soon as possible. We can't move until nightfall."

Suddenly, Jae started to revive.

He swung at me, catching me with a fist on my chin. He pushed away and clamored to his feet. It was like he didn't know us. His eyes looked wildly between Kiran and me as he staggered back.

"Jaevid, just calm down." I raised my hands, hoping he'd snap out of it. "You're hurt. You've lost a lot of blood. We need to take a look at—"

He threw up.

Kiran flashed me a worried glance. Together, we rushed to catch him again as Jae dropped to his knees and started screaming. He yelled like a maniac and hammered against the ground with his fists until his knuckles were banged up and bleeding, too.

It took both of us to restrain him. With Kiran pinning his arms down with a bear hug from the front, I got him in a headlock with a hand over his mouth. Together, we forced him to be still.

"Calm down, you idiot," I repeated. "You keep that up and anyone who might be on patrol around here will be heading straight for us."

His chest heaved with deep, fast breaths. Tears were streaming down his face. I didn't understand any of this. He'd seemed just fine when we left the castle.

I looked to Kiran for an explanation. Maybe he'd seen something I hadn't. "What's going on?"

He shook his head slowly.

Great. So neither of us had a clue.

"Well, we can't stay out here in the open like this." I tried to come up with a way to restrain him—something involving tying him up like a mental patient. Then, out of nowhere, Jaevid went limp again. He stopped struggling and his whole body went slack in our hold.

I thought it might be a trick, but when Kiran loosened his hold, Jae didn't lash out at us. He just laid there, limp as a dead fish, as we slowly let him go.

"Something's not right. You know better than any of us what's going on with him and that forest god, right? So what would set him off like this?"

Kiran's brow furrowed and his mouth mashed together into an uncomfortable, crooked line. He was looking Jae over, thinking. At last, he met my gaze and answered, "Death."

It took a second or two for that to sink in. It took even longer for me to make sense of it. Meanwhile, Kiran and I worked together to get everything prepared for nightfall. I carried Jae into the burned-out, skeletal remains of a building in Barrowton's former city square. It offered some cover from aerial scouts who would soon be launched to search for us.

Kiran unloaded all our gear and supplies, stacking them in a corner and bringing me all the medical tools he could find while I ripped open Jae's blood-soaked shirt and started treating his injury. It was a deep puncture through the middle of his shoulder. It was going to keep him from being much use in combat. Actually, it was a miracle he'd made it this far. He had a lot more grit than I'd ever given him credit for.

"Is he dead?" Kiran appeared over my shoulder, leaning in to watch while I put the final stitches in place.

"No. You think I'd bother to stitch up a corpse?"

He made a 'pfft' sound and walked around to sit across from

me, huddling underneath a coarse blanket he'd swiped from Jae's saddle bag. We couldn't light a fire, even though the evening air was chilly. After I got Jae's shoulder bandaged up and wrapped in a few layers of gauze, I took the blanket from my bag and wrapped him up in it. Then I sat back to think.

Outside, our dragons were hunkering down in whatever cover they could find—lying in wait for further orders. Orders that I wasn't sure I could give. If Jae was out of commission, that meant completing this mission had just become my responsibility. Only, I had no idea where to go or what to do when I got there.

"You know," I started to talk because the silence was crushing me. "Hovrid actually came to me right before this. He asked me to be his new Lord General."

Kiran canted his head to the side. Duh. He didn't know what a Lord General was.

"Basically, the leader of all dragonriders. His number one in command," I explained.

Kiran made an O-shape with his mouth.

"I refused. I mean, not that it wasn't tempting. But something about him … I don't know, I guess it was my intuition that he was after more than just a new Lord General. He wanted me—someone Jae trusted—to turn on him. And then when I actually saw what he was underneath that mask? Gods and Fates, I can't believe I ever doubted Jae for a second."

"If it had been easy to believe, then Hovrid wouldn't have gotten away with it for so long," Kiran replied quietly.

He was a weird guy. Short, you know, because of the whole elf thing. He never said much, or at least never more than was absolutely necessary. And his long, silver hair, multi-hued eyes, pointed ears, and colorful silk clothes were odd, too.

But I was starting to see why Jaevid liked him.

"Why'd you come with him?" I asked.

He glanced up at me then quickly looked away. "There was … someone I was hoping to see."

"A girl?" I guessed.

He didn't answer. But I knew I was right. His mouth scrunched uncomfortably and his brow creased with worry.

"Someone from the prison camp? Or the ghetto in Halfax?" After all, it had to be another gray elf, right?

He shook his head slowly. He had that faraway look on his face. "No," he answered softly.

"Well, I'm sure she's fine wherever she is." I tried to offer him a little hope, since that was in short supply at the moment. "And when all this is over, you can go find her and tell her you helped save the world."

Kiran swallowed hard. "I hope so."

"We can't stay here much longer." Kiran shifted his weight from one foot to the other, peering up at the starry night sky through the charred rafters of our hiding place.

Technically speaking, we should have been long gone by now. We should have sent our dragons off as a diversion while we slipped through the border into Luntharda undetected. But Jae was in bad shape. I didn't know exactly how bad off he was; I'm not any sort of doctor. Although, I could guess that the pale color to his skin, the dark circles under his eyes, and the frantic, shallow way he was breathing weren't good signs.

"I don't see how we can move him like this," I muttered back.

Kiran puffed a frustrated sigh through his nostrils. "I'm going to get a better look. If there aren't any scouts or patrols in sight, we will have to take the risk. The princess is waiting for us."

He didn't hang around for my opinion on the matter. He scurried away across the debris-strewn city like a silver-haired squirrel, leaving me to sit by Jaevid's unconscious body.

Only, he wasn't unconscious anymore.

"H-how late is it?" His voice sounded dry and hoarse. Thanks to the faint, sterling light from the sky, I could see his eyes were open. Even so, he still looked dead. His expression was vacant and his gaze was fixed straight ahead as he lay on his back, not moving.

"Not very. An hour past dark. We're behind, but not by much."

He blinked slowly. "I'm going on alone."

"Like hell you are."

Jae didn't argue. He didn't look at me or make any sound at all.

It wasn't normal, even for him.

I turned away because I wasn't sure how to start or what to say. I had to ask him. Someone needed to, and that someone had to be me because I was his best friend.

"It was Beckah, wasn't it?"

When he didn't answer, I dared to glance down at him again over my shoulder. He hadn't moved. He was still just lying there, staring up at the sky.

The light glinted off something wet sliding down his cheek.

"I failed her," he whispered.

"No you didn't."

He looked back at me, then. His jaw tensed and I saw something crazed cross his face, a primal anger he didn't have the ability or strength to express. It was the look of a broken man. "I promised her, Felix. I promised her I would protect her! And I couldn't do anything to stop—"

"She knew the risks," I shouted as loudly as I dared. "We all did. And we understood what was most important. The only thing that matters right now is getting you and that stone into the jungle so we can put an end to all this. If that means a few of us have to die to get it done, so be it. That's the gamble we all took. And if Beckah were here, she'd be telling you the same thing. This is war, Jaevid. People die—and sometimes it's the people we love."

We stared at each other in silence. I could tell I'd made him even angrier. His face got a little bit of color back—just enough to let me know he still had enough blood in his veins to keep him going.

"Look, I'm not saying you shouldn't be upset. I'm not saying you shouldn't grieve. But don't go off blaming yourself for something that wasn't your fault. I made that mistake already when I thought I'd lost you. I know where that path ends. Trust me, that isn't where you want to be."

Slowly, Jae turned his face away to stare back up at the sky. He blinked owlishly and never said a word, even after Kiran came back. Kiran was out of breath and frazzled, his eyes darted everywhere like a nervous cat.

"I saw them. A scouting party of four dragonriders coming from the east," he whispered. "They're headed straight for us."

"They must be coming from Northwatch."

Kiran bobbed his head eagerly, and then gestured to Jae. "Our time is up. We must move now. Can he walk?"

"I'm not sure. Maybe. But walking might not get us there in time." I glanced at all our piled up gear. Saddlebags stocked with food, medical supplies, and survival gear. All were things I'd been trained to believe I needed in order to survive in Luntharda, and we weren't going to be able to take any of it with us. "You're sure that princess of yours is going to be there?"

"Yes," he answered sharply.

That was good enough for me. "Gather only the weaponry. The rest we'll have to leave behind."

Kiran bounded off again, rummaging through all the bags and laying out our spread of deadly tools. Meanwhile, I hauled Jae to his feet. He was catatonic, staring around aimlessly with a dead look in his eyes. It was starting to freak me out.

I smacked him across the face. "Snap out of it, hero. You've got to get the dragons to draw off the scouts so we can get out of here without being burned to a crisp. You hear me?"

He blinked a few times and finally nodded.

It only took a moment or two before I heard the deep percussion of wing beats. I saw the starlight glint off our dragons' scales as they sailed upward, spitting plumes of flame that would be visible for miles. A few minutes after they wheeled away and disappeared, four more dragons zipped past, flying low and fast in hot pursuit.

The clock was officially ticking.

After I packed what weaponry I could into every nook and cranny of my armor, I gave Kiran the go-ahead to take the lead. He was gonna have to get us out of the city and all the way to the border of Luntharda, because I was on watch to make sure Jaevid didn't pass out again or die before we got there.

I approached him carefully, holding out his elf-human hybrid scimitar with the stag head engraved on the pommel. "I need to know you're still in there, Jae. I need to know you can finish this."

His eyes were clearer when he met my gaze. "Yes, I can."

"Good." I pushed the hilt of the blade into his hands. "Now do whatever magical thing it is you do and let that princess know we are coming for her."

twenty

Kiran ran point, his bow at the ready as he scaled mounds of debris and kept his eyes on the horizon. He found a manageable path for us out of the city, and I had to give him credit—he didn't even stop to consider all the decayed corpses of his kinsmen lying everywhere from the battle. Granted, there were a lot of human remains, too. But if seeing the carnage filled him with any kind of resentment for us or made him second-guess his decision to join our cause, it never showed. He was steady as a rock, focused, running ahead of us without making a sound.

Once we left the city ruins, I got nervous. We were out in the open, plainly visible to anyone who might fly over. There was nowhere to run and nowhere to hide. We were completely on our own, trekking to the border of Luntharda as fast as we could, which wasn't nearly fast enough.

Jae was weak. He leaned heavily against me, stumbling now and again so that I was forced to catch him to keep him upright. That's when I realized … he wasn't going to make it, at least, not at this rate. We were still miles from the border. I couldn't even see the jungle yet.

Suddenly, Jae stopped. He pushed away from me and whirled around, his eyes going wide as saucers as he looked to the sky. In the distance, I heard the low rumble, like thunder from an approaching storm front.

"It's the dragonriders from Northwatch," Jae said. "They're coming this way."

"How long?"

"Five minutes at the most." He blinked slowly.

"Can you hold them off? Get their mounts to turn around?"

He shook his head slowly. "It's the same as before. Hovrid has done something to them. They won't listen to me."

Then his body shuddered, and when he gazed up at the sky again, I saw his irises light up like two green moons. He was using his powers—brewing up another miracle to try and save us.

I knew I should've stopped him. He wasn't up to this. He could barely walk, how could anyone expect him to—

The ground started to rumble beneath us. Jae snarled, baring teeth with incisors pointed like a wolf's fangs. He made a primal, roaring sound and stretched out his hands. Jae made a ripping gesture in the air, as though pulling apart invisible dough with his fingers.

Before us, the ground shuddered open like a cracked piece of pottery. Kiran and I stumbled back to get out of the way, and not a moment too soon. Out of the fissure crawled a creature out of someone's worst nightmare, with eyes glowing like two pits of bottomless, green fire. It looked like an enormous dragon made of roots and earth, held together by raw magic, easily twice the size of any king drake. Horns of twisted roots, scales of shale, claws of crystals, and a hide spotted in moss and plant life. It shook itself free of the ground, as though it had been imprisoned there for an eternity, and let out an earth-shaking screech.

I couldn't keep my mouth closed or take my eyes off it. The dragon spread its huge wings. Each beat was like a mighty clap of thunder. I had to shield my face, as the force of it taking off blew debris everywhere. Once the monster was airborne, we watched in total silence as it soared towards our approaching attackers—ready to intercept them.

"What the heck is that thing?" I heard myself ask.

"Another distraction," Jae replied hoarsely. "But it won't last long. We need to hurry. I've asked Mavrik and Nova to hold them off as long as possible."

I saw him start to wobble. He staggered, and I rushed forward to catch him under the arm before he could collapse.

"I called out to the jungle. Araxie and Jace … t-they're … w-we have to …" Jae tried to speak, but his voice was lost as he took in deep, ragged breaths. His head lolled against me, and I could see that his skin was more ashen than before. Casting that magic, drawing from that power, was costing him too much.

"We can't let him do that again." I growled at Kiran. "He's killing himself a little more every time he does."

Kiran nodded in agreement. "Let's move."

We took off as fast as we could across the rolling prairie. Kiran stayed right beside me, watching our backs with his bow at the ready and his eyes on the sky. Behind us, I could hear the sounds of aerial combat. Dragons snarled and bellowed. The night lit up with plumes of dragon flame erupting into the darkness.

Jae was right. His earth-dragon didn't last long. It made for an amazing spectacle, but it didn't hold up well against fire. Once it caught a few good blasts of burning dragon venom, it only had minutes left before it came crashing back to the earth to smolder and crackle in a giant heap.

Then they were on us. With a skull-rattling boom, a dragonrider touched down right before us. His sword was drawn. His mount's scales glittered in the starlight like black diamonds. I saw the dragon's plated chest heave and its head recoil as it took in a mighty, venom-spraying breath.

She came out of nowhere—my girl. Nova blitzed down out of the sky and smacked right into them at full speed, legs outstretched and jaws open wide. The impact threw the rider from his saddle and he hit the ground with a nasty-sounding crunch. The two dragons rolled across the ground like two brawling cats, snarling and hissing. My girl was bigger, stronger, but her opponent hadn't come to the fight alone.

Three more dragonriders dove in at her at once, overwhelming her and burying her under a heap of scales, claws, and teeth.

I yelled for her. I heard her screeching, screaming in panic.

A sudden explosion of flame sent her attackers retreating back. Mavrik landed beside her, his teeth bared and his black spines bristling as he took up a protective stance between them—daring one of the other dragons to make a move. It gave Nova a chance to recover. She shook herself off and joined him in squaring off with their enemies.

I never saw what happened next. We descended the hill on the other side of the fight and kept going. I couldn't stop, or look back to see if she was all right, I just had to trust that she would be.

It was a race against time, and we were definitely losing. I saw the shadows of the other dragonriders against the gentle light of the stars as they made low, zooming passes over us.

They were coming, growing closer by the second. They were just looking for the perfect place to rally and corner us.

I didn't stop to look at them. I kept pressing forward, running as fast as possible while basically dragging Jae's unconscious body along. Kiran was shouting in elven, firing arrows at the dragonriders who swopped in close to us.

Suddenly, ten of them landed in front of us. We came skidding to a halt, staring into the swords, teeth, and flame of an enemy that outnumbered us. Then a dozen more landed behind us. Kiran took a protective step in towards Jae, his bowstring taut with three arrows ready to fire. The dragonriders moved as one, enclosing us in a circle.

Because I was one of them, I knew that next came the inferno. They'd bathe us in an onslaught of venom that wouldn't even leave bones behind.

"Well? You gonna just sit there and chat about it or are you gonna do something, ladies?" I shouted at them. With my free arm, I drew my sword. No way in hell was I going down empty-handed. I clenched my jaw, squared my stance, and waited for the axe to drop.

It came out of nowhere.

A hailstorm of arrows from the sky rained down all around us, hitting the ground only feet away from Jae, Kiran, and I. But not a single one struck us. They sent our enemies scurrying for cover, however. Three dragons bellowed in pain, one dropping immediately after taking a well-aimed arrow to the back of the skull.

Next to me, Kiran started cheering. He raised his bow in the air, and I looked up to see why. A small group of gray elves on shrikes went streaking past us, quicker than shooting stars, chasing down the dragonriders and locking them in combat. Well, all save for two.

Two shrikes landed before us. They moved so fast it was like they'd materialized out of thin air. Their scales shimmered like mirrors, reflecting the starry sky. Their bony jaws snapped and their eyes gleamed, eyeing us down. Each was carrying a rider wearing a long battle headdress fitted with white horns.

One I knew right away. I'd seen her before, although not up

close. She had to be the gray elf princess I'd heard so much about. She pulled back the mask on her headdress, letting her long, white hair spill freely down her shoulders. Her eyes reminded me of a wolf's—unpredictable, wild, and secretive.

The other rider removed his mask.

My mouth fell open.

"Don't just stand there like an idiot, Farrow," Jace Rordin was yelling at me over the noise of combat, outfitted from head-to-toe in full gray elf battle-dress. "Get on!"

"You have got to be kidding me."

With Kiran giving me cover, firing arrows at any dragonrider who came too close, I dragged Jaevid the last few feet and flung him over the princess's saddle. The shrikes weren't large, not nearly as big as a dragon, and I wasn't even sure they could take the weight of two riders. But it's not like we had any time to test it out.

Once Jaevid was secure, the princess took off without us. I climbed onto the back of Jace's shrike. The creature tensed, moving like a feline and preparing for takeoff. Kiran backed up a few feet and gave me a smirk and a dragonrider's salute.

"Wait!" I shouted. "What about him?"

"No room," Jace yelled back.

We took off, streaking away from the ground and leaving our gray elf companion standing there, watching us with a knowing grin on his lips. What I would have given right then to have some of those powers—to tell Nova or Mavrik to look after him.

But I'm not the one who works miracles.

"Hold him down," the gray elf princess spoke sternly. She scooped up a glob of something green, pasty, and smelly onto her fingertips.

By the dim light of a small oil lamp, Jace and I struggled to hold Jaevid still while she forced his mouth open and fed him more and more of the stuff. It must have tasted bad because Jae fought us hard, but when she finished, he was already looking better. His color wasn't so corpse-like and he was breathing more steadily.

Jace and I stood back, giving the princess some space while she tucked a blanket around him snuggly. All around us, gray elf warriors rushed to and fro, mustering their arms in preparation for the coming attack. Their makeshift compound was pathetically tiny. They had maybe three hundred fighters, not counting the ones who were obviously children that normally would have been way too young to fight.

We were only a mile inside the jungle, if that. They didn't expect their aerial force to hold long. More dragonriders and legions of ground infantry would be headed straight for this jungle, ready to raze it to the ground.

"Is this really all the soldiers they have?" I murmured to Jace, who was looking more concerned than I'd ever seen him. Not good.

"Yes," he replied.

It wasn't nearly enough, which I guess he knew. "Then we can't stay here for long."

"The temple is two days away, on foot. Longer, if Jae can't walk there himself." He growled quietly.

"Why not take the shrikes?"

"It's too dangerous, the altar is calling to the stone. The closer you get with it, the stronger the pull. We already had to evacuate the village. The shrikes will go mad if we try to take them anywhere near it."

"Jace, we don't have two days." I stepped in his way so he had to look at me instead of Jaevid and the princess. "There has to be another way."

"T-there is." Jaevid interrupted us. He sounded so weak I almost didn't recognize his voice. "I made a way."

"What are you talking about?" The princess looked as puzzled as the rest of us.

Slowly, weakly, Jae pushed the blanket off himself and unbuckled the vambrace on his left arm. When he rolled his sleeve up, I could see he was wearing a bandage. He winced as he tore it away and showed us his arm.

The gray elf princess gasped sharply. Her eyes went as wide as two moons.

There was a mark on Jae's arm—a black tattoo with a strange, swirling design. The skin around it was inflamed. It must have hurt badly, because Jae couldn't stand to wrap it back up himself. The princess had to help him with it. While she did, I could see tears pooling in the corners of her eyes.

"Why would you do such a thing?" she scolded him in a soft whisper. "You cannot trust those spirits."

"I didn't have a choice," Jae was smiling that stupid, self-sacrificing smile that made me want to punch him in the neck. "I had to be sure we made it."

"What is that? What's going on? What exactly did you do?" I demanded.

"He's made a pact with the foundling spirits," the princess explained. "They're the direct descendants of Paligno, his firstborns. They have no loyalty or love for humanity—or my people, for that matter. Whatever bargain Jaevid has struck with them no doubt came at a terrible price."

I glared down at my sneaky, scheming, moron of a best friend. "Is that true?"

"Felix, I had to. Surely you can see that now. Without their help, we don't stand a chance."

I cursed and turned away. "What was the price, then?"

He didn't answer.

"Was it your life?"

When Jaevid still didn't reply, I had to take a walk to keep from losing my temper. I didn't make it far, though. There was a commotion in the camp; gray elves ran past me, hurrying toward the sound of calling voices coming from the jungle border.

Over the white-haired heads of strangers, I saw a man standing head and shoulders above everyone else. He was dressed in dragonrider's armor and bled from an open gash on his brow. I saw him looking—searching through the crowd—until our eyes met.

"My son!" Prax started shoving through the gray elves thronging around him as though he were some sort of deity.

He embraced me. In fact, he nearly choked the life out of me. His breathing sounded ragged, like he was trying to hold it together. Before I could get a word out, he grabbed the back of my head and kissed my forehead. "I saw your dragon. Gods, I feared the worst."

"My dragon?" I wasn't sure what he meant.

The look on his face, the dimness in his eyes, made my chest suddenly feel constricted. I couldn't breathe.

"No. Not Nova. I just saw her. She was fighting. She was with Mavrik. They were going strong."

Prax bowed his head. "I'm sorry, boy."

twenty-one

My dragon was dead.

My girl. My Nova. Before I could even fully process that information, things began happening all around me that kept me from being able to let it sink in. Our comrades in Emerald Flight had arrived just in time. They were helping the gray elves hold the line and keep the dragonriders at bay. But according to my father, that wasn't going to last long. So the gray elves began to muster, to rally and prepare for the inevitable.

Hovrid's forces were moving. Northwatch had emptied and was headed straight for us. Eastwatch, too. Every minute that passed brought them closer and made our chances of success that much slimmer.

Prax had left our friends behind, locked in combat, to find me.

I guess he knew I wasn't going to leave Jae's side. He explained the situation to the rest of us while the gray elf princess stitched up the open wound on his forehead.

"We need to get going." Prax winced as the princess finished her stitching. "Once they hit the border, they're going to come in like an unending flood. They won't stop until there's nothing left. What they can't kill with blades and arrows they'll drench in dragon venom. It's going to be a massacre."

"We are prepared to do what we must to see the stone safely returned." The princess didn't look the least bit concerned. She flashed Jace a meaningful glance as she stood and picked up her war headdress.

"That's very noble, but I think you're missing the point." Prax countered. "Say you make it to that temple. Say you even manage to put the stone back where it belongs. What's going to keep the forces from Maldobar from running you into the ground and taking it right back? I think we both know they've got you pinned into a corner. If these are the only fighters you've got left, then the war is as good as over already. We may have the stone now, but we can't keep it. They're going to take it back and there's nothing we can do to stop them."

There was a tense silence. I had my suspicions that the princess, Jace, and probably everyone gathered here to make a final stand was relying on one thing—one person—to make sure that didn't happen.

And that person was Jaevid.

None of us, however, seemed willing to say that out loud. We didn't know what he could do, or if he could do anything to keep history from repeating itself. He was trusting in that deity, and we were trusting in him.

"It's time," Jaevid appeared behind us like a phantom, dressed in his long, black cloak and resting his hand on the pommel of his scimitar. He was standing on his own, which was a vast improvement from before the princess had rammed that salve down his throat.

"Time for what?" Prax glanced around at the rest of our group for an explanation.

Jaevid pulled the cowl of his cloak down low over his head. "Our escorts have arrived."

While the gray elf forces continued to assemble and prepare for the proverbial meat grinder that was headed their way, Prax, Jace, the gray elf princess, and I followed Jaevid away from the camp. We went deeper into the jungle. Gradually, the sounds of the camp faded behind us. The air grew hotter, thicker and heavier with moisture. There was no light except from a single torch the princess was carrying. I'd heard Jace call her Araxie a few times. They must have had something going on, because he seldom left her side.

We stopped when Jae did. He ordered us to douse the light. Darkness swallowed us, and I couldn't keep myself from gripping the hilt of my sword. Alien sounds echoed everywhere. The calls of birds were like eerie laughter. Leaves rustled. Twigs snapped. My pulse was pounding in my eardrums.

Right in front of me, Jaevid stood perfectly still. I could barely see him through the gloom, because his eyes were glowing again—bright green like emerald fires.

I stepped in closer to him, letting my shoulder bump his on purpose. "I'm sorry, you know, for what I said before … about Beckah."

He didn't look at me, but I could see the corner of his mouth twitch in a smile. "There's nothing to forgive, Felix. You were right."

Somehow, that didn't make me feel any better. "Doesn't happen often, does it? Me being right?"

"There's a first time for everything, I suppose."

That made me laugh. It gave me hope. Even with those glowing eyes, the real Jae—my friend, my brother—was still in there somewhere. "As fun as it is, guessing what the heck you're doing and how you plan to pull this off, I'd sure love to know what's going on here. What are we waiting on?"

He let out a sigh, as though he were steadying himself. "When I made a deal with the foundling spirits, they promised to give us their protection and help to reach the temple."

"You heard what Prax was saying to us, didn't you?"

Jaevid nodded. His expression had gone solemn and steely.

"He has a point, Jae. All of this could be for nothing if the armies of Maldobar reach that temple. They could slaughter every last one of us and take the stone back. Then there'll be nothing to stop the curse."

"Nothing except you," he said.

"Me? What can I do? I hate to be the bearer of bad news here, but I'm not the one with magical powers."

"Magic isn't what started this war, Felix. And magic isn't going to be what ends it, either," he explained, so calmly that he might as well have been discussing our dinner options. "You have something I'll never have, something that you said would take me a lot further in life than sword fighting or air combat techniques ever could. Something that has saved men's lives and reputations countless times."

"Jae—" I knew where he was going with this.

"Charm," he interrupted.

"I was talking about girls," I clarified. It was embarrassing that he even remembered that, but he was taking it way out of context. "I seriously doubt a bunch of blood-hungry dragonriders and infantrymen are going to stop and listen to me try to schmooze them."

He turned to face me. The colored bands of his eyes were still glowing brightly, making me wonder who I was actually talking to—him or that gray elf god. "Hovrid is dead. The throne of Maldobar is empty. In truth, it has been empty for a long time. And once I put the stone back, Paligno's curse is going to break. I have his assurance of that. The people who were deceived and enchanted into following his orders are going to have their eyes opened. They're going to see what's really been happening. They're going to be confused, angry, and filled with shame for what they've done. They are going to need a new king, someone to guide them toward a peaceful future. There is only one person worthy and capable of making sure that happens. And that person is you, Felix."

I swallowed. "But I'm not even a legitimate noble. I'm a bastard child. The duke wasn't my real father."

"It doesn't matter. You're all Maldobar has and everything it needs. You're the natural selection, being the heir of the next most powerful noble family in the kingdom. But you're also the best selection, because you know there can be peace between Maldobar and Luntharda. You have a way with people. They listen to you, even if they don't know you. You're going to need that charm of yours."

"I don't know how to be a king," I protested weakly. It sounded like a pathetic excuse, even to me. The idea of a crown—any crown—being placed on my head was horrifying to me.

Jaevid gave me a reassuring punch in the arm. "I'm sure you'll figure it out. Just promise me you will do everything you can to make sure the peace is lasting."

I told him I would, although I had no idea how I was going to keep that promise. I was too caught up in the way he was talking, the way he phrased things. It wasn't like him. It wasn't normal.

It almost sounded like a goodbye.

I was trying to wrap my mind around the idea of being the king of anything. How was I going to tell Julianna? What was she going to say? What if I died, too? Did that mean my mother would be the next queen? Gods and Fates, I hoped not. She might've been worse than Hovrid.

All of a sudden, Jae reached out his hand into the dark, empty air before us, almost as though he were inviting a dog to sniff it. Only it wasn't a dog.

A large, strange-looking creature appeared before him. It materialized out of nowhere, silently taking form and looming over us with an unsettling sense of intelligence winking in its eyes. With tall, black ears, a tapered snout, and a slender body, it looked a great deal like a fox. Granted, an enormous fox. But its jet-black fur was mottled with feathers. It had long tail feathers that dragged over the ground, and there were faint silver, swirling markings all over its body that were only visible when it moved. Two black wings were folded at its sides, and when it looked at me, I got a falling sensation in the pit of my stomach.

More creatures appeared. They were smaller, about the size of horses, and while they definitely had vulpine faces and ears, their bodies were a mutant mixture of bird and fox. Their feathers came in a variety of vibrant colors and their glowing eyes seemed to peer straight through me. One with bright green, blue, and yellow feathers hedged towards me with its head down, ears back, and snout twitching vigorously.

"They're going to help us get to the temple," Jae explained. He was already sitting on the back of one, holding onto fistfuls of its scruff for balance. "Don't be afraid."

"How do we know they won't turn on us?" Araxie glared suspiciously at the one that had apparently chosen her as its passenger.

"*We are not bound to the stone,*" the big, black fox-monster's voice hissed through the air as though it were insulted. It was so loud I had to cover my ears. "*We came before it.*"

Araxie winced, but she didn't falter. She had a lot of nerve. She eyed her mount skeptically, and then finally conceded with a frustrated snort.

The rest of us mounted up, trying to balance on the backs of the twitchy, anxious creatures that yipped and chirped to one another like they were complaining or telling jokes about us that we couldn't understand.

I grabbed a meaningful fistful of my mount's scruff. He could badmouth me all he wanted to his buddies, but I wasn't about to let him drop me. It was a good idea, too, because the way they maneuvered through the jungle wasn't anything like a dragon flew. It didn't even compare to a shrike, really. They flew like a flock of owls, completely silent except for the eerie yipping sounds they made to one another. They leapt from branch to branch, using their wings to flutter and soar between the gaps.

Okay, I sort of liked it. It was smooth, fast, and graceful. I could feel the power emanating from the creature—a being that was probably older than all the mortal kingdoms in the world. Its strange, feathery pelt was as soft as silk between my fingers.

The jungle awoke with the rising of dawn, but we didn't stop to marvel at it. We raced through a living labyrinth of green, riding hard all day without stopping. We passed twisting rivers, hidden cliffs, waterfalls, lagoons, canyons, flowers as big as carriages, and groves of trees covered in weird-looking spiky fruit. Everything was more wildly beautiful than I'd ever imagined. Being a dragonrider, I'd always imagined this place would be dark, swampy, and filled with terrors with jagged teeth. That couldn't have been further from the truth.

The road appeared out of nowhere. It was a path made of mismatched, pearlescent white stones. They began sparsely, but the nearer we got to the temple grounds, the more they came together to form an overgrown avenue. We burst through a line of trees that had been planted close together to form a sort of fence. And there it was—the temple. We'd reached it in what seemed like mere hours. It should have been impossible. But then again, I'd witnessed a lot of unbelievable things lately.

The foundling spirits landed before it. They huddled close together, their feathers bristling and their eyes glinting with anxiousness. I remembered what Jace had told me about being near this place. The closer we got with the god stone, the more intense the madness would be amongst the animals. Maybe the foundlings weren't affected by it, but it definitely seemed like they could sense it. It had them on edge.

I could sympathize. I felt it now, for the first time. It was like a weight on my chest, or an intense, thick heat that made it difficult to breathe. I glanced at Jaevid. He was already looking at me. When our eyes met, he nodded across the empty, crumbling courtyard, away from the temple, to an enormous pit.

"Let's get this done." I climbed down from the fox spirit's back. Jae did the same.

Together, we started for the pit. Out of the corner of my eye, I saw him holding onto that roundish lump under his robes—the god stone. It was almost over, I kept telling myself over and over. We were here. We had time.

And then, all of a sudden, we didn't.

They came from every side, bursting through the trees. Wood splinters showered everywhere. It was an onslaught of shrikes from the air, giant elk-looking beasts and boars charging at us across the ground, along with all manner of jungle monsters I'd never heard of. Some were as big as bears and resembled tusked, stony-skinned gorillas. Others were giant lizards with color-changing scales, long, whipping tails, and snapping, toothy jaws.

We were outnumbered, surrounded, and at a serious disadvantage. I saw Jae's expression twist into a look of rage. His eyes gleamed brighter. His teeth became pointed and he ripped his scimitar from its sheath. I rushed to stand back-to-back with him, with my sword already drawn.

"Never a dull moment with you, eh?" I smirked as one of the lizards lunged at me. I drove my sword through its neck with one swing.

"I aim to please," Jae snarled back. He was squaring off with a shrike. It struck first and he reared back, bashing it over the head with the blunt end of his scimitar. Once it was down, a flourish of his hand summoned vines that burst from the ground, wrapped around it, and held it down while he sliced through its chest.

One of those giant, scaly gorilla beasts charged straight for us, bellowing and swinging its fists.

"Head's up," I yelled, as I ducked into an evasive roll.

Jae did the same, skidding off to the opposite side. We came up at the same time, our blades moving in unison, and took out the beast's stumpy hind legs as it barreled past us.

The monster went down with a boom. Immediately, Jae brought his hand up in a sharp gesture, summoning more vines from the ground. They burst straight through the ugly beast.

"Got any more of those rock dragons up your sleeve?" I asked, as I ran back to get in formation beside him. "We can't keep this up forever."

The foundling spirits were helping. To their credit, they were keeping the biggest and baddest of the monsters away from us. If not for them, we would have been completely overrun.

Even so, if Jace was right, the entire jungle was focused squarely on us right now. We were standing in the eye of the storm, and eventually that gray elf princess was going to run out of arrows.

We were only yards away from the edge of the pit. I could see Jae's eyes focus there with intent. That was our destination. I just had to get him there.

"Go! I've got your back!" I shouted over the roar of battle.

"We all do," Araxie chimed in. She darted past me and planted a well-aimed arrow right between the eyes of another lizard.

Jaevid didn't question us. He took off, and I ran after him. He deflected the creatures attacking from the front, and I did my best to fend off the ones that were chasing us toward the pit. When we got to the edge and I caught a glimpse at the spiraling staircase that went round and round the edge of it, I yelled a curse. It would take us forever to get to the bottom.

If we went down like normal, completely sane people, that is.

Jaevid grabbed me and jumped out into the open air. I didn't have time to react or brace myself. I couldn't even scream, because as soon as I got a good breath, we were caught out of midair. One of the foundling spirits had swooped in out of nowhere, caught him by the back of his clothes, and was carrying us down into the deep darkness.

We went down … down … down—until I was sure we had to be getting close to the bottom.

My feet hit first. Jae let go of me then and I lost my balance, landing on my rear at the bottom of the pit. Overhead, the opening was so far away it looked like a small circle of light the size of a full moon. I heard sounds of commotion echoing from above, the occasional shriek and cry of the jungle animals, and the shouts of our friends.

A hand appeared in my face. "We don't have much time," Jae said, as he hauled me up to my feet again.

With a flourish of his wrist, Jae brewed up a bit more of his magic to light the way. Before, I'd seen him use an orb of light that hovered over his palm. This time, however, he summoned some sort of creeping plant that grew in long tendrils along the floor and then climbed the walls. It had tiny blooms on it and when they opened, they glowed with a soft light that reminded me of stars. Those shining flowers led the way to a gaping tunnel.

I shivered. Something about it gave me a creepy feeling. It was almost as though I'd been here before, somehow—although I knew I definitely hadn't.

The foundling spirit started following us. It wasn't until I got a better look at it by the light of Jae's magic, glowing flowers that I realized it was the same spirit I'd ridden here.

"She feels bad about Nova," Jae said quietly.

I glanced at the spirit again, watching it creep along behind me on four birdlike legs. It looked like some sort of fox-griffin, although instead of being mixed with an eagle it was mixed with a parrot. Unique, pretty, but totally weird.

"So it's a she?"

Jae dipped his head. "Her name is Pasci."

"Pasci, huh?" I eyed the foundling spirit, watching the way she was sniffing at me with her long snout twitching and her tall ears perked up at the sound of my voice. "Well, tell her I'm not exactly emotionally available for another relationship yet. I only just lost Nova."

"If it's any consolation, she didn't suffer."

I stared at the back of my best friend's head. I felt the urge to hit him for talking about that right now. Of course, it was a little comforting to know that. I just … wasn't ready to feel anything about it yet.

Just like I wasn't ready for us to reach the end of that tunnel, either. Because a better part of me, a smarter part, knew something bad was going to happen there. You didn't find anything happy in a damp, dark cave like this. This place had a powerful silence that made my skin prickle.

In the center of a round, empty chamber, I saw the same altar made of a single slab of milky, white stone that I'd seen in my dream. I saw the bones laid out on it, and my heart started to pound against my ribs. The heat of the curse was so alive in the air I could feel it like the crackling heat off a furnace.

Jaevid was strangely calm. He walked toward the altar, brushing back the cowl of his cloak. His hand went to that round, stone-shaped lump under his robes. I could hear him muttering, whispering under his breath as though he were talking to someone. Then he stopped, turned, and gazed back at me.

I could see it from a mile away—the look he gave me whenever he was about to do something reckless, stupid, and potentially life-threatening.

His hand moved and he took out the stone. Out of pure reflex, I turned away and shielded my eyes. He'd told me not to look at it—not even for a second. I cringed and braced myself, waiting for something to happen.

I heard a horrible cracking sound.

Someone screamed.

Jace and Araxie were running toward me through the tunnel. Araxie was shouting in protest, her face pale with horror.

I dared to look back at Jae, just in time to see him rear back and smash the stone against the edge of the altar.

Crack!

Araxie was still screaming for him to stop, with Jace struggling to hold her back.

Crack!

Next to me, my foundling spirit friend, Pasci, was shrieking and yelping, spinning in circles. She began to cower with her ears pinned back and her hide shivering.

Crack!

The god stone shattered into a million tiny pieces.

"What have you done?" Araxie was hysterical. Jace fought to keep her at bay.

Pasci howled. Somewhere beyond the cave, I heard a mismatched chorus of similar panicked sounds coming from the other foundling spirits.

Jaevid collapsed to the floor, barely catching himself against the edge of the altar. I dropped my sword and ran to him. The pieces of the god stone crunched under my boots as I grabbed his shoulders and tried to hold him up. He was limp. When he looked up at me, I could see that he'd lost all the color in his face.

"No. No, Jaevid. Not here. Not like this," I smacked his cheek to try and revive him.

His head lolled to rest against me. "It's okay, Felix. It's done. It's over now."

"What are you talking about? Nothing's done. You just broke the stone, you moron!"

"No. Look." He raised a hand and pointed shakily to the altar.

The bones were melting away. The white skeleton of that animal was slowly dissolving into a fine, white mist that shimmered in the light as it faded away.

"It's going to be okay now," Jae rasped. He reached into his vambrace and pulled out a dirty, rumpled piece of cloth. It was a handkerchief with two dragons stitched on it. He handed it to me. Then he grabbed the pendant around his neck—the one he always wore—and with a swift jerk broke the resin string. He laid it carefully in my hand, too.

"I'll be wanting these back. You'll keep them for me, won't you?" He asked with a strange, distant smile. All the while, his skin was turning whiter by the second. Only, it wasn't just his skin. His clothes were beginning to turn white, too.

"Jaevid, what's happening?"

"There has to be a stone. Paligno's essence has to walk the earth to keep the balance and to keep things living and growing. His mortal body perished here, but his essence was contained within the god stone. Now ... it will be contained within me. There will be no more lapiloques, and no more god stone. From now on, it will only be me."

Araxie had gone silent. She stood next to Jace, tears streaming down her face and smearing the war paint under her eyes. Next to her, Jace was scowling. His brow was furrowed and his mouth was open, but he didn't say anything.

"This isn't goodbye." Jae closed my hand around his belongings.

I bit down hard. "It better not be."

He tried to stand. I had to basically carry him to get him up on the altar. He sat there a moment, looking at his own hands as though amazed. Second by second, they were turning the same milky hue as the stone he was sitting on. Shaking his head, he muttered under his breath as he turned and shakily lay down on his back.

His eyes traveled slowly around the cave before finally staring back at me. "It's so quiet now. I wish you could hear it the way I can."

"Way overdue, isn't it?"

"You have no idea. I'm so tired, Felix,"

I took his hand and gripped it fiercely. "Rest, then. I'll be here when you wake up, ready to do something else amazing and dangerous."

He squeezed my hand back. His legs had turned to solid, white stone. "Take care of yourself, brother. Watch over our friends—our family. And please ... tell Mavrik this wasn't his fault. Tell him to have a good life. Tell him I said 'thank you.'"

"I'm sure he'd rather hear all that from you," I replied.

"I had to shut him out of my mind. Otherwise ... he'd try to come here and find me. I couldn't let him take that risk. I couldn't lose him, too."

"Fine," I agreed as I clenched my teeth. "But only if you tell Beckah hello for me."

Jaevid smiled weakly. He let go of my hand just as his fingertips started turning to stone. I watched him grow stiff. I watched his eyes glaze and become fixed. His chest rose and fell slowly, one last time.

"*When you need me, I will return.*" His voice didn't come from his lips. His body had already turned into solid stone. Instead, the sound came from everywhere. From the air around us, from inside my own mind.

In an instant, Paligno's curse broke over us. I could feel it— the sudden rush of freedom, of relief, of cool serenity. Peace that surpassed anything I'd ever felt flooded that place. It filled every corner of my soul and brought tears to my eyes.

It was finished.

We were free.

twenty-two

I stood nearby, watching as the gray elf princess pressed her lips to the cold, stone surface of Jaevid's forehead. Between her broken sobs, I heard her speak to him in her native language, brushing her fingers over his face. Jace lingered next to me, still solemn and silent. His forehead was creased with concern and his arms were folded over his chest as he gazed down at all that remained of his student, my friend, and our last hope.

The curse was broken. The stone had been officially taken out of play. But that didn't mean the war was over. Jaevid had left the last task in my hands. He'd seemed so sure that I was capable of it. I told myself that I could trust him; I'd always been able to trust him. He wasn't a liar, and even if I screwed everything up, he would be back. This wasn't goodbye.

It still hurt, though.

Araxie was still trying to pull herself together as we walked back through the tunnel. Jace was holding her hand, which definitely betrayed that they were together. She'd just let her head fall onto his shoulder, leaning against him some as we left the tomb in silence … when the earth began to shudder violently under our feet.

Jace and I exchanged an alarmed glance. Time to go.

We sprinted for the exit, dodging falling rocks shaken free from the tunnel's ceiling. Suddenly, what looked like giant roots burst through the walls of the tunnel. One whooshed right past me, narrowly missing the end of my nose. We dodged them, ducked down, and wove our way out to the pit where a lifetime's worth of steps stood between the surface and us.

Not good.

Something huge erupted from the ground beneath our feet, catching all three of us entirely off guard. I heard Araxie shriek and Jace yell. We were tossed with incredible force through the air like ragdolls. I tried to grab onto something, anything, but I was tumbling end over end.

A pair of big, strong talons closed around my arms, catching me under the shoulders. In the blink of an eye, Pasci had me. She yipped triumphantly and zipped through the air with me dangling under her. She sped out of the pit and into the open sky, just in time as an enormous tree exploded out of the pit behind us.

I saw Jace and Araxie running toward me, covered in dirt with equally panicked expressions on their faces as the tree grew bigger and bigger, dwarfing all the others in the jungle—which were already giant by anyone's standards. But this one was a behemoth.

It swelled, sprouting more limbs, breaking through the canopy and unfurling leaves the size of houses. The trunk completely covered the pit, as well as most of the courtyard around it. The roots fanned out, snaking across the ground to wrap around the various structures on the temple grounds. Nothing was crushed, or destroyed, but the tree's roots seemed to wrap it all in a protective embrace.

And as abruptly as it had begun, everything became still again.

Jace, Araxie, and I stood gaping up at the tree. No one said a word. The trunk had to be at least two hundred feet in diameter. It towered over the jungle, disappearing above the canopy and out of sight.

"That's one way to make sure no one goes down there, I suppose." Jace muttered.

I scowled. "But ... how is he supposed to come back with that thing in the way?"

I expected Araxie to offer some expert opinion. Being the resident gray elf royal, she might have had a better idea than the rest of us. She was a little distracted, though.

While Jace and I were staring up at the tree, scratching our heads, she whirled around and drew back her bow, hissing a few angry words in her native language.

Too late, I realized we were completely surrounded.

The Maldobarian infantry had us pinned on every side. They

stood all around the perimeter of the temple grounds, swords drawn and shields raised. The worst part was … they had my father. Prax had been forced to his knees with the sharp edge of a blade held to his throat.

The pressure in the air was palpable. The soldiers seemed rattled and anxious. I spotted more than one pair of wide, frightened eyes fixed upon the tree that had just spontaneously popped out of the ground. Not something you saw everyday in Maldobar. No doubt these guys had already fought through all manner of jungle hell to get here in the first place. Looking through their ranks to take a quick inventory, I saw a few gray elf hostages who must have made it much easier to find us—in fact, there was one gray elf warrior in particular that I happened to know.

When he saw me staring at him, Kiran gave an annoyed eye roll and shrug. Typical. Even with a dagger at his back and his hands in shackles, he still had an attitude.

"Drop your weapons immediately!" A soldier with a general's insignia stitched in gold onto the breast and shoulders of his uniform stepped forward. He sounded confident, but I saw fear written all over his face. "Where is the traitor? The one called Jaevid Broadfeather? Produce him at once!"

"Sorry. Can't do that," I called back, keeping my sword drawn and firmly in hand. He could have it when he pried it from my cold, dead fingers.

"Soldier, I strongly suggest you take inventory of your army here. We have you outnumbered and surrounded. You cannot escape. You cannot win this," the general threatened. "You're guilty of high treason, and murder as well. But if you give up peacefully, I'll see that you are treated well on your way back to answer for your crimes."

"Jaevid Broadfeather is dead."

You could have heard an ant sneeze.

Kiran's face went completely pale.

"He sacrificed himself to put the stone out of our reach— yours and mine. No one else can have it now. It's gone for good," I continued. "He did it to break the curse that has been spreading across our lands, making the animals turn on us. He did it to break the hold our real enemy had on you. He gave up everything so that we could live. He set us free."

A few of the soldiers were lowering their weapons. They were listening to me, so I kept talking. Charm? Pfft. This was downright insanity. All I had to go on was Jae's confidence that I could do this, and his warning that the people of Maldobar would be in a vulnerable state now that Hovrid's hold on them was broken.

"I know you can feel it, just as I can—the peace that's here now. Think about it. Do you even remember coming here?"

They glanced at one another, looking bewildered and rubbing their eyes like they were waking up from a dream.

"I know you must be confused. You must feel lost, like you've just come out of a nightmare," I said, and more and more of the soldiers began lowering their arms. The one holding a blade to my father's neck let him go, and Prax immediately got to his feet.

"Over two decades of war and bloodshed have brought us here. We've all done things—terrible things that we'll have to live with. No one is blameless because every single one of us was deceived by a man we believed we could trust; a man who called himself our king. I'm asking you to see him for what he truly was—a liar and a murderer."

The general narrowed his eyes at me dangerously. "Who are you to levy such an accusation?"

"I am Duke Felix Farrow, high noble and the only rightful heir to the throne of Maldobar," I declared. "And it is by that authority that I command you to stand down, lower your weapons, and release your captives."

"What happens now?" Princess Araxie was sitting across from me, the light of the small fire pit between us making her eyes shimmer like opals.

Sitting beside her, King Erandur still looked haunted by the news that both Jaevid and the god stone were gone. His eyes were wide and fixed on the crackling flames, as though he were lost in his own mind.

"We start over." I sighed, rubbing my fingers around the things in my pocket—Jaevid's things. "He said he's coming back. And I, for one, believe him. So all we can do now is wipe the slate clean and rebuild. Neither of our kingdoms are in a good state, as it stands."

That was putting it lightly—*extremely* lightly. But I knew everyone sitting around that fire pit was acutely aware of how tense things were outside. Jace, Kiran, Araxie, and I were resting inside the treetop hut reserved for the king and his guests. But outside, it was a different story. The remains of the gray elf forces were housing the riders and infantry from Northwatch who had come here to kill them. Evil imposter king aside, there was a lot of bad blood in the air. A lot of distrust. A lot of anger. Tensions were high and it wouldn't take much to fan the flames. I'd dispatched my father to keep an eye on thing, walk the grounds, and make sure no one put a toe out of line at least for the rest of the night.

We all deserved at least one quiet night.

"Perhaps, then, what we need is a gesture of good faith." Erandur spoke up suddenly.

Araxie looked stunned, like she hadn't expected her father to be so accommodating.

"Your man Jace wishes to stay here in my kingdom. He's already expressed that desire to me, and I have granted it. If you were to appoint him as an ambassador, I could make him an official member of my court. He would become a presence here representing your efforts to work toward peace," the king continued.

I nodded. "A good idea."

"We should send an ambassador of our own to Maldobar, as well," Araxie suggested.

"Kiran," I said suddenly.

He looked at me out of the corner of his weird, color changing eyes.

"If he's an acceptable candidate to you, that is. I've gotten to know him well enough to trust him. Jaevid had a lot of faith in him, too. He speaks our language and has firsthand knowledge of our customs. I think he'd be a good fit."

Araxie was rubbing her chin thoughtfully. She looked at Kiran hard—studied him from head to toe like she was searching him for some hidden flaw. It even made me a little nervous. She definitely had a steely way about her, like a she-wolf who wasn't going to tolerate any members of her pack embarrassing her.

"True. But he is young and impulsive. It took him two years to pass his trials and become a scout. Are you up to this task?" she asked him outright.

Kiran straightened. His expression was determined. "I can do it."

"Then you will have your chance. Serve your kingdom well, young warrior," Erandur decreed and put a hand on Kiran's shoulder. It made the young gray elf blush.

We ate a meal of grilled meat and dried fruit in silence. Not that there wasn't anything to talk about. But if any of the others felt the way I did, then they were too overwhelmed by the task before us to even try talking about it. Right about now, the small company of riders I'd sent back to Northwatch would be arriving bearing the news that the war was over … and that Maldobar had a new king. It wouldn't take long for that news to spread. Maybe there would be riots. Maybe they'd burn the royal castle to the ground in rebellion.

But then again, maybe not.

Regardless, there wasn't a single thing I could do about it from here. And honestly, I wasn't worried about riots and castle burnings. I was worried about the only thing that mattered: what was Julianna doing right this second?

After dinner, Erandur and Araxie retired to their private quarters. Jace tagged along at the princess's heels like a faithful guard dog. As much as I would have liked to give him a hard time about that, I had a shadow on my heels as well.

Kiran followed me as I wandered out of the hut onto a balcony overlooking the jungle. I leaned against the railing and let the cool night air blow over me. The lights from other tree huts shone like floating orbs all around us. There were fragrant, floral smells on the wind and the musical calls of birds echoing in the night. It was strange, but beautiful. Once again, this place wasn't anything at all like I'd thought it would be.

Far below, I could hear the commotion of the camp. I wanted to be down there, amongst the other riders, drinking ale and having a good awkward laugh with our new pointy-eared friends. But here I was, having responsibilities. Geez, when had that happened?

"You seem troubled." Kiran came to stand next to me.

I rubbed the back of my neck. "You would be, too, if you had the eyes of two kingdoms looking to you to fix two decades worth of damage."

He gave me a challenging smirk. "Do you think you can peacefully unite our kingdoms?"

"I don't know," I admitted. "But I think I can try. You think you can convince your kinsmen who were sent to prison camps to die that they can trust me?"

His sarcastic expression started to fade.

I patted him on the back. "Relax. We've both got our work cut out for us. So we'll just have to take it one miracle at a time. But I'll make a deal with you, Kiran. I need someone working for me I know I can trust. So you stay with me, watch my back, and help me make sure this peace lasts, and I promise that together we will do whatever we can to make this right for your people."

I held a hand out to him.

Kiran drew back for a moment, as though he were unsure of the gesture. He studied me, my hand, and finally reached out to grasp it firmly. "A deal."

"You mean 'deal' right?"

"Yes. A deal."

"No, no. You just say 'deal' and then we shake."

He narrowed his eyes suspiciously.

I laughed and shook on it. "Don't worry about it. It's a deal."

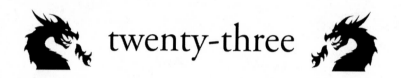

twenty-three

It wasn't at all what I expected. Not just any tackmaster lived here. Ulric Broadfeather was held in the highest esteem by Blybrig Academy as the very best money could buy. He should have been able to afford a much nicer place. But as Sile, Roland, and I rode up to the front drive on horseback, I got the feeling we weren't going to be welcomed in with open arms.

The house looked nearly abandoned and the message painted on the front door read "TRESSPASSERS BEWARE." The gardens were overgrown and wild looking. The roof was in bad need of repair and the front door was sagging on the hinges. If not for the smoke rising from the chimney, I would have just assumed it had been left to rot.

After months of searching, I'd finally managed track Ulric

down. Not that he was in hiding, per say, but every time anyone mentioned his name there was an awkward pause and sudden reluctance for anyone to say anything about him. His crime was common knowledge now. And so was his insanity. Both had probably driven him out of business. No one wanted anything to do with him now.

I looked to Sile to make the first move. This whole errand had been his idea. It was some kind of personal vendetta, I figured. Roland and I were just here to bear witness in case things got ugly. Roland had even suggested to me that he wasn't sure if Ulric would even agree to see Sile at all.

The woman who answered the door was as thin as a broomstick. Her hair was frayed and her apron was stained and tattered. She cracked the door just wide enough to peek at all of us. When she saw Sile, she went pale and I thought she might faint.

"No! Go away! He doesn't want any visitors!" She screamed and tried to slam the door.

Sile jammed the toe of his boot into the doorway before she could close it. "Let me in, Serah," he growled deeply. "I'm standing here with your son and the King of Maldobar. I suggest you don't turn us away."

Slowly, the trembling woman moved away from the door. But when Sile pushed the door open, she darted away into the dark, disheveled parlor like a frightened mouse. Roland and I followed him inside.

Hiding in the dark corners of the house, I spotted the pale, frightened faces of two young girls cowering behind the woman. These must have been the twin sisters I'd heard Jaevid mention once or twice. They were as gaunt and wild-looking as their mother.

There was an odd, musty smell like sour laundry. I wasn't sure what to make of it until we found Ulric. He was sitting on the dirt floor of the cellar, wrapped up in old blankets that reeked like they hadn't been washed for months. The mattress on the floor was in the same state, and there was a waste bucket that was nearly full to the top of ... some pretty nasty stuff.

I'd seen Jaevid's father before, once or twice, at the academy. But the man we found crouched on his knees, scratching at the walls with his fingernails hardly looked like anything more than a haggard shell of a human being. His beard was long and as filthy as the rest of him. His eyes were bloodshot and glazed. He looked thin and fragile, as though he were slowly wasting away to nothing but bones and skin. He didn't even look up when we came down the steps.

"Ulric," Sile said as he ventured closer.

But if Ulric was even aware of our presence, he never let on. He was scrambling around on his knees, muttering under his breath. He kept repeating something over and over, although I couldn't quite make out what it was.

"Ulric, I came here to tell you something." Sile touched him on the shoulder.

Instantly, Ulric bounded to his feet with alarming speed and started screeching at the top of his lungs, "Soon! It's coming! I know it! I can see it. I can smell it in the air."

Next to me, I saw Roland's jaw tense and he looked away.

Ulric was pacing back and forth and rubbing his hands together. That's when I noticed the marks he'd been making—there were hundreds of them covering every square inch of the stone walls of the cellar from floor to ceiling. They looked like symbols in some language I didn't recognize, but they looked far too precise to be nothing at all.

Suddenly, Sile caught him by the arm and forced him to stop, all but pinning him up against the wall. "Listen to me now. I came to tell you your son is dead. Do you understand me? Jaevid, your son, paid for your crime with his blood."

Ulric was shaking like a leaf. He looked at Sile, Roland, then at me. "Son? What son? I have no son."

Sile's eyes flickered dangerously. "I have kept my word and it's cost me much more than I can say our friendship has been worth. We are finished now. Roland is taking those women from here. You can die here in this hole, if you choose, but you won't take anyone else with you."

"Finished … finished." Ulric was whispering again.

With a curse under his breath, Sile let him go and nodded to Roland. It was time to go. Whoever this person was, the god stone had addled his brain until there wasn't much left.

Sile and Roland started for the stairs. As I turned to follow, I heard Ulric scramble back over to the wall and begin etching and scratching with his nails again. He was still muttering, laughing, and taking in frantic crackling breaths.

"Nothing is finished. It's coming soon. I can see it. I can feel it. The legacy of the God Bane ... the harbinger comes!"

"Master—er—I mean Your Majesty! It's nearly time, you should be inside getting ready!" Miss Harriet came hurdling across the yard with all her skirts in her arms. Her puffy face was flushed and her hair was flying everywhere. She looked like she'd just weathered a hurricane.

Behind her was my new bride, following along and covering her mouth to hide her smirk. Julianna waited until Miss Harriet finished giving me grief over my appearance before she hurried away to make sure all my attire for the coronation was still in order—though she'd only just left it. We were preparing to leave my estate and head to the royal city of Halfax. Rumor had it there was a golden crown on a red, velvet pillow waiting there with my name on it.

Everyone was waiting for us to arrive. Supposedly, the whole city was in an uproar, ready to welcome their new king and queen. Prax had sent me several letters describing how the entire castle had been redecorated. It was as though the people of Maldobar were desperate to purge every trace of Hovrid from their land.

"Harriet's dreadfully proud of you." Julianna said, giving me a coy smile as she wandered over to drape her arms around my neck. "As am I, Your Majesty."

"Hm. You know, it's significantly less annoying when you call me that for some reason." I grinned and looped an arm around her waist to reel her in closer.

She giggled and blushed.

I enjoyed kissing her now even more than before. Something about her having my last name made her taste even sweeter. It didn't take long for her gaze to wander away from me, though, and over to the three statues that loomed before us.

One was older than the rest. It was the one I'd commissioned in Jaevid's honor. On his right side was a much newer one that had only been put in place a week or so before. It was carved into the shape of a young woman with long, braided hair, wearing the armor of a dragonrider and standing proudly with a bow in one hand and a sword in the other. It seemed only fitting to put her there, at his side. I was sure that was what she would have wanted.

Next to her was one last structure, a large granite box with a single dragon scale set into the top. That was where I had ordered Nova's ashes to be placed. It just felt right to keep her with me, here, on the same cliffs and breathing the same air as her wild kin.

"I know Jae would be very proud of you too, Felix." Julianna added in a quiet, cautious voice, afraid of upsetting me.

I smiled. "Maybe so."

"You've already seen to it that all captives of war on both sides be freed, including the gray elf slaves. So many families will be reunited." She was smiling, too. "Yes. I believe that would make him extremely happy."

"Tearing down all the gray elf ghettos has made a lot of other people unhappy, however," I sighed at the thought. There was a lot to fix, a lot that had to be changed if we were ever going to move forward and heal. Jaevid had sacrificed everything for this chance, though. I wasn't about to waste it.

"People are always afraid of change." Julianna had a contemplative glint in her eyes as she stared at Jae's statue. "But that doesn't necessarily mean change is bad. Change is necessary, even if it frightens us. Without it, we would never grow."

"Maybe you should just give my coronation speech instead. You're better with words than I am."

She swatted playfully at the back of my head. "Felix Farrow, don't you dare try pushing your responsibilities off on m—"

I stole another kiss before she could finish, making her blush and pout.

For a long time, we stood together in the gardens of my family estate. We stared at the statues of Jaevid and Beckah, standing side-by-side against the backdrop of a gray sky. The winds picked up, and in the distance I could see the waves frothing and capping. There was a storm brewing, unusual for this time of year.

"What do you suppose he meant?" Julianna was whispering again.

"About what?"

"About returning to us when we need him." She turned to look at me with worry in her eyes.

I didn't want to tell her that I was concerned, too. After that encounter with Ulric ... I was still rattled and trying to assure myself that you couldn't put any faith in the ravings of a madman. Still, something about it sat wrong in my mind. And when I thought about Jaevid's parting words, I was even more nervous. I still had absolutely no idea what he'd been talking about. I was restless at the thought that there might something else—something worse—coming our way.

"Whatever he meant, there's nothing we can do about it right now except continue to do everything we can to rebuild," I replied. Reaching over, I took her hand in mine and held it firmly. "And as for Jaevid ... I've decided to believe in him the way believed in me. He thought I could rule Maldobar and change things for the better. I think we haven't seen the last of him. I think that if anything threatens this kingdom again, Jaevid is going to have something to say about it."

Julianna gave my hand a little squeeze. It hurt. I'd accidentally cut open one of my palms on that jagged black crystal that was set in the royal throne while battling that stupid pig. It still hurt, even if it was hardly more than a gnarled pink scar now. The soreness hadn't gone away.

I could see a difference in the way Julianna regarded Jae's statue, as though he baffled her. "It's nearly impossible to believe what he could do. A timid, gentle, halfbreed boy from the gray elf ghetto?"

Something caught my eye, a glimmer on the horizon reflecting the light from a break in the clouds. The shimmer of dragon scales. I couldn't be sure from so far away, but I thought I recognized the familiar silhouette of a certain blue dragon—now free of his saddle—sailing proudly on the stormy winds.

"No, not impossible," I corrected her. "But definitely unexpected."

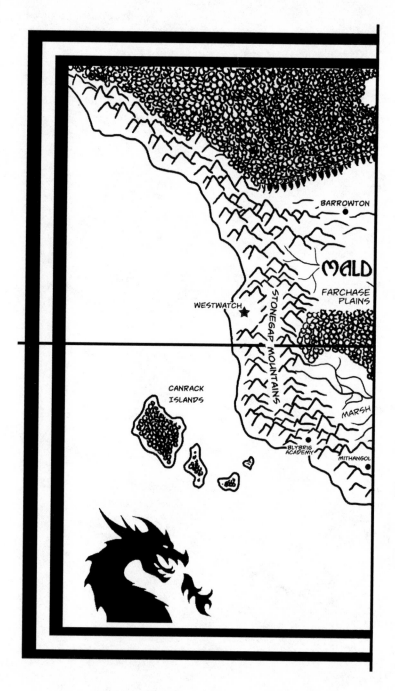

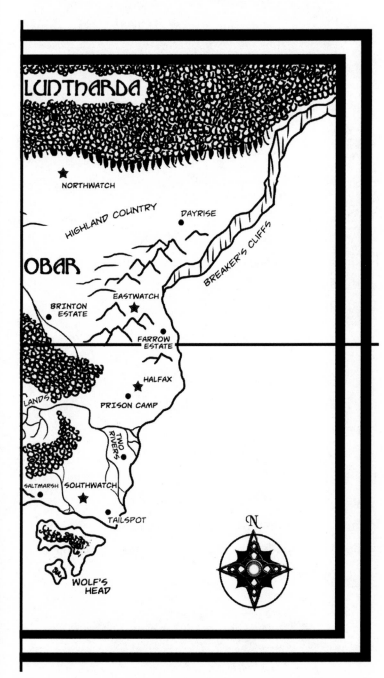

ACKNOWLEDGEMENTS

I'd like to express my deep gratitude for all my faithful (and incredibly patient) readers for supporting the series. I feel truly blessed to have been able to share Jaevid's journey with you all!

Also, thanks for not killing me for the cliffhangers.

A special thank-you to my agent, Fran Black. I can't thank her enough for all her hard work, guidance, and dedication. She's a rock star!

To Georgia McBride, thank you for taking a chance on my timid little halfbreed dragonrider, his blue dragon, and me. We are eternally grateful!

A big thank you to my parents, grandparents, and family—but especially my loving husband. I had never had anyone support my love of writing as diligently as he has. From helping me with details and dialogue, to dropping everything to make sure I make it to signings and events, Keith Conway, you have made me fall in love with you all over again.

NICOLE CONWAY

Nicole Conway is the author of the children's fantasy series, THE DRAGONRIDER CHRONICLES, about a young boy's journey into manhood as he trains to become a dragonrider. Originally from a small town in North Alabama, Nicole moves frequently due to her husband's career as a pilot for the United States Air Force. She received a B.A. in English from Auburn University, and will soon attend graduate school. She has previously worked as a freelance and graphic artist for promotional companies, but has now embraced writing as a full-time occupation.

Nicole enjoys hiking, camping, shopping, cooking, and spending time with her family and friends. She lives at home with her husband, two cats, and dog.

Introducing

Savage

Book 1 in
The Dragonriders Legacy Series
(unedited)

Nicole Conway

ONE

The jungle was quiet, but my bare feet made a squishing sound on the damp moss that covered the enormous tree limbs. Everything was still dripping with cold dew. The first rays of morning sunlight bled through the canopy overhead, turning everything a surreal shade of green.

I crept as quietly as I could, squeezing my bow tightly in my fist. My heart was pounding. I was already sweating.

All of a sudden, a brightly colored parrot burst from the foliage and fluttered across my path. I lost my footing and wobbled, flailing my arms to regain my balance. My stomach lurched. I opened my mouth to yell.

And then she grabbed my belt from behind.

Enyo dragged me down into a squat. Together we watched the

bird disappear into the distance. Then she shot me a hard look. Her eyes sparkled like aquamarines in the dim light.

I scowled back at her. It wasn't my fault. The stupid bird had come out of nowhere.

I wrenched out of her grip and slung my bow over my shoulder, crawling down a steep turn in the limb and leaping over into the next tree. That was how you moved in Luntharda—scurrying from tree to tree like a squirrel. The ground wasn't impassable, but it was extremely difficult terrain. Not to mention it was practically writhing with things that would have been happy to make a breakfast out of a pair of novice hunters who weren't *technically* supposed to be this far away from the city.

"This isn't going to work, you know." Enyo muttered as we scaled a network of vines, climbing higher and higher.

I ignored her, but I couldn't out run her. Even if I was taller, she was much faster. Together, we ran along the boughs, leaping, dodging, and climbing until I knew we had to be within earshot. I stopped first and Enyo skidded to a halt beside me. She was grinning wickedly.

I was glancing around for the perfect spot right above the narrow, well-beaten trail that zigzagged through the underbrush below. Faundra left those trails when they moved between their favorite grazing spots.

I found it—the exact, ideal spot where an overgrowth of giant lichen made a great place to hide. I slipped my bow off my shoulder and took out an arrow, making sure to check the fletching and the shaft for damage before I set it in the string.

"Say you do actually kill one this time. Say we even manage to field dress it and get it back to the city. Do you really think Kiran is going to be okay with you running off without him?" Enyo whispered as she tucked herself into the lichen beside me. I could feel the heat off her skin when her arm brushed mine.

"Well obviously if I did it without him, then I don't need him in the first place, right? I'm not a kid anymore," I growled under my breath. "He's holding me back on purpose."

That was debatable, really. Gray elves went through puberty around fifteen. Their hair turned from black to white as freshly fallen snow, and their bodies matured. After that, they were considered adults and could choose a profession, get married, and basically do whatever they wanted. I was sixteen. I should have been treated like an adult, too.

There was just one problem—I wasn't a gray elf. And to make matters worse, my adoptive guardian, Kiran, didn't want me trying to make my first kill yet. He didn't want me going anywhere without his presence or permission. He treated me like a child.

"Maybe because you never listen," Enyo muttered under her breath. Maybe she thought I couldn't hear her.

I narrowed my eyes at her. "Just shut up. Why did you even come?"

She glared back. "Well if you die, someone should at least be able to explain what happened."

"Pfft." I snorted and looked away. "Just stay out of my way."

Enyo pushed some of her long, coal black hair behind one of her pointed ears. "And stay here—I know, I know."

A twig snapped.

Immediately, we both fell silent. My heart was pounding and my palms started to get sweaty. This was it, the chance I'd been waiting for.

One by one they started emerging from the morning mist. The herd of faundra traveled quickly with their littlest fawns grouped in the center to shield them from predators. The does were as big as horses, some even seven feet tall, with their white pelts flecked with soft gray markings. They had long, powerful legs and one kick to the face would crush your skull like an egg. But they weren't the ones you really had to watch out for.

The stags were even bigger. Their shaggy pelts had stark black swirls and a blaze right down the front of their snout. Their heads were crowned with sweeping white antlers that had ten razor sharp points. You definitely did not want to be on the wrong end of those.

"Beautiful," I heard Enyo whisper faintly.

I smirked.

Then we saw him—the alpha male. He was bigger than the other members of his herd by far. He had a single black stripe that went from the end of his snout, down his back, all the way to his tail. He was older, so his pelt was thicker around his neck like a mane, and all the other black marks on his hide had faded away. His horns sloped back to almost touch ends with four extra points on each side.

I was so excited I could barely breathe. When I drew my bow back, my hand wouldn't stay still. It made my arrow point bounce all over the place.

Enyo placed one of her hands on my back.

I closed my eyes for a moment and tried to remember everything Kiran had taught me. I took a deep breath. I listened to the jungle. Then, slowly, I opened my eyes again and took aim straight for the alpha male's heart. My hand was steady and my bowstring taut.

All I had to do was let go.

Something caught my eye. It was fast, like a flickering shadow darting through the underbrush.

I got a bad, sinking feeling in the pit of my stomach that made all the tiny hairs on my arms and neck stand on end.

Clenching my teeth, I tried to ignore it. I tried to fight it. But I couldn't.

The cold chill came over me, making my body jerk beyond my control. The bowstring slipped, and my arrow went flying. It zipped through the moist air, grazing leaves and lodging deep into the side of a doe. She bucked and bleated, sending the rest of the herd into a frenzy. They bolted in every direction, disappearing like ghosts into the jungle.

But the doe I'd shot was badly wounded. I knew she couldn't run far. Without thinking I ran for the trunk of the tree and started my descent, jumping down from branch to branch.

"Reigh! Stop!" Enyo was screaming at me.

I ignored her. There was no stopping now. When my feet finally struck the forest floor, I went to the spot where I'd shot her. There was blood on the ground and more droplets speckling the leaves and ferns, leading away into the undergrowth.

Enyo seized my wrist suddenly. Her face was pale with fright. "We can't be down here. It's too dangerous." Her whispering voice trembled.

"I can't just leave a kill lying out there," I argued.

"Something will have heard them," she pleaded. "Something will smell the blood!"

"Go back to the tree and wait for me, then." I snatched my arm away from her and pointed. "I'm finishing this, with or without you."

Her expression faltered. She looked back at the tree, then to me, with her eyebrows crinkled and her mashed into a desperate line.

"I said go!" I yelled.

It startled her. She backed away a few steps, then turned to run.

***

I tried not to think about all the rules I was breaking as I dove into the foliage, alone, to track down my kill. The blood trail wasn't hard to find even among all the towering fronds and enormous leaves of the plants. I'd never stood on the jungle floor alone like this before. I felt insignificant, like a tiny insect, as I looked up at the giant trees. In fact, everything seemed bigger now that I was this close to it. The air seemed cooler, too. The canopy was so far away, like a distant sky of endless green leaves. It gave me chills.

Or maybe that was just my *problem* acting up again.

I crept through the undergrowth, traveling fast and trying to stay out of sight as I followed the blood trail. The drops were getting bigger and closer together. She was slowing down. It wouldn't be long.

And then I saw her.

The doe was lying in the middle of a small clearing between two big ferns. She was motionless, but I could see her side rising and falling with the shaft of my arrow sticking straight. She was still alive.

I quickly shouldered my bow and drew my hunting knife. As I got close to the edge of the clearing, I hesitated. I did a quick glance around, waiting to see if anything or anyone else was nearby.

But everything was quiet. Everything was still.

The doe bleated loudly when she saw me. Her legs kicked and her eyes looked around with wild anxiety. Standing over her, I could feel my hand beginning to shake again. I had to kill her. I had to end her suffering—preferably before she gave away my position to every dangerous predator in a five-mile radius.

I put my knee over her snout to hold her head still. She was too weak to fight me off. Her milky brown eyes stared straight ahead as

I drew back, ready to plunge my dagger into her heart.

Then I heard it; a deep, heavy snort from the edge of the clearing. I looked up just in time to see him stride free of the underbrush, his white horns gleaming in the morning light. The alpha male had come back for her.

Our gazes met. His ears flicked back and he stamped a hoof. I tightened my grip on my knife. I tried to think of what to do—any fragment of a lesson Kiran had given that would help me right now.

There wasn't one.

The stag lowered his head, pointing all those deadly horns straight at me and charged.

I scrambled to my feet and ran for the nearest tree. I could hear his thundering hooves on the ground, getting closer and closer. I wasn't going to make it. I was fast, but he was much faster.

The second before I could grab onto the lowest handhold, I heard a bowstring snap. The alpha bellowed. I dared to look back, just in time to see him fall and begin rolling. An arrow was sticking out of his haunches. He tumbled toward me, rolling like a big furry boulder. I tried to climb, but it was too late. The massive stag smashed right into me.

The impact knocked the wind out of me. Something popped. One of my arms suddenly went numb. I was being crushed between a tree and a very angry faundra stag. Something sharp sliced right across my face. It must have been one of his horns. I felt the warmth of my own blood running down my face.

"Reigh!" I heard Enyo's voice.

So did the stag. He staggered back to his feet, shifting his weight off me. I could breathe again, but I was seeing stars. I crumpled to the forest floor in a daze.

"Don't just sit there! Climb!" Enyo yelled again.

The stag was charging straight for her, even with an arrow sticking out of his flank. She clumsily drew back another, her whole body trembling with terror. Her eyes were stuck on the shaggy monster galloping straight for her. I could see her hesitating, trying to decide if she should fire or flee.

She wasn't going to make it either way.

Something inside me snapped, like the last raindrop before the dam broke.

I screamed, yelling her name at the top of my lungs. The chill came over me again, a coldness that rushed through every vein, making my body jerk and my eyes tear up.

But this time I didn't fight it. I clenched my fists and let it take me.

Time seemed to slow down and stop altogether. I could feel my pulse getting slower. My puffing breaths turned to white fog in the air. Before me, darkness pooled, amassing into one dark, inky puddle on the ground. It rose up like a flickering column of black flames, and took the form of *him* …

The black wolf I called Noh.

He looked at me with a smiling canine mouth and red, wavering bogfire eyes.

"Kill it," I commanded.

"*With pleasure*," his hissing voice replied.

TWO

I couldn't remember a time in my life when Noh hadn't been there. Ever since I was a little kid, he'd always been right there, hiding in the back of my mind, like a memory from a former life that refused to fade. And almost as soon as I'd noticed his presence, Noh had absolutely terrified me.

It wasn't that he'd ever tried to hurt me. Somehow, I didn't think he could have even if he wanted to. But I could feel his presence just as clearly as I could sense his intentions—and they weren't good. He thrived on my anger, my sadness and confusion. Whenever Kiran and I had an argument, he would start creeping around the corners of the room, slipping soundlessly from shadow to shadow, almost like he was waiting for something.

Waiting for me to finally lose it.

I didn't know what he would do. Frankly, I didn't want to know. And Kiran had warned me over and over that I had to keep myself under control, I had to make sure not to go too far. The repercussions could be severe. Noh might hurt someone, and it would be my fault. I was the only one who could see Noh. I was the only one who could hear him, and the only person he listened to. I could control him—for now. But Kiran worried that if I let him off the chain, if I let him have his way, that might not be the case anymore.

Then no one would be able to stop him from doing whatever it was he wanted to do. Stuff I couldn't fathom and didn't even want to try to imagine.

The worst part was knowing that eventually it was going to happen. Somehow, someway, I was going to mess up. I always did. That's me—Reigh—Luntharda's number one screw up. It was just a matter of time before I lost it and Noh did something . . . unforgiveable.

***

My body was heavy. I couldn't move. I was delirious, feeling nothing but a cold like pinpricks on my skin. I could hear the deep, constant sound of my heartbeat. So maybe that meant I wasn't dead.

Then there was a voice—someone shouting right over me. "Reigh? Reigh!"

A strong hand smacked my face.

My eyes popped open. I bolted upright and choked, sucking in a deep breath.

"It's all right. Breathe. You'll be fine." I recognized the voice. It was Kiran. He was sitting right next to me, studying me with a concerned furrow in his brow.

"E-Enyo …" I tried to speak, but I was barely able to catch my breath. I felt weak and dizzy, as though I'd nearly drowned.

"She's fine." Kiran put a hand on the back of my head and leaned in close, poking experimentally at the open wound on my face. It hurt so bad my eyes watered.

"You'll need stitches," he decided aloud. "One of the stag's horns had blood on it. I feared the worst."

That's right. The stag had nicked me. In my daze, I'd almost forgotten.

I looked past Kiran to the place where the doe should have been lying. But she was gone. There was no trace of her or the stag anywhere. Across the clearing, a few other gray elf scouts were checking Enyo. She was unconscious, but her cheeks were still flushed with color. She was alive.

My body sagged with relief. I met Kiran's knowing gaze. The hard lines in the corners of his mouth grew deeper when he frowned.

"Is he still here?" he asked quietly so that no one else would hear.

I glanced around, checking for shadows. Noh was gone, for now. I shook my head slightly and winced. My arm—my whole shoulder—felt like it was on fire whenever I tried to move it.

"Good. Now get up." He patted the top of my head; a gesture that passed as his gruff, awkward effort at parental affection.

I struggled to stand. My arm was killing me. I couldn't bear to move it, and Kiran had to help me get up. He dusted the leaves, moss, and twigs off my clothes and picked up my bow. Across the clearing, one of the other scouts had picked up Enyo and was carrying her back with the others toward the nearest tree-path.

I followed with Kiran walking right behind me. I could feel his gaze burning at my back. Anyone else would have thought he was just back there making sure I didn't stumble and fall to my death because of my injured arm. I guess that could have been part of the reason, but that wasn't all of it. He was probably worried about Noh showing up again. I was worried about that, too. Worried—and confused about what had happened to the doe and the stag.

Kiran managed to keep his temper in check until we got back into the city, behind the private walls of the home we shared. He walked me through the front door of the clinic we ran together, a Healing House for the sick or wounded. Like an angry specter, he haunted my steps as I walked up the stairs to the fourth floor where we lived.

Then he let me have it.

***

"Have I taught you nothing? Did you ever hear a single word I said?" Kiran stared straight at me, expecting an answer.

I couldn't decide what was more terrifying, that he was about to pop my dislocated arm back into socket or that he was using the human language to scold me this time. He only did that when he didn't want anyone else to overhear what we were saying.

Kiran hadn't said much of anything while he cleaned the wound on my nose. The gash was deep, and it had taken fifteen stitches to close it. Now I was going to have a brutal looking scar from one cheek to the other, right across the bridge of my nose. Painful? You bet. And I had a feeling Kiran had intentionally taken longer than usual to close it. Part one of my punishment.

Now it was time for part two.

I swallowed, tensed and ready as his fingers probed around on my shoulder. Whenever he poked too hard, it hurt so badly I thought I was going to die.

"And this time you took Enyo with you," he went on. "You risked her life, as well. She is a child, Reigh. A *child*!"

I looked away. "I told her to go back."

He gave my shoulder a sudden, violent jerk. It snapped, and I screamed. But the tingling numbness in my joints was gone. I could move my arm again. It actually felt … better.

"You are a reckless, thoughtless boy." He growled as he began to rotate my arm, testing to see if it really was set properly. Then he sternly wrapped my whole shoulder in a bandage. "Everything you do, every decision you make, has consequences. Why don't you understand this? You only think of yourself. And that is exactly why I do not let you take your place as a warrior."

I glared at the woven grass mats on the floor. "Is that why you're ashamed of me? Or is it because I'm human?"

Kiran stopped. "I am not ashamed of you."

"Then it's because I'm a monster?"

"You aren't a monster, Reigh."

I raised my burning gaze up to him. "Then what am I? Who else do you know who can feel if someone is dying? Who else has a bad spirit living in their head? Noh killed the elk didn't he?"

When I started to shout, Kiran raised a hand. I closed my mouth and glowered back down at the floor. Right. I wasn't supposed to get angry. We wouldn't want my dark friend showing up again.

"Is that why you won't let me call you father?" I asked.

He didn't answer. He never did. We'd had this argument before—lots of times, actually. And that was where it always stopped.

Kiran wasn't my father. He was a gray elf who had taken me in when I was a baby, although I didn't understand why. Clearly parenting wasn't his thing. He avoided people like others avoided the plague. And while he did try to be warm to me, it was like he didn't know what to say. So instead he just didn't say much at all.

According to him, I'd been abandoned as an infant. Someone had left me lying on a rock just inside the boundary of the jungle, alone and vulnerable. Luckily, he had heard me crying before a hungry tigrex or snagwolf could make an easy meal of me. Kiran had taken me in, raised me like a son, but never once allowed me to call him my father.

I still didn't understand why.

He was plenty old enough to be my father. He'd earned his scars almost forty years ago, fighting in the Gray War. Of course, he never talked about any of it. But sometimes I overheard others telling the stories during the great feast. They talked about how he'd ridden on the back of a dragon, fought to end the war, and stood alongside the princess. Some said he'd even called the lapiloque by name.

I didn't know if any of that was true, although sometimes Kiran would sit for hours in front of the fire pit, completely silent, just watching the flames slowly die. Those were the nights when I saw the darkness in his eyes I didn't understand.

And sometimes, when he didn't think I was paying attention, I would catch him staring at me that way, too.

What I did know about him was that he was strange, even by gray elf standards. He'd never married, never had any children of his own, and he didn't have all that many friends. Not that he wasn't well-thought-of in our community—his reputation from the war basically made him a local legend. He was regarded as a hero. But that didn't seem to matter much to him. He never smiled, he never danced, and he never talked about his past.

"Drink this," he said and pushed a cup of strong smelling tea into my hands. It was an herbal remedy to treat swelling and pain, and it tasted so bitter I could barely swallow it. But every awful sip made the soreness in my shoulder subside.

"She's okay, isn't she?" I dared to ask only once his back was turned. "I didn't hurt her, too, did I?"

Kiran paused. He let his hands rest on the top of the chest where he stored all of our medicines. When he turned around, his expression was wrinkled with a sour frown. "She was unharmed," he replied. "But her mother will break her bow for this. She will have to start her training over to earn another one."

I looked down again. Great. So basically, she was alive, but she was still going to hate my guts from now on.

"Did she see what I did?" I couldn't make my chin stop trembling so I bowed my head, hoping Kiran wouldn't see. "It's just, you know, I don't have a lot of friends and Enyo is the only one who …"

I couldn't finish.

"No. I don't think she knows what happened."

A sniffle escaped before I could choke it back in. With a sigh, Kiran sat down next to me and put his arm around my shoulders, pulling me over to lean against him. "I found you before the others did. You were right. Noh did kill them. But I disposed of the carcasses. No one will find them. No one will know what happened. You'll be fine, but this cannot happen again. We were very fortunate."

I nodded shakily. Yeah, we we'd been insanely lucky. Noh had never killed anyone or anything before. I'd always been able to stop him. "I just couldn't control it. I just—I didn't know what else to do. I had to save her."

He patted my head. "I understand."

"It's getting stronger. I see him almost every day. He won't leave me alone."

Kiran didn't answer.

"What's wrong with me?" I asked quietly. "What am I?"

His answer was barely a whisper, "I don't know."

***

It was close to midnight when I gave up trying to sleep. My mind was restless, and the moonlight pouring through my open window was too bright. I couldn't stop thinking about the elk, the feeling of letting Noh go, and how the wound on my face was absolutely killing me. I got up and took the bandage off my shoulder to stretch and flex my arm. It hurt, too, but the herbal remedy me helped a lot. By tomorrow it would be as good as new.

Pulling on a long, silk tunic with baggy sleeves, I buckled my belt and dagger around my waist. I carried my sandals downstairs, careful to hold my breath when I crept past Kiran's room. He had ears like a fox and slept on the first floor in case we got any late night emergency calls.

I grabbed my bow and quiver off the hook and slipped out the door of the clinic. Above me, a wooden sign hung with the words "HEALING HOUSE" painted in green elven letters. Our clinic was right smack in the middle of the market district. All around me the lights of the city twinkled in the night. Oil lamps flickered against colored glass windows and towering buildings made of cool alabaster stone.

Mau Kakuri was the largest gray elf city that had been rebuilt after the war. Some called it the "city of mist" because it stood against a steep mountainside where a curtain of waterfalls poured down into a shallow river that ran through the middle of the garden district. The falls provided a constant haze of cool, crisp mist that hung in the air, trapped beneath the dense jungle canopy. Sometimes, if the sunlight broke through the trees just right, it made dozens of shimmering rainbows.

The streets, arched bridges, tall stone buildings, and elegantly spiraling palace towers were all built atop the mossy rocks and around the plummeting water. This was where the royal family had chosen to live, where the ancient archives were kept in the caverns behind the falls, and where I had lived my entire life. I was one of only two humans in Mau Kakuri, and we were so far from the boundary of Luntharda and Maldobar, so deep within the dense jungle, that odds were I'd never seen another one ... ever.

I took the quiet back road to the edge of the city. I wasn't sure she'd be there. After all, Enyo was probably furious with me. She might never want to speak to me again. But I was willing to take that chance.

At the end of a long, narrow path that zigzagged treacherously up the side of the cliff face behind a few of the falls, I found her.

She was sitting in our usual spot, her bare feet dangling over the edge of the mossy rocks. The water poured over the edge before her, a constant veil from the city below.

It was tricky to get to her. The boulders were slick and the edge was steep. But I'd come this way so many times that I could have done it with my eyes closed.

"Did you come here to apologize?" Enyo wouldn't look at me as I sat down beside her.

"Would it help?" I hesitated and studied her profile.

She didn't look thrilled to see me. "No. And I'm not sure I would believe it, anyway."

I chewed on my lip.

"Your nose looks awful," she said.

I poked at the fresh stitches gingerly. "Hurts, too."

"Good."

We sat in uncomfortable silence for what seemed like a long time. Then, I took my bow off my back and placed it gently on her lap.

She stared at it, ran her fingers over it, and then slowly raised her eyes to meet my gaze. "You're giving it to me?"

I nodded once.

"But you'll lose your place to become a warrior. You'll have to start all your training over."

"Yeah, well, I'll probably have to do that anyway." I shrugged. "Kiran doesn't think I'm ready. He thinks I'm selfish and probably stupid, too."

Enyo smirked and nudged me playfully with her elbow. "I kind of agree."

"As long as you don't hate me, that's all I care about." I sighed and sat back, resting my weight on my hands. "But I am sorry, you know. I shouldn't have brought you along."

I heard her snort sarcastically. "I saved your life! You'd be dead without me."

"As if."

"You're such an idiot, Reigh." She socked me in my sore shoulder.

I whimpered and rubbed my arm.

After a few seconds of sitting there, watching the falls and listening to the constant rumbling of the water, I saw her look my way again. She was still rubbing her hand along the bow I'd given her as though she were anxious about something.

"Do you remember what happened? After the stag charged for me?" she asked at last.

I tried to avoid her probing stare. "Do you?"

"No," she said quietly. "Everything got hazy. I was so afraid I must have fainted. I just remember … feeling so cold. When I woke up, I was at home. No one would tell me where you were. I thought you were dead, Reigh."

I swallowed hard.

"Was Kiran angry with you?"

"No more than usual."

She nibbled on her bottom lip. "My mother was furious. She

said that we both should have died. It doesn't make any sense, does it? Why would the stag just decide to let us go? And what happened to the doe?"

I didn't want to answer any of her questions. Lying had never been one of my finer skills.

"My mother said it was a miracle," she said softly, like it was some kind of secret. "The spirit of the lapiloque saved us."

I stared at her. Then I couldn't help it. I laughed out loud. "Seriously? You think the ghost of some dead god saved us?"

Enyo made a sulking face. "Don't say it like that, it's blasphemous."

"Right." I rolled my eyes.

"He's not dead, Reigh. I know it."

"How? How can you possibly know that?"

I watched her expression become dreamy, almost like she was lost in her own private fantasy. "I can't explain it. I just do."

"That's ridiculous, even by your standards."

She glared at me. "Haven't you ever just believed in something, Reigh? Even though you couldn't see it or touch it?"

I thought about Noh and my body instantly got chilled.

"He's not just a myth. He's real." She spoke with such conviction; I almost wanted to believe her. "And I believe he's coming back."

THREE

Things were quiet for a while. I kept a low profile, following Kiran's orders to stay in the city and out of trouble. He didn't want me out of his sight. This was part three of my punishment, I guess. Part four was when he took the stitches out of my nose.

Meanwhile, rumors swirled through the crowded markets and bustling public baths about how Enyo and I had miraculously escaped being mauled to death by a faundra stag. Some of our local friends even came by the clinic to ask me about it and check out my battle scar, although Kiran forbade me to tell them any details. Most people agreed with Enyo's theory that the spirit of the lapiloque had somehow intervened and protected us.

Only Kiran and I knew differently.

In fact, Kiran didn't act like anything had happened at all.

He went on running the clinic, treating patients for snake bites, broken bones, cuts, and all the usual daily ailments like usual. He doubled my load of chores probably to make sure I didn't have any spare time to do anything stupid, but I didn't mind it. Staying busy helped pass the time … and kept me from wondering what Noh was doing. He'd been unusually quiet since the incident.

I ran errands on foot through the city squares, buying ingredients so I could spend the evenings grinding herbs and making medicines. During the day, I changed bed sheets, washed bandages, scrubbed Kiran's surgical tools, and helped him make the delivery kits for the midwives. He was the best healer in the city, so his schedule was always packed and there was rarely a day when we didn't have a line of patients going out the door.

But on some mornings, before the sun rose, Kiran left me in charge while he went out with the other warriors to lead scouting parties that kept a close watch on the city's outer perimeter. Every able-bodied warrior had to take a turn doing that. Well, every one except for me.

For extra money, Kiran tutored some of the younger warriors, too. He taught them to fight and to shoot a bow, throw a dagger, or wield a scimitar with deadly accuracy. And all I got to do now was watch him leave from the clinic doorway.

Before the incident, he'd at least let me be a sparring partner. I was his best student with a blade. Being left at the clinic was beyond boring, not to mention totally unfair. But without a bow, I was going to have to wait until he decided I was trustworthy enough to be trained again.

Never, basically.

"Everyone else my age has already gone on their first hunt or done a patrol. They've brought down graulers, battled tigrex, and I'm just sitting here," I moaned.

Kiran was ignoring me, crouched at our fire pit stoking the coals so he could cook our dinner of roasted fish and potatoes.

"It's embarrassing. They're making fun of me, you know. All those warriors you're training call me names sometimes."

"I'll ask them to stop," he answered calmly.

"Right. Because getting my father to tell them off is really going to make them not treat me like a little kid," I scoffed.

Then I realized what I'd done.

Kiran pointed a heated, punishing stare in my direction. "I am *not* your father," he growled.

I cringed and bowed my head slightly. "I know."

He went on working quietly, almost as though he were trying to ignore me. At last, he got up to shove a few small silver coins into my hand. "Go and buy bread. No wandering. Come straight back."

I managed to keep it together until I got outside.

As soon as I was a safe distance from the door, I kicked the crap out of the first small tree I came across. I wailed at it hard, breaking the trunk and stomping it into the ground over and over until I was out of breath.

When I stopped, my face was flushed and my heart was racing. I raked some of my long, dark red hair out of my eyes and sat down on the front step to cool off. I squeezed the coins in my fist and thought about all the things I could have done with them instead of buying bread.

Maybe I could pay a seer to tell me who I really was. As enticing as that seemed, I was pretty terrified of what a mystic might see if they looked at me too closely. Nothing good, that's for sure. Good people didn't have bad spirits following them around.

Kiran didn't have to say it. I already knew why he didn't want me calling him "father." If I started doing that, it meant he had to claim me as his own. And I was the kid no one wanted. My own parents had left me to die—probably because someone had tipped them off about the monster I was destined to become.

"*A spider is only a monster to a fly.*" A familiar, whispering voice echoed through my mind.

Coldness sent shivers over my skin.

"Go away, Noh," I muttered. "Leave me alone."

I saw his red, glowing eyes smoldering in the shadows nearby. He materialized from the gloom and began to approach me, the edges of his pitch-black body wavering like licking black flames. He always took that form, appearing like a wolf with tall pointed ears and a long bushy tail, but I knew he wasn't. Noh wasn't an animal at all. He was something else entirely.

"*I cannot leave.*" He padded over to lurk cautiously nearby.

"Why not?"

"*Because we are one, you and I.*"

"What is that supposed to mean?"

His toothy maw curled into a menacing smile. He vanished

into a puff of black mist without answering.

"Reigh?"

I looked up and saw Enyo climbing the steps toward me. She had a confused frown on her face.

"Who are you talking to?"

I shook my head and grumbled, "Myself."

Her expression became sympathetic. "You had another fight with Kiran?" she guessed.

I nodded.

Enyo stood over me, tapping my foot with hers. "Come on. I want to show you something." There was an excited edge to her voice.

I couldn't resist. I got to my feet, cramming Kiran's coins into my pocket, and followed Enyo into the city. The sun was setting as we ran along the narrow passes between buildings, scaling garden walls, darting over bridges, and climbing terraces to get to the rooftops. Enyo was light on her feet, springing the gaps from one roof to another like a cat. It was fun, and I couldn't keep from grinning as I landed and kicked into a roll, leaping immediately to my feet to keep running.

The moonlight broke the canopy, hitting the mist in the air and sparkling like a swirling shower of diamonds. The farther we ran, the brighter the air seemed. Skidding to a halt at the edge of the last residential rooftop, the palace loomed before us with its slender spires bathed in silver light. Behind it, the waterfalls made a constant roaring sound.

Enyo sat down and began taking off her sandals.

"What are you doing?" I squatted down next to her.

"Shh! We have to be quiet. Now hurry and take yours off, too," she whispered.

***

I left my shoes next to hers and followed as she started climbing down the side of the building. There was a high, white stone wall separating the palace from the rest of the city. It only had one gate, and I didn't think we were going to just go waltzing through it.

But Enyo had found her own way inside.

Between two young trees was a place where the roots had cracked the stone, breaking it just enough for a small person to slip through. Enyo had obviously been here before, because she'd taken the time to dig out the ground around the hole so I might be able to squeeze through.

"You first," she whispered. The moonlight shimmered brightly in her multicolored eyes. She was grinning from one pointed ear to the other.

I had a bad feeling about this.

As I wriggled and squirmed my way through the hole, I prayed to whatever god might be listening that I wouldn't get stuck. Then I felt my body come to a screeching halt.

Yep. Definitely stuck. The gods hated me.

I tried to turn and flail, but it wasn't any good. My shoulders were wedged in tight. Behind me, I could feel Enyo trying to help. She was pushing on my rear as hard as she could. This was a new low. I could imagine the look on Kiran's face as he dragged me out of that hole by the ankles. I'd never hold another bow as long as I lived.

Suddenly, with one great push from behind, my shoulders popped free and I launched out of the hole and onto the soft grass. I landed right on my face.

I sat up sputtering and brushing my hair out of my eyes. Then I got a good look around. I was sitting in some kind of garden. Before me was a small pond surrounded by willow trees. Through the wavering fronds I could see stone archways and open hallways leading away into the palace. There were statues everywhere carved into the shapes of different animals, and beautiful flowering water plants grew in the still water.

Voices echoed from across the pond. I saw fluttering of white fabric. And then Enyo grabbed me from behind, dragging me into a hiding place behind one of the statues. She pressed a finger to my mouth as a warning. We had to stay quiet.

"She is so fragile, Jace. We must do something. She won't survive on her own," an old woman's voice pleaded. "If we take her to the temple, perhaps he will hear our prayers. I can't just sit back and do nothing."

"Araxie … I'm just as worried about her as you are," a man's deep voice answered. "But it's been so long. Nothing has changed. I think we need to look to our own medicines and methods—the things your people have relied on all these years."

"You don't believe, then?" The woman stepped into view. I could see her clearly through the trees, her long white gown billowing around her. She was wearing a golden crown nestled into her snowy white hair.

The man moved in closer and took her hand. He was taller, wearing dark green and silver robes with a circlet of silver on his head.

I sucked in a sharp breath. I knew who they were.

I'd never seen the king and queen this close before. They were much older than I expected. The queen's face was creased with age and her hair so long it nearly dragged the ground.

The king was a human, like me—the only other one in the city. He was tall and stern looking. Age hadn't bent him or made him frail, probably because he'd been a dragonrider before leaving the human kingdom of Maldobar. At least, that was what everyone said whenever they told the old stories.

With a square-cut white beard and long hair that was salt-and-pepper colored, he definitely walked like a warrior as he moved to put his arms around the queen. The way his eyes sagged at the corners made him look exhausted, though.

"I can't lose another one. She is my only grandchild, Jace. The last of our bloodline. I can't bear it," the queen's voice weakened. She started to cry and the king held her close at his side, slowly walking with her back into the palace.

Once they were gone, Enyo and I exchanged a glance.

"Is that what this was all about? Eavesdropping on the royal family?" I whispered.

Enyo scowled. "Of course not. I want to show you something." She grabbed my wrist and dragged me out of our hiding place.

Across the garden, on the other side of the pond, stood a large, flat stone tablet made of bone white marble. It had been polished until it was completely smooth and engraved with an intricate picture. It was a scene, like a glimpse from a nearly forgotten past, depicting a young man in strange armor holding a round object in the air over his head. I'd never seen him before, but I immediately knew who that man was.

I'd heard the stories, after all. Everyone had. With his human stature and pointed ears, wearing a carved pendant around his neck and the cloak of a dragonrider—it could only be one person.

The rest of the scene carved into the stone was just as detailed. There was an elven maiden on one side of him, and a human king on the other. Both were kneeling in great respect while their armies placed their weapons on the ground.

"It's from the end of the Gray War. When the lapiloque took up the god stone and destroyed it so it could never fall into evil hands again." Enyo was smiling again, her expression filled with wonder. "You see? He was real."

"Just because someone carved it on a piece of rock doesn't make it true."

"And just because you don't believe in him doesn't mean it's not," she countered.

I stuck my tongue out at her. "What is it with girls and falling for these hero types, anyway?"

Enyo's cheeks turned as red as ripe apples. "I never said I'd fallen for him!"

"You didn't have to," I teased. "Just look at those rippling arms he's got, eh? I bet you dream about him."

"I do not!" She started after me with her fists tight.

I backed up and laughed, darting out of the way as she took a swing at my face. "I bet you can't stop thinking about what it would be like to get whisked away on the back of his dragon."

Enyo dove at me again, rearing back and trying to land a punch wherever she could. Then suddenly, she stopped short. I saw her face go pale and her eyes grew wide, focusing on something—or someone—else.

I felt the chill a second too late. My breath turned to white fog in the air. Slowly, I began to turn around.

Noh was standing right behind me, his red eyes smoldering like coals against the night. Only, this time he didn't look like a wolf. He looked like a human teenager with long, unruly hair. He had a squared jaw, a thin frowning mouth, and … the same long scar across the bridge of his nose that I now had.

He looked *just* like me.

Only, instead of dark, muddy red hair his was black. His skin was deathly pale, and his eyes had no center—just bottomless pools of vivid red light.

For an instant, I was captivated. I stood there marveling at the sight of him until I saw his attention shift. He was looking at Enyo appraisingly, and I could sense the change in his mood. He licked his lips hungrily.

"No." I shouted and stumbled away from him. "You can't have her. Leave now!"

Noh tilted his head to the side slightly. He studied Enyo for a second longer and then looked back to me. The corners of his mouth slowly curled into a menacing smile.

"I mean it! Leave!" I shouted louder, throwing my arms out as I planted myself between him and Enyo. "I won't let you touch her. You don't get to hurt anyone unless I say so!"

"*As you wish, my master.*" He started to chuckle and grinned so wide I could see his pointed canine teeth. With a flourish of his hands, he bowed at the waist and swiftly began to dissolve, vanishing into fine black mist.

The sound of his laugh was still hanging in the air even after he was gone. I tried forcing myself to calm down, but I was angry and panicked. I couldn't think straight. Enyo had seen him. No one else had *ever* been able to see him before, not even Kiran.

The situation was changing from my private problem with one random bad spirit to … something I didn't even have a name for.

"R-Reigh?" Enyo's voice trembled.

"It's fine. It's nothing," I said quickly.

"Nothing? Are you insane?"

I bit down hard on the inside of my cheek.

"Reigh, you have to talk to me! Who was that?" she grabbed onto my arm so I would look at her. "What's going on?"

I jerked away and started for the hole in the garden wall. "Nothing! You didn't see anything! Just forget it ever happened!"

Enyo stepped in front of me, planting her hands on my shoulders and forcing me to stop. "Tell me what's going on!"

I wanted to. I really did. But as often as we argued, there was one thing Kiran and I both agreed on: no one could ever know about the things I could do. I was dangerous. And while he called me master, Noh was becoming more and more difficult to control. He had an appetite for murder, a hunger for death that couldn't be sated. If he stopped listening to me, if I lost control of him altogether, then no one would be able to stop him from feeding.

I couldn't risk it—I couldn't let him hurt Enyo.

"No," I growled at her fiercely. "Get away from me. Never come near me again."

Her eyes widened. Her mouth opened, but no sound came out. Slowly, she took her hands off me. "You don't mean that. I know you, Reigh. You're my best friend. Please, just talk to me—"

I shoved her out of my way. I pushed her hard enough she fell back onto the grass. "You're wrong. You don't know anything about me. I'm not your friend. I can't even stand the sight of you. Stay away from me, Enyo. I mean it."

When she didn't answer, I started running.

I dove for the hole in the wall and crammed myself back through it as fast as I could. I staggered to my feet on the other side and began sprinting through the city streets, past the empty market squares with gurgling fountains and down dark alleys crowded with wooden crates. I didn't bother going back for my shoes.

I ran for home.

FOUR

He knew.

As soon as I burst through the door, barefooted and without any bread, Kiran knew something bad had happened. In an instant he was on his feet and racing down the steps to shut and lock the front door of the clinic. He doused the lamps downstairs and came back up to do the same in our living quarters. I watched him blur around me, his expression grim as he shut all the windows and closed the drapes.

Our home became as dark as a tomb with only the fire from the hearth casting a warm glow around the living room. Long shadows climbed the walls, making me anxious. I was too afraid to look at them closely—terrified that they might begin to move or take the shape of Noh again.

"Tell me what happened," Kiran commanded in a quiet, eerily calm voice. He was standing in front of me, holding onto my shoulders so I couldn't turn away.

I tried. But when I opened my mouth, nothing would come out. Questions whirled through my brain. Was I losing control? What if I couldn't get Noh to leave? What if he hurt someone? Would Kiran abandon me, too? Where would I go? What would I do? Would I ever find a home again?

My throat felt tight. I squeezed my eyes shut and bowed my head, trying to silence the whispering doubts.

Suddenly, Kiran pulled me in and wrapped his arms around me tightly, holding me like I was a small child again.

"It's all right, Reigh," he said. "Whatever happened, I'll fix it. You're going to be okay."

I buried my face against his shoulder. Regardless of what he said, he couldn't fix it—not this time. And when I told him what had happened, I think he began to realize that, too.

Whatever I was becoming, I wouldn't be able to hide it for much longer. Noh was getting stronger, and for better or worse, he and I were bound somehow. I didn't know how or why, but he was here because of me. I couldn't get rid of him. I couldn't even hide him anymore.

Kiran sat across the fire pit from me, quiet despair creeping into his features as he stared at the flames. For a few minutes, he didn't say a word. We sat in silence, watching the flames hiss and dance in the darkness. Dinner was finished and while it smelled good, but neither of us had touched it.

Then a sound echoed through the house.

Knock, knock, knock.

It was coming from the clinic downstairs. Someone was at the door. Kiran jumped up and snatched his scimitar off the hook by the door. I started to get up, too, but he snapped his fingers and gestured for me to stay put. I did—at least, until I heard him open the front door. Then I crept to the edge of the stairwell to listen. It was a long way down to the first floor, but sound bounced off the stone walls of our home like a cave. You could hear a whisper from four stories up.

"We apologize for the late hour, master. We bring word, an urgent request from the Queen," a young man's voice stammered with nervousness as he addressed Kiran.

My stomach did a backflip. I wondered if Enyo had been caught on the castle grounds.

"What is it?" Kiran demanded.

There was a rattling commotion and the sound of the door shutting. Whoever it was, Kiran had let them inside.

"News from the border. Maldobar is under siege. Northwatch burns and a company of human soldiers has retreated into the jungle. They are headed this way, but they travel with many wounded and no supplies. It is doubtful they will survive to reach the city," the young man reported. "Her Majesty would like you to lead a rescue mission to intercept them with supplies and guide them safely here. Your knowledge of the human language and customs would be essential."

"Leaving when? I have responsibilities to my patients here," Kiran spoke sharply.

"Immediately. The errand is most urgent. It's believed that one of these men is a member of Maldobar's royal family."

There was a tense silence. I waited, holding my breath, until at last I heard Kiran let out a growling, frustrated sigh.

"Very well. I'll need some time to make arrangements for my boy to stay with someone. Bring shrikes. We leave at dawn," he answered.

There were a few mutterings of gratitude and the retreating sound of footsteps. The front door snapped shut and I heard Kiran coming back up the stairs. Quickly, I slipped away into my bedroom. I left the door cracked and flopped down onto my bed, jerking the blankets up to my chin.

I pretended to be asleep when I heard Kiran push the door open in a bit further. He sighed again, whispering something under his breath that I couldn't make out. Then pulled the door closed and I heard his footsteps fading away down the hallway toward his bedroom.

Minutes passed and I waited until the house was quiet. Kiran hadn't come back out of his room. I figured he was either busy packing or stealing a few hours of sleep before he had to leave.

I got up and opened my closet, digging through my stuff until I unearthed a backpack made out of soft, tanned leather. It was stocked with a few basic supplies, two days' worth of rations, and something else—something Kiran didn't know I had.

I pulled the long, curved blades out of the bag and held them firmly in my hands. The soft leather grips felt at home there, as though they'd been made especially for me. They hadn't, of course. These blades were a lot older than I was. Each pommel was plated with silver and set with chips of mica to make the shape of a snarling snagwolf's head.

The gray elves called these weapons "kafki," and only the finest fighters for the royal family had wielded them. Each blade was twelve inches long and curved, like a pair of small shovels. But that wasn't what made them unique.

The twin blades weren't made of metal. They were made of wood that was as white as bone and harder than stone—wood from the most dangerous predators in all of Luntharda. Greevwood trees were legendary, even among the gray elves. They were subtle monsters, not something you'd think twice about until one had its roots around your neck and was slowly digesting you.

Gruesome? Definitely. But their wood was as prized as it was hard to gather. Once you cut away the bark and exposed the white meat of the tree beneath, you only had a short time to be able to cut and mold it. After that, it became harder than iron. The elves liked making knives, swords, and scimitars from it because they couldn't be broken and they never went dull. The perfect material for making pointy, sharp, deadly things.

And I hadn't come by these by chance. They were a gift, and Kiran didn't know anything about them. I was afraid that if he ever saw them, he'd take them from me.

It wasn't that weapons were forbidden to me. After all, Kiran had given me my first bow and taught me everything I knew about how to handle a blade. He'd trained me to wield a spear, a scimitar, fire a bow, how to throw daggers with lethal proficiency, and even how to fight with a human-styled sword. But I doubted if even he had any experience with kafki. They were considered an ancient weapon, used more for decoration now than anything else, and being made of greevwood meant they'd probably belonged to someone royal a long, *long* time ago. So if Kiran caught me with them, he would probably insist on giving them back to their rightful owner.

Only, she was definitely dead. So giving them back wasn't really an option.

I dug through my wardrobe for my scouting clothes—the best thing for traveling in Luntharda when you didn't want to be spotted. I'd never worn them before, so they were still new and creased, fresh from the tailor. They'd been waiting for me at the bottom of the drawer for a year.

I took off my casual clothes and put on the black undergarments. I tucked the sleeveless black silk shirt into the matching long black pants. I bound each of my legs from my ankle to my knee with a strip of thick, black canvas, making sure to tuck my pants down into it snuggly. It was padding for running, skidding, rolling, leaping, and climbing through the trees. I did the same with my arms, binding from my wrists to my elbows with several layers of the wrapping.

The outer tunic was made of something thicker, and it was

midnight blue with a silver border stitched into the elbow-length sleeves and around the base. It came down to my knees and was split up the sides so I could move easily. Over it, I buckled a light, black leather jerkin and a belt with sheaths for the two greevwood kafki. I laced up my nicest pair of sandals—the ones with soles made especially for gripping even the slickest of tree limbs—and threw my pack over my shoulders.

The night air rushed in when I opened my bedroom window. I climbed out onto the ledge, looking back behind me at my childhood bedroom.

There, I hesitated.

Basically, I had two choices.

Kiran was going to leave at dawn. He was going to strike out into the jungle, leading a group of warriors to help those human soldiers. And once again, I was going to get left behind. So either I could stay here, hiding in the clinic like a coward and trying to keep Noh at bay and pretend there wasn't something wrong with me.

Or I could do what Kiran didn't have the guts to do:

I could kick myself out.

He was probably hoping this would all blow over, that I'd regain control of Noh, or that he might even leave altogether and I'd get to finish out my life as a normal person. But deep down, the truth wasn't something either of us could change. Noh had killed once. He would do it again, and whether I liked it or not—whether it was fair or not—I would be the one to blame.

No one here would be safe from Noh unless I was gone.

Clenching my teeth, I looked out across the sleeping city of Mau Kakuri and knew I couldn't stay here anymore. Whatever was happening to me—whatever connection there was between Noh and I—I couldn't risk him hurting anyone else. This city couldn't hold me. Kiran couldn't protect me. That left only one option.

It was time to break free.

***

This was my only chance. I had a few hours to get a head start before Kiran figured out I was gone. He wouldn't be able to look for me, not right away. He'd gotten orders from the Queen, so he was obligated. I had to be long gone by the time he wrestled with his better sense and decided to ignore it and come looking for me anyway.

I acted casual so I didn't draw any attention, strolling down the stone paved streets to the edge of the city. There, the jungle rose up before me like a swelling tidal wave, ready to drag me under. Dense, dark, deep, and dangerous, you had to be a special kind of stupid to go out there alone at night.

No one had ever accused me of being all that smart, anyway.

I got a thrill of panic and excitement as I crossed the border, leaving the city behind me and stepping into the wild. Wherever I wanted to go, whatever I wanted to do—no one could stop me now. I was my own man. No crusty old gray elf could tell me what to do anymore.

I ran for the trees and struck out toward Maldobar. It would take days to get to the boundary line, and that was if I didn't stop or get eaten by something first. But I made up my mind right away; that's where I had to go. I wanted to see it for myself, the land where I was born. A kingdom filled with people with round ears like mine, and where dragons ruled the wide, open skies.

It sounded good at the time.

I kept up a fierce pace, sprinting along the tree-paths until my lungs burned and there were miles between Mau Kakuri and me. The sun was rising, and Kiran would just be figuring out that I was gone. I pushed those thoughts from my mind and listened to the jungle. I couldn't hear the rumble of the falls or smell their moisture in the air anymore. Instead, I heard the birds calling to another as they fluttered through the trees. I spooked a shrike that was napping in a sunny spot, warming his wings. He hissed at me as I darted by.

Finally, I stopped to catch my breath and to check my bearings. The jungle was a tangled mess of dense greenery and entwined tree branches. Getting lost would have been easy for anyone. But the first thing Kiran had ever taught me was how to navigate. It's the first thing all gray elves learned because if you couldn't find your way back home, you were basically guaranteed to get eaten by something.

The elves had their own system of roadways along the broad

limbs of the trees, far above the jungle floor. They marked them with symbols engraved into certain places on the trees. A circle meant a road leading north. A circle with a horizontal line through it meant east, one with a vertical line meant west, and one with a single dot in the center meant south. Easy, right?

But those were just the main pathways that led between major cities. There were plenty of other destinations in the jungle like temples, mineral springs, hunting grounds, burial sites, and things like that. There were also warnings of things to avoid—like a grove of greevwood trees that had sprung up too close to a city or village.

Of course, young novice warriors and scouts weren't supposed to leave those marked paths. But if you ever found yourself lost in an unknown part of the jungle, far from a city where someone might hear you calling for help, there was always the tree.

Kiran told me that the humans navigated using the stars. Because of the dense jungle canopy, we didn't get to see the stars often. Or the moon, either, for that matter. However, if you climbed high enough to peek out of the canopy, you could see the tree from almost anywhere. Day or night, winter or summer, the tree was there. It never changed—never dropped its leaves in fall or grew an inch in springtime.

Paligno had planted that tree when the last lapiloque had died—or at least, that's what everyone else believed. They said it had just sprung up, willed to being by the ancient god of life to cover the lapiloque's burial place. Regardless of how it had gotten there, that tree had grown to a size that towered even over all the other giant trees in Luntharda. It loomed over the canopy, and it could be seen for miles and miles. It was a fixed point, which is all you needed to navigate.

I'd only seen the tree once. When I was ten, Kiran had taught me how to climb up to the very top of the canopy and hoist myself through the barrier of leaves and brambles. Up there, the air blew freely, the sky was endless, and the sun was like a warm caress on my skin. I could see the tree from Mau Kakuri. It wasn't all that far away. It was closer to the boundary line with Maldobar than the city, though, and Kiran said few people went to see it now. It was out of great respect for lapiloque that they let him sleep in peace, leaving the temple grounds untouched and the area around it free of civilization. They all believed so sincerely that one day he would rise again.

A load of crap, really. If there was one thing I knew for certain, it's that dead people stayed dead.

OTHER TITLES IN THE SERIES

FLEDGLING
AVIAN
TRAITOR

Find more books like this at http://www.Month9Books.com

Connect with Month9Books online:
Facebook: www.Facebook.com/Month9Books
Twitter: https://twitter.com/Month9Books
You Tube: www.youtube.com/user/Month9Books
Tumblr: http://month9books.tumblr.com/
Instagram: https://instagram.com/month9books

Fledgling

NICOLE CONWAY

Avian

NICOLE CONWAY

Traitor

NICOLE CONWAY